FATAL TRADE

FATAL TRADE

BRIAN PRICE

This edition produced in Great Britain in 2021

by Hobeck Books Limited, Unit 14, Sugnall Business Centre, Sugnall, Stafford, Staffordshire, ST21 6NF

www.hobeck.net

A CIP catalogue for this book is available from the British Library.

ISBN 978-1-913-793-39-5 (pbk)

ISBN 978-1-913-793-38-8 (ebook)

Cover design by Jayne Mapp Design

Printed and bound in Great Britain

 Created with Vellum

Hobeck Advanced Reader Team

Hobeck Books has a team of dedicated advanced readers who read our books before publication (not all of them, they choose which they would like to read). Here is what they said about Fatal Trade.

'This is one of the best police procedurals I have read this year … I loved it!'

'[I] enjoyed this immensely.'

'I was hooked by the second page … brutally compelling and with brave, hard-hitting realism.'

Are you a thriller seeker?

Hobeck Books is an independent publisher of crime, thrillers and suspense fiction and we have one aim – to bring you the books you want to read.

For more details about our books, our authors and our plans, plus the chance to download free novellas, sign up for our newsletter at **www.hobeck.net**.

You can also find us on Twitter **@hobeckbooks** or on Facebook **www.facebook.com/hobeckbooks10**.

To Jen

Prologue

Glasgow 1999

TONIGHT WOULD BE THE NIGHT. Martina knew it. The early evening had been quiet, with no punters using her services, but she expected one of her regulars to come along at any moment. He was rich and married, but something about sleazy sex with a young woman in a back alley turned him on. Tonight he would regret it.

Tall, thin, and wearing a PVC miniskirt that almost showed her knickers, she was tottering on high heels, looking vulnerable but desirable at the same time. She saw him pull his BMW into the side of the road and watched him get out.

'Waiting for me, Candy, are you? That's a good girl,' she heard him leer.

Without speaking, Martina led him into the alley. As he fumbled with his trousers, she opened the small handbag hanging from her shoulder. The darkness obscured her actions, and she felt him flinch as she held the blade of a knife against his genitals.

'You are going to move very slowly towards that lamp post,' she hissed. He complied, his terror almost palpable. 'Now put your arms round it and hold your thumbs together. If you try anything, your wife will be very disappointed next time you try to screw her.'

She wiggled the blade slightly to emphasise her point. She pulled a plastic cable tie, already formed into a circle, from her bag and slipped it over his thumbs, pulling it tight so he couldn't escape. She grabbed his phone, wallet, cash and car keys and persuaded him, with further threats of intimate mutilation, to give her his PIN numbers. Before she left, she yanked his trousers and pants down and wrote 'Pervert' in lipstick across his spotty backside. He wouldn't be found for hours.

Her next target was Piotr the pimp. He was the one who'd put her on the streets when the trafficking gang had deemed her too old, at nineteen, to satisfy the customers who preferred younger flesh. He lived on the first floor of a block of luxury flats in an area of the city where an expensive car would attract little attention. She knew he would be in. He didn't get out on the streets until much later, when he could extract 'commission' from his string of girls, leaving them little to show for their night's work. He would also supply users with the heroin they craved. Martina never touched the drug. She had seen what it could do to women on the game, destroying them physically and leaving them with barely enough money to survive on.

Knocking on Piotr's door, she feigned distress.

'Petey, Petey baby. Help me. I'm hurt.'

The irritated pimp opened his door and released the chain when he saw her hunched over and clutching her belly. His scarred face and the absence of several teeth testified to many years of brawling. His muscular build and aggressive manner suggested that he would usually win.

'What do you want, you stupid tart? I'm busy. Get back out there and make me some money.'

'I can't. Let me in. It was McQuarie's boys. They attacked me.'

Furious at the thought of his rival moving in on his turf, Piotr turned away for her to follow him into the flat. She straightened up and swung her hand, quickly but smoothly, towards his tattooed neck, a move she had practised endlessly. The blade of her knife slowed slightly as it penetrated the layer of muscle, then slipped easily into his carotid artery. He was dead within seconds.

Martina sat back in her seat and watched the lights of Glasgow slip past as the train gathered speed. She was relieved and exultant; everything had gone to plan. The bundles of notes retrieved from the safe in Piotr's bedroom sat comfortingly in her bag along with her passport, which the traffickers who brought her to Scotland had passed on to him.

She delighted in being virtually unrecognisable. It was such a relief to abandon the streetwalker's clothes, dumped with her blonde wig and the knife in a commercial waste bin behind Glasgow Central Station. Instead, she was wearing Piotr's jeans, T-shirt and hoodie, which just about fitted her, albeit with his belt tightened a few notches. She would buy herself some shoes when she reached London, but in the meantime, with two pairs of socks Piotr's trainers would suffice. She felt a sense of freedom in looking unremarkable, the brash lipstick and eye makeup replaced by subtle tones that complemented her light brown hair. She no longer needed to strut as she walked or wear the heels that made her feet ache.

Martina smiled to herself when she thought of the hapless punter she had robbed. Her last action in Glasgow had been to use a phone box on the station concourse to tip off the local paper about 'something worth photographing' in the alley. His BMW, left on double yellow lines near the station, was sure to attract parking tickets and could even be towed. He would have some explaining to do when his wife found out.

As the train crossed the border, she reviewed her plans. For the first time since she was duped into coming over from Poland, she felt free. She looked back over the years of abuse in the filthy brothel run by Callum Mackintosh, and then her time on the streets pimped out by Piotr, and shuddered. She had known girls like herself who had crumbled into helplessness. Many were addicts. Some were dead. But she had determined, early on, that she would rise above it all. And this was happening, at last. No longer would she be the victim. She would be the victor. With the money from the punter, taken from three different ATMs, plus her own savings and Piotr's cash, she had around eighteen thousand pounds. Enough to kick-start a new life and launch her towards her ultimate goal: revenge.

Chapter One

THE SMALL, grey-haired woman grimaced as she entered the police station, dragging a tartan shopping trolley containing her husband's head.

'What are you useless buggers going to do about this?' she demanded, reaching into the trolley and heaving a cardboard box onto the counter.

'Good morning, Madam,' replied Dana, the young civilian support officer, looking askance at this strange woman and her parcel. 'How can I help?'

'I told the copper in the police car about it. He just laughed and said I was imagining it. Just 'cos I look old, doesn't mean I'm mad.'

'I'm sure it doesn't,' soothed Dana, although her expression didn't quite match her words. 'May I take your name? And what have you got in there?'

'Take a look for yourself. Then maybe someone will believe me.'

Dana reached for the box and started to open it, looking increasingly uneasy. An odd smell pervaded the reception area, and there was a suspicious brown stain along the bottom edges. As soon as Dana lifted the lid the smell grew worse. She glanced inside. All the colour drained from her face, her legs gave way and she threw up spectacularly over her computer keyboard.

'Sarge!' she screamed, fumbling with the keypad on the door behind her. 'There's a head in this box.'

Three uniformed officers rushed into the reception area and were greeted with a belligerent stare from the visitor, whose folded arms and tapping foot signalled her impatience with the proceedings.

Dana dashed to the toilet, where she spent the next hour, comforted by a fellow civilian.

PC Hartley peered into the box and paled. 'It is a head, Sarge, a bloke's head.'

Sergeant Robertson confirmed the fact, locked the door to the police station and phoned the duty Detective Inspector.

'There's an old lady in reception with a head in a box, ma'am. Can you come down?'

'On my way,' replied DI Fiona Gale.

While the officers waited for the Inspector, a female constable checked on Dana. PC Hartley took the grey-haired woman gently by the arm, leading her to an interview room. 'Come along, dear, someone will get you a cup of tea. That'll be nice, won't it?'

'I'll have the tea, but don't be so bloody patronising. I'm not senile. That's my husband's head, and I want to know what it was doing on my doorstep.'

Fiona, a rather plump woman in her late forties with short dark hair, whose smart skirt suit and brisk manner spoke more of efficiency than warmth, arranged for the box and its contents to be taken somewhere safe and cool. Hartley removed the vomit-coated keyboard and swabbed down the reception counter with disinfectant, an expression of disgust on his face.

'Looks like we'll need a new receptionist. That one's lost it.'

Fiona was on the verge of reproving him for his lack of sympathy when her phone rang. 'Yes, sir. A human head in a box, brought in by a woman. DC Cotton is speaking to her now. It all seems to be under control, but the civilian receptionist is traumatised. Will do.'

She turned to Hartley.

'The Chief Superintendent is on his way down. Find a new keyboard and make sure the place is tidy and open for business by the time he gets here. And you can stay on reception for the time being.'

'Yes, ma'am.'

DC Mel Cotton, trim and fit-looking, entered the interview room bearing tea and biscuits. The room, which was comfortably furnished, in contrast to the rooms where suspects were interviewed, was used for talking to vulnerable witnesses: children, and people traumatised for one reason or another. Nevertheless, it was still fitted with a discreet alarm strip and unobtrusive video recording equipment. Its occupant was pacing up and down, her wiry frame restless and her expression one of annoyance.

'Hello. I'm Detective Constable Melanie Cotton' she said,

with a pleasant smile. 'Please sit down. Can I have your name and address?'

'Ellen Wilkins. Mrs. And I live in the ground floor flat, Anstruther Buildings, Tiptree Road, Mexton.'

'OK, Mrs. Wilkins. I'm going to have to caution you and record this interview. Don't worry, you're not under arrest.'

'I should think not. I didn't put it there.'

Mel recited the caution, switched on the recording equipment and settled back in her seat.

'Tell me what happened, please. Take your time.' She smiled encouragingly.

'This morning, about seven, there was a bang on the door. I answered it, but there was no-one there, only the box. I took it into the flat, opened it and had the shock of my life. I'd thought I'd never see anything of George again.'

'You don't seem that upset about it, if you don't mind my saying so.'

'It's shocked me. Of course. But I've had worse. I was a paramedic. Once you've seen the result of a lorry smashing into a coachload of kids at sixty miles an hour, anything else seems trivial.'

'And George was your husband?' Mel wondered how Ellen Wilkins could be so calm after such a shocking event. Perhaps she hid her distress well.

'Oh, I hated him. He fell in with some local villains, drank, started to hit me and then blew all our savings. I haven't seen him in four years or so, and the planet's better off without him. The only thing he left me was his name. We never actually got divorced. I suppose I'm a widow, now.'

'So what did you do after you'd opened the box?'

'I rushed into the street. My mobile was out of charge, so I hoped I could borrow a phone off somebody. Wonder of wonders, a police car was coming up the road, so I flagged it down. I said my husband's head was in a box in my kitchen, and the copper just laughed and told me to go home and take my tablets. I suppose he thought I was barmy. It was raining, and I was in my dressing gown and slippers, so I expect that's why. No excuse for rudeness, though.'

'We'll speak to the officer concerned, I promise you. Why didn't you borrow a phone and dial 999 then?'

'Waste of time. I'd've probably got the same idiot coming back. So I got dressed and brought the head to you. Seemed the quickest way to get something done about it.'

'I realise you were shocked, but perhaps it would have been better if you'd let us collect it.' Mel saw little point in lecturing Ellen on the need to preserve forensic evidence, but felt she had to say something. Ellen shrugged.

'Can't help that. At least you lot are taking me seriously now.'

'Yes, we are. I'll need the keys to your flat, please. It's now a crime scene, and you can't go back there until we've processed it. I'll take your fingerprints and a DNA sample for elimination in a moment. Now, I need to know exactly what you did, from the moment you heard the knock on the door until you spoke to the police officer.'

Ellen repeated her account of the events of the morning, her voice beginning to tremble.

'Did you see anyone suspicious, or any strange vehicles, when you ran out of the flat?'

'No. There was no-one else about until the police car came along.'

'How about the previous day? Anything unusual happening?'

'Nothing. Nothing at all.'

'Have you been threatened by anyone?'

'No. I'd've mentioned it, wouldn't I?'

'Yes, of course. I'm sorry to keep you, Mrs Wilkins, but I just need a quick word with my boss. Will you be OK?'

'As long as someone shows me where the toilet is. All that tea's gone right through me.'

Mel smiled and said she would send someone to look after her.

Chapter Two

MEL REPORTED the substance of the conversation to Fiona. Mel respected her and enjoyed working for her – she seemed fair and efficient, although perhaps a little distant. But Mel hadn't been in CID long enough to see how good a detective her senior officer was. The DI immediately dispatched a forensics team to Ellen's flat.

'So, what do you make of her, Mel?'

'Ellen's clearly a tough one. Cynical. Not fazed by blood or body parts. She was honest about her dislike of the victim. And she's certainly not mad.'

'Could she have killed him?'

'I doubt it. She would have chucked the head in the canal rather than bringing it to us, if she was involved. I think she's telling the truth.'

'OK, thanks Mel. Get as much as you can on George Wilkins from her. We need to know more about the family and George's associates. Uniforms will do door-to-door, but I'm not expecting anything solid from them. The doctor will have to certify death.'

Mel chuckled at this.

'Yes, I know it's bleedin' obvious, but there are procedures. Can you ask neighbouring forces if they have come across a headless corpse? I'll let the DCI know. He'll want to take charge of the case.'

'Yes, ma'am. I'll get Ellen to sign a formal statement and arrange for someone to run her home. I've already asked Tom to run a PNC check.'

'Good. Thanks.'

Mel suppressed her excitement as she returned to the interview room. Gruesome though the head was, this was why she had become a detective. She hadn't minded being on the beat, although the unremitting greyness of much of the town was depressing. But she had soon realised that she really wanted to use her brain to track down criminals rather than chase shoplifters and break up fights. This was her first murder as a detective, and she was determined to make her mark. And, as a woman in CID, she knew she would have to work extra hard.

'Have you anywhere else to go, Ellen?' she asked. 'Any relatives?'

'I could stay with my daughter, Jenny, for a bit, I suppose.'

'Anyone else?'

'I have a son, Stephen, but he has…problems. He was a sweet boy but he became ill and doesn't keep in touch. I do miss him.'

Mel didn't push the point but made a mental note to follow up on Stephen Wilkins.

'I expect they'll be upset to hear about their father.'

'Not likely. He was a rubbish dad. Either working or down

the pub most of the time. Didn't have much to do with them. I raised them virtually on my own. That's why I look seventy when I'm only sixty. Then I retrained as a paramedic. I used to be a nursing assistant, but I didn't want to go back to wiping arses and mopping up sick. I'd had enough of that with the kids. Don't get me wrong – I love them both, but I was fed up of basic care and wanted something a bit more rewarding.'

Mel refrained from pointing out that modern nursing involved very much more than dealing with body fluids.

'What did George do for a living?'

'He was a mechanic. Brilliant with cars. Had a series of good jobs, but, when the recession hit, the garage he was working at closed down. He started doing odds and ends, fixing up old bangers to sell, and also did some driving work. The blokes he hung around with seemed pretty dodgy, but I don't remember many of their names. He'd always liked a pint, but then the serious drinking started. He never drove drunk, though. Funny,' she looked wistful, 'he swept me off my feet when we met. Then he started knocking me to the floor.

'When I found out he'd spent all our savings at the bookies I threatened to go to the police and chucked him out. Before I knew it, he'd sold the house and used the money to pay off his debts. I never saw a penny, and there was no point suing, even if I could've afforded a lawyer. So the children and I moved into the flat. That was about eight years ago. We were happy then. He popped in a couple of times to collect some papers and things, but the last time he came was four years ago, as I said.'

'OK. If you can remember the names of any of his associates, that would be a great help. I'll write up the details of what you've told me and get you to sign a statement. Then we'll drop you off at Jenny's. We can fetch some things from your flat if you need them. We'll probably want to speak to you again. Here's my card. Please get in touch again if anything else occurs to you. I'm very sorry about the unpleasant experience you've had.'

The shock of the morning's events began to hit Ellen as she sat in the back of a police car taking her to Jenny's. Just as she did when attending road accidents as a paramedic, she had pushed the horror to the back of her mind and got on with things. But there was always an emotional payback. The flashbacks. The sleepless nights. The sudden bouts of nausea. As the car passed her own flat, she shuddered at the memory of her grisly find. She knew she wouldn't sleep much tonight. Reporters were gathering on the pavement like magpies on fresh roadkill, their raincoats flapping in the wind. She was glad she would be staying somewhere else.

Chapter Three

In a comfortable flat on the outskirts of Mexton a man and a woman sat talking. But the conversation was far from comfortable.

'The fucking numpty's gone too far this time. He'll have the polis all over us,' the man raged.

'It's not that bad, surely. There's no current link between Charles and George. They'll never find the crime scene, and Charles's men won't say anything.'

'They'd better not. Put the word out. If anybody says anything about this, I'll personally rip his tongue out and shove it up his arse. What about your tame copper? Can he bury it?'

'Too big for him. Too public. But he could misdirect things if needed,' the woman replied.

'Probably not enough. There might be a better way. I'll have a word with my contact. What about Charles? Has he outlived his usefulness? Should he be retired?'

'No, not at this stage.' The woman looked thoughtful. 'He

may have started this shitstorm, but if no-one identifies him, there's no need for drastic measures. His skills are useful.'

'Well, keep a close watch on him. There's too much at stake.'

'I will. And I'll get daily updates on police activity so we can act if we need to.'

'Keep me informed. And you will tell me if Charles becomes a problem, won't you?'

'Of course. At once.'

The woman left the flat, her mind in turmoil. The man made her shudder, but she would keep on working with him for the moment. She had plans, which hadn't included helping to clear up after a very public murder. But she would handle it. She always did.

'Come in, Fiona. Come in, please.' Detective Chief Inspector Bob Hawkins called DI Gale into his office and invited her to sit. She was a little nonplussed because he rarely called her Fiona. She looked at her boss, taking in his thinning hair, his middle-age spread and his drinker's complexion, and wondered what was up.

'A puzzle, this one. The head, I mean. What do you make of it?'

'Too early to speculate, sir. We've no witnesses, no forensics and no obvious motive. It looks as though it was meant to frighten Ellen Wilkins, but we don't know why. We're chasing up a number of leads, but there's nothing to show so far.'

'Hmmm. By rights I should be SIO on this. But I've got another murder on the go, that domestic stabbing, and I'm supposed to be delivering a training lecture to a group of probationers next week. There are no other DCIs available, so

I wondered if you would like to take the lead on it? Could be good for your career.'

Fiona was flattered. It wasn't usual for a DI to take the role of Senior Investigating Officer in a high-profile murder case. She didn't think her record was that good, but perhaps she'd made a better impression on her bosses than she had realised.

'I'd love to, sir. I'm sure I can handle it.'

'That's excellent. You can always call on me for help, at any time. And I want to be kept informed at every stage. I'll authorise a budget for forensics – try not to exceed it, but let me know if you really need any more. There's some money available for overtime, as well, if you want it. I'm also giving you a bit more help. DS Paul Jessop is joining us from the Met, and he can lend you a hand until we find a permanent place for him. So, rally the troops and get stuck in.'

'Yes, sir. Thank you for the opportunity. I won't let you down.' Fiona left Hawkins's office full of excitement. The first murder investigation for which she would be responsible. If she got a good result she could apply for Hawkins's job when he retired – he only had a few years to go, surely. She straightened her jacket, smoothed down her skirt and headed for the incident room, keen to make a good impression on her team.

When Fiona left, Hawkins picked up his phone and dialled.

'Just to let you know, sir, DI Gale is running the investigation into the head. That's right. Career development. She should be fine, but I'll be keeping an eye on her. A close eye.'

Chapter Four

Wednesday 2nd October

ELLEN's gruesome find prompted a torrent of press coverage. The *Mexton Messenger*, with its penchant for inaccuracy, reported that a head had been left on the doorstep of 'Miss Eileen Wilson', while the *Sun* ran the headline, 'Off his nut'. Other papers were more restrained but, since they had little real information, speculated wildly about organised crime, revenge murder and the beginnings of a serial killing spree. The press liaison officer was bombarded with calls, which she fielded with the promise of a press conference when more information became available. A few desperate reporters hung around the dilapidated-looking police station, hoping to persuade passing officers to speak to them, but they were brushed away like irritating insects.

The incident room, fresh with the early morning smells of shower gel, aftershave and coffee, hummed with anticipation. Fiona, the murder book open in front of her, addressed the twenty detectives and civilian staff gathered for the morning briefing. She was both apprehensive and nervous; excited at the prospect of working on a murder but fearful of failing. She knew she would be scrutinised not just by her boss but also by her team. If she screwed up, everyone would notice, and if the team couldn't pull together under her command, the failure would be hers. She had to get them on board.

'First off, I must tell you I've been appointed SIO on this one, with DCI Hawkins's support. As you know, it's the first time I've been in this position, so I'm looking to you all to work with me. If you have any concerns or suggestions, please come to me directly. A good result on this will reflect well on all of us. Thank you.'

Several people smiled. Jack Vaughan, an experienced, world-weary Detective Sergeant, ran his hands through his short, slightly greying hair and scowled. Fiona didn't notice.

'Secondly, we've got a name for the investigation. Operation Robespierre.'

'You've got to be joking,' laughed Mel. A couple of other DCs smiled knowingly.

'Yes, I know about Robespierre and the guillotine. But the computer generates operation names randomly. We don't choose them.'

'I think the computer's taking the piss,' said Jack. The others grinned.

'Be that as it may, we're stuck with it, so let's crack on,' Fiona replied tartly. 'We've had nothing from forensics or door-to-door enquiries, but I've had a preliminary report from the pathologist. The victim was alive until fairly recently – the head hadn't decomposed much, although it was smelling a bit. It was removed after death with a saw. The cuts are jagged, suggesting it could have been a pruning saw or something similar. It was rather messy – the job wasn't done by anyone skilled. The head is otherwise undamaged. There were traces of oil, metal filings and grease in the hair. Obviously, we need the rest of the body to determine cause of death. So why would someone send a woman her dead husband's head when they split up years ago?'

'Perhaps she crossed the Godfather but didn't have a horse,' suggested Mel.

'Very funny. But I don't see Ellen being involved in organised crime, and Mexton isn't exactly a hotbed of Mafiosi. It must be some kind of threat. An attempt to frighten her. But why? What did we get from the PNC?'

'George seems to have been a bit iffy,' replied DC Tom Ferris, straightening his glasses and brushing his floppy dark hair from his eyes. 'We had suspicions that he'd been handling stolen cars, but not enough evidence to pull him in. He was arrested over a batch of forged MOT certificates fifteen years ago, but the magistrates believed him when he said someone else had planted them in his garage. His fingerprints weren't on them, and he had a flash brief at the trial.'

'How could he afford that?' Fiona asked. 'He was unemployed and only earning small sums from odd jobs, wasn't he?'

'So we believe. I'll get on to HMRC and see if he filed any tax returns.'

'Well, good luck with that. How about known associates?'

'Some of them are more serious villains. He's been seen with Kelvin Campbell and Charles Osbourne, both of whom are thought to have been involved in planning robberies and handling drugs, although they've never been convicted. They look like upstanding members of the community, in legitimate business, but we believe they're involved in a range of illegal activities.'

Tom paused, and heads turned at the crash of the incident room door opening. A tall man wearing an expensive suit and a supercilious air entered and stood at the back, surveying the team. His eyes lingered on Mel.

'DS Jessop, I presume?' said Fiona, visibly irritated at the interruption. 'I'll introduce you properly after the briefing. Carry on, Tom.'

'OK. George used to hang out in the Fife and Drum, a known haunt of lowlifes, as well as the Maldon Club in town. One other thing. He was in a car we stopped driven by Billy Peel, an enforcer for the Eastside Crew. They were clean, so we couldn't hold them for anything.'

'Who are they?' asked young DC Michael Adeyemi, new to the area.

'The Eastside Crew? Disaffected white kids from the sink estate who model themselves on some of the London gangs,' replied Fiona. 'They're into drug dealing, mugging, protection, pimping and all manner of nastiness. We know who most of the foot soldiers are, but we can't get any evidence against the bigger players. There's little point nicking ten-year-old delivery cyclists for possession of small amounts. Witnesses go all Tommy on us. Deaf, dumb and blind.'

'I've looked into Ellen Wilkins,' said Mel. 'She's got no record, and the local health trust confirmed she worked on ambulances for twelve years. Her daughter Jenny, who she's staying with, is thirty-two, married and lives nearby with two young kids. Ellen's son, Stephen, has come to our attention before. He's twenty-eight, unemployed, and was cautioned for affray a couple of times. He was briefly sectioned a few years ago after attacking his father in a pub. George didn't want us to press charges.'

'Was there any follow-up from the shrinks?' asked Jack.

'Probably not – the mental health service is in tatters,' replied Mel.

'Right,' summarised Fiona. 'We need to find out where Stephen was around the time George was probably killed. That's up to three days ago. We also need to interview Campbell and Osbourne, although I doubt they'll give us much.'

The other detectives murmured their agreement.

'People might have known George on the Eastside – perhaps the neighbourhood officers have someone who might talk to us. Outside chance, though. Ellen may have George's mobile number – track its movements over the past few days. If he was up to something, he would probably have been using a burner, but you never know. Contact DVLA and find out what he drives. Run the plate through ANPR records. Ask around in the Fife and Drum – probably no point, but someone might talk. Don't go there alone, though. Crucially, we have no address for George. Finding out where he lived is a priority. Check the electoral roll and look up the records of Stephen's assault on him – see if he gave an address. Anything else?'

'Ellen might have remembered something more,' suggested Mel. 'I'll "head off" there now, if you like.'

The others groaned, used to her gallows humour.

'Good idea. DS Vaughan will divvy up the other jobs – OK, Jack?'

'Yes, guv. Right, everyone, let's get to it.'

The incident room erupted as Jack gave the officers their tasks. Mel slipped her notebook into her pocket and set off to interview Ellen again. Fiona returned to her office, relieved that the briefing had gone off without a hitch. She believed things were going well, but what really counted was a result. And that, above all, was what she needed.

'Sorry I was late, ma'am. Traffic.' DS Jessop drawled, entering Fiona's office without knocking. 'Pleased to meet you.'

He extended his hand, which Fiona shook with slight reluctance. There was something about his demeanour that set her teeth on edge.

'That's all right. It's your first day. But we start briefings early and on time.'

'Yes ma'am. Of course.' He grinned, and the odour of mints wafted into the room.

'So what have you done before?'

'I've been in the Met for the past seven years. Major crime, vice, robbery. I've done it all.'

Fiona rather doubted that.

'You'll find Mexton a bit quiet after London. Why the move?'

'I fancied a break from the nightmare of the Smoke. Housing costs are ridiculous unless you're a millionaire – or a Chief Super. Also, my ex-wife lives in Mexton and I'll get a chance to see more of my kid, I hope.'

'OK. Good. I'll introduce you to DS Jack Vaughan. He'll fill you in on the investigation and show you round the office. I'd like you to shadow him for a day or two, then I'll work out a proper role for you.'

'Great. I'll tell the girl to get me a coffee and I'll get stuck in.'

'We don't employ girls, DS Jessop, and if you're referring to Mel Cotton, she's a detective constable, not a barista. We get our own coffee, and the machine is in the corner of the incident room.'

Jessop left Fiona's office, seemingly unruffled and without

apologising. Fiona shut the door and wondered what kind of dinosaur she'd been landed with.

'Mum's gone back to the flat. You've just missed her,' said Jenny Carpenter, a worried-looking young woman in jeans and a jumper, when Mel knocked on her door half an hour later. 'She went back to her own place as soon as she was allowed to. My two kids were a bit much for her, I think. They're four and five, a noisy stage, and Mum's feeling a bit fragile. I gave her my keys.'

'I quite understand,' smiled Mel, looking around the living room, which bore all the signs of being inhabited by young children. 'But, while I'm here, did you have any contact with your father?'

'No. Not even a birthday or Christmas card since Mum chucked him out.'

'So you've no idea where he was living?'

'None at all, I'm afraid. Stephen may know – I think he stalked Dad for a while, but Stephen's difficult to talk to. He has issues.'

'He didn't seem to like your father.'

'That's an understatement. He hated him. Blamed him for the split and for denying us a normal family life. You know Stephen attacked him?'

'Yes, we do. He's on my list to interview. Any idea where he's living? Your mum didn't know.'

Jenny gave an address in a formerly prosperous, but now run-down, part of town.

'Did your husband know him at all? We're trying to trace anyone who might have had any contact with him.'

'I shouldn't think so. I never brought Pete home, and Dad

didn't come to the wedding. He's a shopfitter and works away a lot. He's in Bristol at the moment. I can phone him and ask him if you like, but don't get your hopes up.'

'Thank you, Jenny. Please call me if he knows anything. Here's my card.'

'OK. Should I be worried about Mum?'

'I hope not. She seems to be handling a horrible situation well, but I'm afraid I can't give you any more information. Do get in touch if anything else concerns you.'

Jenny showed Mel out, promising to phone her husband that evening. Jack was out of the office when Mel phoned, but she left a message for him and headed off to see Stephen. She was a little nervous about interviewing a possible murder suspect, who could be violent, on her own. Her mother, a uniformed sergeant, had been killed in the line of duty while trying to calm a drug addict carrying a knife. She knew the risks but she was excited at the prospect of making a collar. Her DS was always on her case, and this was a chance to prove herself. Anyway, HQ knew where she was going.

Stephen's bedsit was one of eight in a three-storey Victorian house. Much the worse for wear, its windows and doors needed painting, several tiles had slipped off the roof and sections of guttering leaned precariously away from the eaves. A scrawny cat looked at Mel suspiciously as she approached the door. The smell of decaying rubbish, and the takeaway containers and cider cans strewn along the path, suggested that no-one had put the bins out for some time. The atmosphere was vaguely menacing, and Mel felt unsettled. She wondered what crimes the unprepossessing exterior concealed.

She pressed the bell marked SW, hoping it would be heard over the rap music thumping from an upstairs flat. After a few minutes, a dishevelled figure in a scruffy T-shirt and jeans opened the door. He towered over Mel and scowled, clearly annoyed at the disturbance.

'What d'you want?'

'Stephen Wilkins?' asked Mel, proffering her warrant card. 'Detective Constable Cotton. May I come in?'

'Why? What am I supposed to have done?'

His eyes flicked from side to side, and he couldn't meet Mel's gaze.

'Nothing. Nothing at all. But it's better we talk inside.'

'Come in, then, if you must.'

Mel followed Stephen into the house, noticing the outline of a folding knife in his back pocket. She surreptitiously checked that her baton and pepper spray were within easy reach. Then the door slammed behind her.

Chapter Five

STEPHEN LED MEL UP GRIMY, uncarpeted stairs to the second floor. His bedsit was as untidy as his appearance and smelt of unwashed bedding and stale curry, with an overtone of weed. Dirty crockery filled the small sink in the corner of the room, and the cooker was badly in need of a clean. Takeaway containers were overflowing from the kitchen bin. A small TV was perched on a rickety table at the end of the bed.

'What's this about, then?' Stephen glared defensively at the detective. He didn't invite her to sit.

'I need to talk to you about your father.'

'Why? He's a scumbag. I've not spoken to him for years.'

'Well I'm sorry to have to tell you, but I'm afraid he's dead.'

Stephen shrugged. 'So what? He nearly killed Mum and he wrecked the family. Left us skint. Never had anything to do with us while he was alive, so why should I care about him when he's dead? No loss.'

Mel took out her notebook and probed Stephen's relationship with his father.

'He was all right when me and Jenny were little, but then he began to drink and started knocking Mum about. She put up with it for as long as she could, but then something happened, I don't know what, but he wasn't there any more. Things were better then, although we didn't have much money. I started to get ill, though, and eventually lost it when I saw him laughing with his mates in the pub. I went for him and got put away in hospital for a bit. I'm on tablets but they make me feel fuzzy.'

'So when did you last see him?'

''Bout a couple of months ago, I think. My memory's a bit hazy. He looked like he was doing all right for himself. Had a flash car.'

'Where was that?'

'Somewhere on Blackberry Way. I saw him parking next to a posh house. I remember it 'cos there was a statue in a pond in the garden. A woman with her tits out, pouring water from a jug or something. Didn't see the number.'

Mel decided not to ask what Stephen was doing in that exclusive area of town but pressed him over his more recent movements instead.

'Can you tell me where you've been over the past few days?'

'I'll try. Things are a bit of a blur. Sunday I reckon I was in all day watching TV. Monday I was using the library computer to apply for jobs most of the morning so's they don't stop my universal credit. I haven't got one of my own. Went for a walk in the afternoon, can't remember where, and spent the evening watching telly. Tuesday I was here most of the time. Popped out to get some food and fags in the afternoon. Before you ask, no-one saw me apart from the staff in the library and the bloke in the corner shop. I don't mix with people, as you might have guessed.'

Mel realised that Stephen was probably more of a danger to himself than anyone else, although she would confirm his alibi where possible. She would be able to check the log on his universal credit account if it became necessary.

'OK. Thank you, Stephen. Here's my card. If you think of anything that might help us find out what happened to your father, please let me know. Oh, and I wouldn't take that knife out in public if I were you. You could get into trouble.' She felt it inappropriate to recite the 'I'm sorry for your loss' mantra and left Stephen in his dismal bedsit, wondering whether he'd been let down by his family, his doctors or both.

―――――

Mel made a detour on her way back to the station and drove along Blackberry Way. Neat, owner-occupied, thirties-built detached homes contrasted sharply with the neglected and seedy rented accommodation in Stephen's neighbourhood. Even in the rain they looked appealing. A few expensive cars were in evidence, and the gardens were immaculate. The house with the statue in the pond was easy to find. A recent-model BMW and a Porsche in the drive underlined the affluence of its owners. The house was clearly well cared for, the paintwork flawless and the shrubs in the garden neatly trimmed. She made a note of the house and car numbers, resolving to check occupancy and ownership when she returned to base.

Chapter Six

WHEN SHE GOT BACK to Ellen's flat, Mel found her wiping
fingerprint powder from the front door, an expression of
resigned irritation on her face. She was obviously house-
proud. The flat was clean and well-maintained. Although the
decoration was dated, it was in good condition, and the furniture, far from new, had been looked after. The kitchen was
spotless – all traces of the bloody parcel that had sat on the
table the previous day had been thoroughly removed. When
asked, Ellen knew nothing about the Eastside Crew but
confirmed that George had known Osbourne and Peel.

'Yes, I remember the two names. Never heard of Campbell. It was meeting those lowlifes that started him off,' she
recounted. 'He drank more and was doing all sorts of driving
jobs at odd times of the day and night. He never said what he
was doing, and told me to mind my own business when I
asked. I suppose I didn't really want to know.'

'Did he ever bring anything back to the house? Anything
suspicious?'

'No idea. He could have brought back a sawn-off and a

couple of pounds of heroin for all I knew. At four in the morning I was hardly going to make him a cup of tea and ask him how his day had been. He might have put stuff in the garage, but everything was cleared out when the house was sold.'

'So, have you thought any further about why someone left you his head?'

'Of course I have. A bit hard to ignore, isn't it? No idea though. I suppose you've not found anything?'

'We're pursuing several lines of enquiry,' replied Mel, diplomatically.

'In other words, you've no clue either.'

Mel smiled ruefully, finding Ellen's directness refreshing rather than offensive.

'We've got a couple of leads but nothing concrete so far. It seems odd that you were targeted when you haven't seen him for years. It must be because of something that happened before you split up.'

'Well, I've no idea what.'

'OK. You have my card. Please get in touch if you think of anything.'

⸻

The incident room was busy with detectives working at computers and talking on phones when Mel returned to the station, although much of the activity seemed hardly productive. Jack took her aside and berated her for interviewing Stephen on her own.

'What's the idea of swanning about like Jane bloody Tennison? Just because your dad was a DCI, it doesn't mean you can do as you like. You can get hurt just like the rest of us. For all you knew, Stephen Wilkins could have been a murdering lunatic. I thought you'd learned your lesson when that twat nearly strangled you in the Memorial Gardens. Don't take chances again, right?'

'Oh, come off it, Sarge. He was fine. He's damaged and depressed, not dangerous. He's never assaulted a police officer. I'm not surprised he had a go at his father after what George did to the family. We have to take some risks in this job.'

'Yes, but you didn't know that. He could have been dangerous. I would have thought you'd have known better after what happened to your mum.'

The reference to Mel's mother made her boil over.

'My mum was just going off shift when a meth addict wandered into the station. He was off his head and waving a knife. She tried to calm him down and it seemed to be working. Then he flared up again and slashed her throat. She was doing her duty! What should she have done? Hid in a back room until the addict had gone away or killed someone else? It happened during my training and I nearly jacked it in. But with Dad's support I stuck with it and was determined to do a job that would have made my mum proud of me. And that's what I was fucking doing.'

Jack's tone softened somewhat and he held up his hands in a placatory gesture.

'OK, OK. I meant no disrespect. But we are a team, so don't go into any more potentially dangerous situations without backup. Clear?'

'Yes, Sarge, sorry,' she said, but inside she shrugged it off, wondering when he would stop being such a prick. She sat at her desk to update her investigator's notebook, fuming quietly, until DC Martin Rowse brought her a coffee. His infectious grin and easy manner always cheered her up, although he'd been looking pretty haggard of late, having recently become a father.

'Don't mind Jack. He's only looking out for you. A burglar put one of his trainees in a wheelchair when he went after him alone, so he's a bit over-protective. It's OK to be self-reliant, but perhaps you need to listen to him?'

'Yes, but I'm not a kid. I see your point, I suppose. And thanks for the coffee.'

With Fiona in a budget meeting it fell to Jack to summarise progress so far. He straightened his jacket and addressed the team.

'As we expected, no-one from the Eastside has talked. Campbell's whereabouts are unknown, but Osbourne lives on the outskirts of town. One of those exclusive estates full of stockbrokers, CEOs and financiers. Billy Peel is on bail on an ABH charge. We don't know where he lives, and we don't expect to get much from him even if we can find him.

'Ellen doesn't know George's mobile number. Mel checked the voters' register for the house in Blackberry Way. A Marnie Draycott is listed as living there as well as George Wilkins. The Land Registry shows that it's owned by Maldobourne Holdings, a property company with a local address. The Porsche is leased by the same company from a dealership in town, and the BMW is registered to Marnie Draycott.

'First priority, then, is to visit the house and talk to Ms Draycott,' continued Jack. 'Mel – can you do this with Martin? Hopefully he'll keep you out of trouble. We've no real grounds for a search warrant but see if you can take a look around.'

'OK, Sarge. We'll call in around seven.' Mel ignored Jack's comment.

Jack Vaughan was not happy. He sat at his desk, absent-mindedly scratching the thin scar that ran underneath his chin, and pondered. He'd mentored several young DCs during his eighteen years on the force but had never come across anyone as determined and headstrong as Mel. He welcomed her enthusiasm for the job, but she had a lot to learn. She hadn't been in CID long and was still finding her feet. Perhaps he had been too hard on her, but she shouldn't have visited a potential suspect on her own. Apart from anything else, whatever Stephen said would have needed corroboration. He, Jack, would have to keep a close eye on her and perhaps be a little more approachable. He was supposed to be mentoring her, after all, but she rarely came to him for advice.

Another problem was DI Gale. He had worked with her for several years, initially when they were sergeants together, and later with her as his boss. He didn't resent her promotion. He didn't fancy the paperwork that came with the DI post and preferred to get stuck in to the nuts and bolts of an investigation. But he knew that efficient paperwork and skilful management-speak had got Gale the job. He respected her administrative skills but didn't think so much of her as a detective. She wasn't incompetent or unpleasant, but he felt she could be a little warmer and more open. Perhaps it was the divorce that made her slightly humourless, he speculated. It had happened while they were still sergeants; her husband had left after claiming she cared more about the job than him. Before that she was much more friendly and outgoing. Maybe she hadn't got over it. But given her lack of spark as a detective, what on earth had Hawkins been thinking when he put her in charge of the case? She would never hack it.

The new DS, Jessop, didn't help, either. Jack found him arrogant and sexist, bragging about his experiences in the Met and making lecherous remarks about Mel and the other females on the team. It was obvious from the start that Gale didn't like him and he had little respect for Gale or his other colleagues. He would need watching.

Chapter Seven

'SOMEONE'S DONE ALL RIGHT for themselves,' Mel murmured, as she and Martin walked up the gravel path at 67 Blackberry Way. Not a stone was out of place, the brass door knocker and letterbox were polished to a mirror sheen and even the statue in the pond was spotless and free from algae. Mel knocked on the door, half-fearful of tarnishing the brass.

'Police, are you? What do you want?'

Marnie Draycott knew who they were before they produced their warrant cards, despite Martin's casual jacket and faded chinos. She was tall and expensively dressed, with elegantly manicured nails, an impressive figure and perfect make-up.

'May we come in, Ms Draycott? It's about George,' Mel asked.

'He's not here. Haven't seen him for days. Try the Maldon Club. That's where he usually is this time of day.' Her impatience was obvious.

'I don't think the doorstep is the best place for this,' insisted

Mel. A reluctant Marnie let the detectives in, demanding that they took their shoes off in the hall to protect the cream carpet from dirt. The house was expensively furnished and immaculately kept, but didn't feel at all homely. There were no books, photos or personal touches in the lounge, and it looked like an illustration from an estate agent's brochure, advertising a prestigious new development. The scent of Marnie's expensive-smelling perfume was overlaid by cigarette smoke.

'So what's this about?'

'I'm afraid George is dead, Ms Draycott. I'm sorry. I presume you were his partner?'

Marnie's face froze, her expression hinting at anger rather than sadness.

'What? When? How?' She reached for a cigarette and lit up, dragging urgently on the burning tobacco.

'I can't give you the details, I'm afraid, but his remains were discovered yesterday morning. When did you last see him?'

'Sunday. He went down the club in the evening and didn't come back. I assumed he'd picked up some young tart and gone back to her place.'

'Did he do that sort of thing often?'

'Now and again. The spark in our relationship died a while ago, and the bastard was always seeking pastures new. I'm sorry he's dead, though. I used to like him.'

'What did he do for a living?'

'This and that.' Her tone was evasive. 'Odd jobs for people.'

'What sort of people? And what sort of jobs?'

'People in the entertainment industry. Whatever they wanted doing.'

'Illegal things?'

'I couldn't possibly comment. What he did was his business.'

'Can you think of anyone who would want to kill him?'

Marnie thought for a while, smoking furiously.

'Some of the people he's worked for – and I'm not naming anyone – can be a bit particular about loyalty, if you know what I mean. He could have upset someone, but not that much, I'd have thought. Not enough to kill him.'

'We noticed that the house belongs to a company, Maldobourne Holdings.'

'Does it? Never heard of them. I thought George owned it. Perhaps he was renting.'

'Can I ask what you do, Ms Draycott?'

'I'm a management consultant. I help companies sort out their problems.'

Mel wondered what exactly that entailed.

'Is it OK if I use your toilet?' asked Martin.

'Of course. But if you're looking for an excuse to snoop around, you needn't bother. Help yourself. If I refuse, you'll only get a search warrant.'

'Thank you,' said Mel. 'We need the number of George's mobile phone so we can track his last movements.'

The officers searched the house while Marnie sat smoking and drinking coffee. A desk drawer in a back room yielded a pile of statements from three different banks, and a laptop, the password helpfully written on the underside, joined them in evidence bags. The room was clearly George's, the rows of football videos testifying to his interest in the beautiful game and the set of weights in the corner suggesting he at least tried to keep fit.

'Hang on a bit,' said Martin, as the detectives were putting on their shoes to leave. 'Those videos. No-one uses VHS any more and we didn't see a video player anywhere.'

'Perhaps they're there for sentimental reasons. But we'd better take another look,' replied Mel.

The videos proved to be empty cases. Two had traces of a white powder in the corners, while a third contained a plastic bag holding a rag with blotches of a distinctive-smelling oil on it. Mel bagged each case up separately, wondering where she'd come across that smell before. Behind the row of videos was the box for a mobile phone, which she also took.

As they were leaving, Marnie provided George's mobile number and grudgingly gave her permission for the officers to remove the collected items.

'Thanks for your help, Ms Draycott,' said Mel. 'Please get in touch if you think of anything that might help us. George died violently. Very violently. He deserves justice.'

Marnie shrugged, took Mel's card and said nothing as she closed the door on them.

Once the detectives had driven off, Marnie picked up her phone and dialled.

'The police have been. About George.'

'What did they want?'

'They asked the usual stupid questions and took his laptop and a load of old videos. I didn't give them anything.'

'I'm sure you didn't.' The speaker hung up.

'Gun oil!' exclaimed Mel, in the car. 'It's gun oil.'

'What are you talking about?' Martin looked confused.

'The smell on that rag. I remember it from when they showed us round the station armoury during our induction process. Forensics will need to check it, but I'm sure that's what it is.'

'That's a weird sort of memory. But well done. So it seems as though he had a firearm at some point. Looks like he was involved in something heavy.'

'Well, I'd guessed that from his wandering head,' Mel grinned. 'And I reckon that white powder's coke.'

'You're probably right. We'll get the lab to look at it. By the way, what do you think about Gale being the SIO?'

'Not sure, really. I know Jack's not impressed by her, but I think she's OK. It's a big responsibility.'

'Hmmm. Proof of the pudding, I suppose. She's a bit distant, and I get the impression she's unhappy. But that needn't stop her doing the job.'

'Jessop's a bit of a twat, though. He stands too close, and I'm sure he drinks.'

'Yes. I know what you mean. I hate his self-satisfied smirk and the way he can't keep his eyes off you. He asked me if you had a partner.'

'What did you tell him?'

'I said you were going out with an ex-SAS cage fighter whose jealousy was legendary.'

'Idiot,' Mel laughed. 'Still, I'd rather go out with a parking meter than with him.'

Once they were back at the station the two detectives spent a couple of hours writing up their notebooks and preparing to present their findings at the following morning's briefing.

Mel returned to her flat around nine thirty, humming an old Oasis tune to herself. It was too late to cook, but she made herself a tuna salad, passing a few spare lettuce leaves to Ernie, the Red-footed Tortoise who lived in an enclosure in the corner of her living room. When still in uniform, she had rescued him from the flat of a drug dealer who had overdosed on his own merchandise. What he was doing with a tortoise was anyone's guess, although Mel had half suggested that the animal might have been left as collateral against a drug debt. She didn't really believe that, but readily adopted the tortoise. She researched his needs via various reptile care websites and provided him with suitable accommodation, including a heat lamp to compensate for the chilliness in her flat. In some ways he was the ideal housemate – quiet, tidy and undemanding – although she sometimes felt it would be nice to live with someone who had better conversational skills.

She sometimes wished she hadn't been an only child. It might have made her self-sufficient, but she would have liked to have made friends more easily. She realised she hadn't had many boyfriends, compared with other women she knew, although she was perfectly presentable and good company. But when she was younger, blokes were wary of dating a copper's daughter, and her last adult relationship failed when she suspected her partner of dealing cannabis. She would be a bit more cautious in future.

Chapter Eight

London 1999-2004

ALTHOUGH EXPENSIVE, renting a decent flat in London was essential. Martina intended to use it as a base for discreet escort services, and a scruffy bedsit in Hackney would not have fitted the image. She had planned ahead. A significant chunk of her earnings on the streets, not disclosed to Piotr, had gone towards creating a new identity. Over the years she had acquired a new passport, driving licence and National Insurance number in the name of Marnie Draycott, which enabled her to open a bank account. These, and a set of forged references from landlords, were enough to convince a letting agent that she was a suitable tenant. Within a week she was ensconced in a comfortable flat in Pimlico.

The skinny streetwalker in Glasgow metamorphosed into an extremely attractive and confident young woman. With a proper diet, her figure filled out and her skin cleared. She had her hair styled and tinted a rich auburn. She joined a gym and got herself fit. Some decent clothes came next. When she put her mind to it she could look stunning, and she had no trouble attracting clients. Initially, she took work through an escort agency. It was a safer prospect for someone new to the city. She also looked for business in the bars of expensive hotels, but before long she was working for herself from home as her reputation spread, although she still took the occasional agency job.

Before her capital was depleted completely, she began to turn a profit. It was enough money to live on, but she needed more. She was good at her job, and the word about her experience and versatility soon spread. Slowly her client base began to accumulate the sort of men she had been looking for – lawyers, members of parliament, police officers and people famous in the media – and eventually she could afford to turn away less-desirable customers.

Then she moved up a gear, taking on other women, plus the occasional man. While she was still prepared to keep her own regular clients sweet, she made it clear that her fees had to go up and she would require a retainer whether they used her or not. The increase was substantial but not so great that the clients couldn't afford to pay. Most didn't mind. She more than satisfied their needs, and they would have continued to use her if her fees had doubled. The word blackmail was never mentioned – she preferred the term 'a non-disclosure fee' – but it was obvious that details of her clients' activities, and preferences, were only a click away from hitting the internet or the news desks of the more salacious newspapers.

Her discretion in attracting, and keeping, clients was matched by her circumspection in recruiting others onto her books. She would not employ anyone who used hard drugs, failed health checks or had a criminal record for anything other than minor offences. Contacts in the police enabled her to weed out unsuitable prospects and also alerted her to any attention from the authorities.

Clients who were violent towards her employees, unless it was consensual and paid for, were immediately banned, with a threat of exposure should they think of talking. In two cases that was insufficiently persuasive and she was forced to take more permanent measures. For one, a devotee of rubber amongst other things, she made an uncharacteristic house call to his fifth floor flat. A dose of Rohypnol in his brandy rendered the offender unconscious, and it was easy to tip him off his balcony. The rubber suit that encased her meant that she left no traces detectable by current forensic techniques, and she took his personal appointments diary in case her name appeared in it. A sheaf of vilely indecent photos of children, left in his bedroom, acted as a smokescreen, diverting attention away from his usual practices. The other offender was found near a gay meeting place on Hampstead Heath, a plastic bag over his head and residues of GHB in his system. The coroner recorded a verdict of accidental death, resulting from a sex game that went wrong.

Chapter Nine

London 2007

MARNIE'S FINANCIAL ASSETS INCREASED, while her physical assets began to decline slightly, requiring higher maintenance. She had other, younger, women to cater for the needs of her clients, but she still looked good, and there were a few, who preferred an older woman, that she continued to service herself. While she didn't mind the physical activity – she was a professional, after all – she still had flashbacks, just before she fell asleep, of the months of abuse by rough and sweaty men in the Glasgow brothel where she was kept when she first came to the UK. Most of the time her memories were a blur and kept under control, as were those of her years on the streets. But sometimes they came back with terrifying clarity and she reached for the sleeping tablets beside her bed, knowing that without chemical help she wouldn't sleep that night.

Her goal was still revenge on the people who had trafficked and abused her, particularly Callum Mackintosh, who had owned the brothel. She paid several private investigators to make discreet enquiries, and when one of them reported that an expatriate Scot was running exclusive sex parties in the Knightsbridge area it sparked her interest. There must be several Scotsmen involved in that type of work, she thought, and the name didn't match that of her target. Still, it was worth checking out.

Unsurprisingly, one of her clients, a prominent lawyer with a penchant for cocaine, whips and leather, appeared on the list of guests that the PI had provided. It was easy to get him to take her to the next party on the pretext that she was looking for business opportunities. A limousine picked the two of them up outside Harrods, and they were blindfolded as soon as they got in the car. Twenty minutes of aimless driving later, they were dropped off in an underground car park and a lift whisked them speedily up to the fifth floor.

The blindfolds were left on until they had been shepherded into a capacious flat. A doorman took their coats and mobile phones, ensuring that they were switched off. The entrance fee, two hundred pounds, was strictly cash, and the doorman explained that entertainment and other services would be chargeable separately. The glass of champagne that he proffered was free.

The large flat in which she found herself was sumptuously furnished. Couches, occupied by barely dressed men and women, were arranged around the walls, and the lighting was subdued, pinks and reds predominating. The windows were heavily curtained, and the air was thick with cigar smoke and expensive perfume. In a corner, a table laden with champagne and expensive spirits served as a bar, attended by a young woman wearing only lingerie. The room resembled nothing so much as Victorian illustrations of Turkish harems, although with more flesh on show.

Marnie had just taken her drink when she spotted a man on the other side of the room, his face partly hidden by a cloud of cigar smoke. It was him. Mackintosh. He looked slightly different. He now sported a beard, his face had changed somewhat, and his formerly flat stomach had turned into a pot belly, but she would recognise him anywhere. His cunning, lascivious eyes and predatory smile were imprinted on her mind and still haunted her dreams. She shivered, and her hand gripped the champagne glass so tightly she nearly snapped the stem, but outwardly she remained calm. She would talk to him later, knowing that he wouldn't recognise her. She looked and sounded completely different now she had changed her appearance and lost her Polish accent. She no longer resembled the cringing, skinny teenager he had abused so many years ago, along with dozens of other girls. In any event, Mackintosh was busy with a couple of nearly naked girls who couldn't have been much older than fourteen.

For the next half hour Marnie wandered around the room, sipping at her champagne. A few people offered her drugs or asked her why she wasn't participating. She simply said she was there 'on business', which seemed to suffice.

The tiny camera in the brooch on her lapel recorded a barely imaginable range of sexual activity, much of it illegal. As well as a full-on orgy in the main room, involving boys and girls as well as adults, couples would disappear into side bedrooms from time to time. Cocaine and cannabis were widely used, and there were pills of various types on offer for those who wanted them. Nearly all the clients were white males, aged from thirty to their late sixties. They were obviously wealthy, judging by their expensive clothes and the cost of entry, and more than well-fed. Most had a predatory manner, taking what they wanted from the entertainment available as if by right, using and discarding people as they pleased.

Marnie's stomach turned over. For all the affluence of the surroundings, it was really no different from the filthy knocking-shop she had been forced to work in when she first came to the UK as a naïve teenager, deceived by promises of work in a hotel. The looks of haunted desperation in the eyes of the youngsters were just the same as those in her own eyes, and the eyes of her fellow victims, in Glasgow. If it wasn't for her long-term goal, she would have killed Mackintosh on the spot and published the film on the internet that night.

She turned to her escort.

'Who's that man over there, with the two girls? I think I recognise him.'

'That's Kelvin Campbell,' he replied. 'He's a serious player, they say, but he keeps quiet about it.'

'Then introduce me to him.'

'If you insist. But I warn you. He's dangerous.'

'So am I. So do as I ask.'

Reluctantly, her escort complied.

'Mr Campbell,' she said, shaking the man's hand and suppressing the urge to vomit. 'My name is Marnie Draycott. I have a business proposition for you. I've heard that you are in the logistics business. My contacts could be useful to you, and I think we can work together to our mutual advantage.' She guessed that he would still be involved in illegal imports of some kind, be they drugs or people.

Campbell's tone was guarded. Marnie realised he would suspect a trap. After all, she could be an undercover cop. But she also knew that the idea of profit would appeal and he would be willing to take it a little further.

'I don't know you or what you do. But I'm interested.' Campbell's voice was refined, but there was a hint of Glasgow underneath. 'Give the doorman your details and the names of three people who can vouch for you. If I'm satisfied, we'll have lunch next week. If not, well, perhaps it wasn't wise for you to come here.'

Marnie knew that three of her clients would say what they were told to, on pain of exposure if they didn't. She left their names at the door along with her card, and would brief them as soon as she got her phone back.

The doorman replaced her blindfold, and she was driven back to the spot outside Harrods where she had been picked up. An MP, a showbiz celebrity who was involved in supplying dozens of his colleagues with coke, and a civil servant high up in the Home Office should be sufficient to establish her bona fides. She made the calls and returned to her flat, satisfied with the evening's work and pleased that she had been able to control her emotions. After all, she had just encountered the man she loathed more than anyone else on earth.

Chapter Ten

Mexton 2019 | Thursday 3rd October

'You're not, are you?' Cathy Merritt, a motherly DC in the Child Protection Unit, looked at Mel with excitement as she came out of the toilet cubicle.

'Chance would be a fine thing,' joked Mel, wiping a thread of vomit from her chin. 'The only male in my life at the moment is a tortoise, and I can't quite see it happening with him.'

'But you have admirers, surely,' Cathy replied.

'Well there's a new DS who can't keep his eyes off my tits, if that's who you mean.'

'Oh, come on. Half the women in the station, and even some of the men, know that Tom Ferris fancies you.'

'Yeah. Tom's nice. But, to set the record straight, I had a tuna salad last night and I think the fish must have been off. Hence the throwing up. Sorry to disappoint you. And anyway, it's far too soon to think about kids.'

'Well, don't leave it too late. I did and now I'm working on behalf of children all the time. Anyway, give me a ring when you're feeling better and we'll go for a drink. It would be good to catch up.'

'I'll look forward to it, Cathy. But now I've got to deliver a report at the morning briefing. See you.'

Mel combed her hair, checked her blouse for stains and headed for the incident room.

Mel and Martin summarised their visit to Marnie Draycott at the start of the morning briefing, Mel suppressing the feeling of nausea when it was her turn to speak. She had just described the contents of the empty video boxes when her phone vibrated. She glanced at the screen.

'Sorry, guv. It's Ellen Wilkins. Can I take it?'

Fiona nodded, reluctantly.

'Mrs Wilkins? How can I help you? You've had what? OK. Don't touch it. We'll get someone to you as soon as we can.'

The team realised that something serious had happened.

'Someone's sent Ellen Wilkins a threatening note. It's bloodstained and says, "You have twenty-four hours to hand it over. Details will follow."'

'You'd better get over there,' said Fiona. 'We'll resume the briefing this afternoon. Report back to me as soon as you get back.'

'Yes, guv.'

As Fiona was returning to her office she spotted Jessop poking around in the pile of exhibits retrieved by Mel and Martin from the Blackberry Way house.

'What are you doing with those?' she called.

'I thought I'd have a look through the laptop, guv. See if I can find anything useful.'

He seemed a little confused, not quite there, and the odour of mints surrounded him like a cloud of Scottish midges. Fiona raised her eyes to the heavens.

'Are you familiar with the acronym FUBAR?'

'Yes, guv. Fucked Up Beyond All Recovery.'

'Exactly. And that's what can happen when someone unqualified fiddles with a suspect's IT. We've had several instances of a drug dealer's phone wiping itself when the wrong person tried to access it. Only the experts can handle seized phones, laptops tablets and whatever. So please leave it alone.'

'Sorry. I forgot. Just trying to do something useful.'

'I appreciate that. Look, it's early days so spend some time reviewing the files and talking to your colleagues. See if a fresh pair of eyes can come up with something. OK?'

'Yes, guv. I'll just get a coffee.'

Jessop sauntered over to machine, hiding the expression of fury on his face.

Mel arrived at Ellen's flat to find her taping a notice to her front door. It read, 'I don't know what you want and I don't have it. So piss off.'

She followed Ellen into the kitchen, putting on nitrile gloves. She eased the bloody piece of paper into an evidence bag and viewed it through the plastic.

'Have you any idea what this note refers to, Ellen?'

'None at all. George never gave me anything to look after and only came here a few times. He could have hidden something, I suppose, but the flat's not that big. You couldn't hide much, and he was never alone here for long.'

'Did he have a key?'

'I didn't give him one. But the spare set disappeared once. He could have taken it, I suppose.'

'I'll arrange for a search team to come and sweep the place, if you've no objections. It might be wise for you to stay with your daughter for a few days until we can get to the bottom of this.'

'I'm not running scared. And her kids drive me mad after a few hours. Video gaming and watching rubbish TV all the time.'

'Typical young kids, then,' smiled Mel. 'Well, we can't force you. But we'll probably give you an Osman warning.'

'A what? That bloke on *Pointless*?'

'It's a notice from us warning you of a potential threat of death or serious harm. You don't have to do anything, but it covers us if anything happens.'

'That's cheerful. Well, I might go away for a bit, but I'll wait till your lot have searched the place.'

'Before I go, I need to ask you a couple more questions. As far as you know, did George own a firearm?'

'Certainly not. I wouldn't have one in the house. I saw what happens when people get shot when I worked at the hospital. Why do you ask?'

'I'm sorry, I can't say. Did he ever use drugs?'

Ellen thought for a moment.

'I think he used to take speed when he was a teenager. He used to boast about staying up all night at raves. He probably smoked weed as well – most of his mates did. But he'd settled down when I knew him – he was working in the garage by then and took his job seriously. I never saw him use stuff. Do you think he was mixed up in something?'

'Again, I can't say. But I think we'll bring a sniffer dog along, just in case.'

'Be my guest. But the idea of him using my flat to store drugs for someone is crazy.'

'OK. It'll probably be tomorrow morning before we can get a team here. I've still got a set of your keys so you can go to your daughter's – which I strongly advise. We'll try not to make a mess.'

Mel looked back at Ellen's front door as she left. She admired the woman's spirit but wished she would take her advice. Ellen was clearly tough. But did she not realise how dangerous these people could be?

Chapter Eleven

ONCE MEL HAD GONE, Ellen made herself a cup of tea and racked her brains. What had that bastard George got her into? Tough as she knew she seemed on the outside, she had been full of dread ever since George's head had turned up. This kind of thing happened to characters in gangster films set in London or LA, not to retired paramedics in unglamorous English towns. In the dark, sleepless hours just before dawn she feared for her life and for the safety of her children and grandchildren. And it was all George's fault. What on earth could he have hidden? And where?

After finishing her drink she paced around the flat, looking for possible hiding places, although she knew the police would be better at searching than she was. The children's rooms were virtually empty, apart from a few boxes of books and other oddments. There were still posters of rock stars and actors on the walls. She couldn't bear to clear the rooms out, and she had stayed in the flat, which was larger than she needed, for sentimental reasons. It was more than she could really afford to pay in rent, but it was where her children had grown up away from George's influence, so she didn't want to leave.

She noticed a poster peeling away from the wall in Jenny's old room. The tape holding it had yellowed and given up the fight against gravity. That was odd, she thought. The kids were never allowed to use tape on the walls – they had to use Blu-Tak to hold up their pictures. Carefully she peeled the remaining section of tape from the wall, and as the poster tumbled forwards she noticed a small, flat, key stuck to the back of it. The key resembled one from the garage at the house she used to share with George. But why would he keep an old garage key? Then she remembered. He used to rent a garage in town for storing odds and ends. It must be for that. But why would he hide it?

Encouraged by her find, she continued her search. There was nothing in the obvious places like cupboards, under the sink or in the toilet cistern. The floors were laminated and hadn't been disturbed, and there was no loft or cellar. She took a screwdriver from a kitchen drawer and tackled the bath panel, noticing that the slots in the screw heads seemed to be slightly damaged. Surely that was too obvious? She had read of stolen goods, drugs and even bodies being stored behind bath panels. Nevertheless, she undid the screws and pulled the panel away. Using a torch, she inspected the space minutely. Nothing. A few spiders' webs, and what looked like mouse droppings, were all she could see.

She was about to put the panel back when she noticed that the floorboard around the waste pipe didn't fit properly. Either the plumber had been sloppy or there was something there. She levered the short section of board up with the screwdriver and spotted the corner of a plastic bag, just visible behind the pipe. Its weight surprised her when she eased it out of the space, and she was shocked to find it contained a small revolver and half a dozen cartridges.

Trembling, she carried the bag to the kitchen table and looked at it with a kind of horrified fascination. Was it loaded? Could it go off accidentally? Not wanting to put her own fingerprints on the weapon, she slipped on a pair of rubber gloves and cautiously opened the bag. She knew nothing about firearms, apart from what she had seen on TV crime dramas, but she could see the copper noses of the bullets in the gun's cylinder. So it was loaded. She didn't know if there was a safety catch or whether it was ready to fire and realised she should call the police immediately to make it safe. Apart from anything else, she knew it was illegal to possess a handgun. But it occurred to her that, if she was in danger, she could use it to threaten any intruder – not that she planned to fire it, of course. She'd have to think about that.

Two miles away, in a nondescript office above an estate agent's, three men were discussing Ellen Wilkins. One, wearing an elegant suit, was tall and thin. The other two, in tracksuits and hoodies, were short and stocky, with solid muscles built up in the prison gym. One had a tattoo of a pit bull on his neck. The other had a shaved head. Their masculine body spray made the room reek. The tattooed ex-con paced around the room.

'She must know where the stuff is. And the shooter, if George kept it. When he talked, he said it was in the flat but didn't say where. We can force her to tell us. She's not as tough as he was. If she knows, we'll get it out of her.'

The tall man looked thoughtful and then spoke.

'Send her another message. Give her a drop-off point and

a time. If she doesn't co-operate we'll grab her and have a serious chat.'

'You'd enjoy that, wouldn't you,' the shaven-headed man chipped in. 'You got off on torturing George and taking his head off when he'd croaked.'

'Everyone needs a hobby – and mine's a useful one,' he replied, smiling slightly. 'There's a grit bin at the back of the Tesco car park, by the petrol station. It's not covered by cameras. Tell her to drop it there at midnight. Alone.'

'Yeah, but I went past her flat. There's a notice on the door. She claims she doesn't have it and doesn't know anything about it.'

'She's lying. George said it was in the flat. After what I did to him, he wouldn't have lied. I'll leave you to it.'

The tall man stepped briskly out of the room, leaving the others to write and deliver the second note.

Chapter Twelve

ELLEN WAS PACING up and down her living room and didn't notice the stocky, shaven-headed man in the hi-vis jacket, with 'Water' printed on it, pushing a note through her door. She couldn't decide whether to hand the revolver and key over to the police, to give them to whoever was persecuting her, or to hang on to them. In the end she compromised. She would leave the key on the kitchen table with a note for the search team and keep the gun. She didn't fancy being at home while the police turned it over. She would go to Jenny's for the night and return the following day, after the search was completed.

When she found the note on her doormat, she froze and grabbed her phone.

Mel ran towards Fiona's open office door. 'Boss! Ellen's on the phone. They've sent another note.' She put her phone on speaker and asked Ellen to repeat what she had told her.

'They've told me to put it in a car park grit bin at

midnight. I don't know what "it" is. I've been through the place and all I've found is a key hidden behind a poster. They said not to call you and to go alone. What should I do?'

'Can you meet us at your daughter's, Ellen?' called Fiona. 'Give us a couple of hours. We'll get someone over there in advance to check that the place isn't being watched. Let Mel have the details of where you're meant to leave whatever it is.'

While Ellen packed a few items to take to Jenny's, Fiona called the team together and described the message Ellen had received. A note of excitement coloured her voice.

'It's short notice but we can set up a stakeout.'

'You're not expecting Ellen to go, are you, guv?' a worried Jack queried.

'Of course not, Jack. We need a volunteer to take her place. Any offers?'

'Well, as I'm the only one here who isn't obviously male and muscular, apart from you, ma'am, it'd better be me,' said Mel.

Jessop looked sceptical.

'I'm about the same height as Ellen,' Mel continued. 'I can wear her coat and mimic the way she walks. I'm hoping the villains don't know her very well so it won't be a problem.'

'Thanks Mel. These are nasty people, so be careful. I'll ask the Chief Super to authorise a firearms team. We'll arrive there around half ten. And you must wear a vest. The supermarket shuts at ten, but the garage remains open and unstaffed all night. I'll talk to the manager and make sure the garage staff are all off the premises by eleven. Shelf stackers in the main store can stay at the back of the shop from then onwards, without their mobile phones. We don't want anyone putting what we're doing on social media. A couple of us can wait in the petrol station kiosk, and we'll have people sweeping the car park, picking up litter and moving trolleys about. Hi-vis jackets are wonderful camouflage.'

'What if someone wants to buy fuel?' asked Jessop.

'We'll spray a bit of petrol on the ground and put up a sign saying it's closed because of a leak. One of us can be putting sand down to soak it up.'

'Is that wise? We don't want an AFO firing a weapon inside a cloud of petrol. The flash would set it off and blow the whole place up.'

'There won't be much. Just enough to provide a smell. And we'll keep any firearms well away from the spill.'

'Let's hope the villains do the same,' muttered Jack. Fiona ignored him.

By quarter past eleven the team was in place, with Mel waiting in an unmarked car a couple of hundred yards away but in sight of her colleagues. One of the store's home delivery vans had been commandeered for use as a control centre, and the tension was building, as was the smell of sweat and stale farts.

At ten to twelve Mel climbed out the car and approached the store from the direction of Ellen's flat. In a plastic carrier bag she carried a shoe box containing an electronic tracker, the assumption being that whatever the villains wanted would be small enough to carry but big enough to have some value. Stooping slightly, she walked through the car park, dropped the bag in the grit bin and returned the way she came. There were no suspicious vehicles in the area, and apart from under-cover police officers, there was no-one in the car park.

'All units stand by.' Fiona's voice crackled over the Airwave system.

Nothing happened.

By ten to one the team was beginning to wonder whether this was all a waste of time. Then two things happened at once. A stocky figure on a mountain bike three sizes too small for him shot across the car park, grabbed the package from the bin and headed towards an underpass that led to a housing estate. Simultaneously, a container lorry pulled onto the forecourt, the driver seemingly oblivious to the police operation. Fiona cursed. The vehicle obscured the team's view of the fleeing cyclist and also blocked the exit, leaving the police unable to follow their quarry. By the time the lorry had been moved there was no hope of salvaging the situation.

A disconsolate caravan of police headed back to the station, some annoyed at the waste of effort but others just glad of the overtime. The package was tracked and retrieved from a garden in the housing estate, ripped open and discarded. Fiona was both mortified and furious. She had seen Jessop's sneering expression and heard him mutter, 'That's not how we do things in the Met.' She went home to write up her report, feeling sick to her stomach. She'd screwed up. Wasted time and resources, achieving absolutely nothing. And where the hell had that lorry come from? The store had promised that all deliveries would be postponed until the morning. Not only did she fear the superintendent's wrath, she was also desperately worried for Ellen Wilkins's safety. If Ellen was harmed as a result of her action she wouldn't be able to forgive herself.

'So the stupid cow went to the filth,' said the tall man. 'That won't do. It really won't. We're going to have to teach her a lesson. Bring her to me tomorrow. We'll have that chat.'

Chapter Thirteen

London 2007

MARNIE'S LUNCH with Campbell was a guarded affair. The participants circled around each other like boxers at the start of a fight, cautious about giving away too much information. Neither of them paid much attention to the food and both drank only water. Preliminaries, and lunch, over, Marnie opened the negotiations by explaining that she had contacts in several customs posts at North Sea ports. They were prepared to overlook any problems with documentation for imported goods arriving from elsewhere in the EU, ensuring they cleared the ports without undue attention or inspection.

For his part, Campbell admitted that there were certain shipments he would prefer not to be examined by customs, and that any assistance with that would be most welcome. While the nature of such imports was not discussed, Marnie had a pretty good idea what they involved. By the end of the meeting it was agreed that Campbell would notify Marnie of a shipment he would like protected and she would arrange it.

A commission on its value was agreed, and the two conspirators left, each satisfied in part but still suspicious of the other.

———

Four days later, Marnie met Campbell again. He handed her an envelope of notes, which she pushed back to him.

'There was nothing illegal in that shipment. So you don't owe me commission.'

'True, but how did you know?'

'It's what I would have done in your place. It could have been a trap. Now that we've tested each other, can we talk business?'

Barriers lowered, at least partly, Marnie and Campbell spent the afternoon discussing how they could work together. Campbell had come up with the idea of using a specialist freighting company, whose main business was the transport of delicate electronic equipment and similar, to move certain other goods into the country. For her part, Marnie said she was building up a network of officials at the ports who, because of bribery or blackmail, would co-operate in letting shipments through without official scrutiny. Clients of her escort agency, in various government agencies, had been persuaded to provide the names of vulnerable people at the ports, and it had proved easy to compromise them.

'Also,' Marnie explained, 'I have a number of police officers under my control. They're not at the docks, but they could be useful for any inland activities.'

'Well, I am looking to diversify,' replied Campbell. 'Take over more of the supply chain, as it were. Let's see how things work out with the current proposals and we can talk again.'

———

For six months, the arrangements between the two ran smoothly. None of Campbell's illicit shipments was intercepted, although one was nearly discovered by an over-zealous customs officer who Marnie dealt with. Marnie received the agreed commission from Campbell, although she couldn't be sure she was being paid what she was entitled to. That didn't matter, as the aim was to get closer to Campbell, which was working extremely well. Then Campbell invited her down to his place in the country.

'Have you ever shot?' Campbell asked Marnie, as he packed a supply of cartridges into his jacket pocket and picked up a gleaming twelve-bore shotgun. 'It's great fun.'

'I can't say I have,' replied Marnie, thinking of the killing methods she had used in the past. Shooting hadn't been one of them, as guns were hard to get hold of and also noisy. 'Perhaps you'll show me.'

The two of them spent the morning blasting away at pigeons on Campbell's estate, with varying success. Marnie was pleasantly surprised to find that she enjoyed the feel of the shotgun in her hands, the kick against her shoulder and the smell of the smoke. She became quite proficient with the weapon, hitting her chosen target more often than not. Her choice wasn't always the unfortunate wildlife. She deliberately missed on occasions, not wanting to upstage Campbell, who clearly regarded himself as a superior marksman. Male egos could be so fragile, she thought.

After lunch they got down to business.

'Just down the road,' began Campbell, 'is Mexton, a medium-sized town with an undeveloped market for my merchandise. It has a notorious sink estate, unemployment is rising, yet at the other end of the scale the more affluent residents have money to spend on recreations that would be frowned on by the authorities. Both are potentially untapped markets. If you have any contacts in the local police, they could be useful and we can work together. If not, we can keep things as they are.'

Marnie put her coffee cup down with uncharacteristic force.

'Let's cut the mealy-mouthed language. You're importing drugs, and you must think I'm stupid if you thought I wouldn't realise it from the outset. I've no problem with that. People should be free to use whatever they want. You may be running whores as well. Again, no problem. I do have people in the police who will do what I tell them, but if we're going to work together, we have to be frank with each other.' She deliberately didn't use the word honest.

Campbell smiled. 'So I didn't underestimate you. I made some enquiries. I have friends in Glasgow, one of whom recognised your photo despite your efforts to change your appearance. He's clever like that. It seems you were on the game for a few years, using the name Candy Lush. When your pimp was stabbed to death, possibly by yourself, you disappeared from Scotland and changed your name to Marnie Draycott.

'You set up an escort agency in London, building up an impressive list of important clients. Some of them are under your control. By blackmailing them you built up your network of contacts. One of your clients, a barrister with a penchant for violence towards women, fell off his balcony in mysterious circumstances. Another ended up dead in a gay cruising spot, despite the fact that he was vigorously hetero. You should know that, following our first meeting, I sent one of my colleagues along to pose as a client. He enjoyed himself – at my expense – but reported nothing untoward. So, I know more about you than you realised. What do you know about me?'

Marnie, relieved that Campbell didn't recognise her as one of his former victims, was anxious not to give too much away. She had to maintain the pretence that her only interest in him was business. But she also had to convince him she was sufficiently connected to be trusted.

'I, too, still have friends in Glasgow. They tell me you were known as Mackintosh there and left Scotland, in something of a hurry, after your business partner committed suicide and your wife disappeared. I believe you dabbled in drugs and girls, but my pimp never mentioned you. Down south you set up a business running sex parties and providing young flesh for very particular clients. The drugs came along as a sideline and became a growing interest – they're more portable and can't go to the police. You have something of a reputation for, shall we say, firm business methods. People don't cross you. Is that enough?'

'Well, it looks like we're in business. I'll open some champagne, shall I? Oh, and you were right about my business methods. Cross me and I'll kill you.'

Marnie looked coolly back at him.

'Yes, we're in business. And it's mutual.'

Chapter Fourteen

Harwich 2007

Mike Apsley regarded his junior colleague, Dave Colton, across the desk in the customs office. There was something not quite right about him. For a start, his car was a little bit flashier than his pay grade would normally permit. OK, Dave could have got the necessary funds quite legitimately. Or he could have taken out a cheap car loan. The vehicle was not that ostentatious, after all, but it still niggled Mike. He was alert to these things. Then there was his colleague's eagerness to deal with shipments of technology for a company called Maldobourne, whatever time of day or night they came into port. Again, there could be a perfectly reasonable explanation. Perhaps Dave was trying to develop specialist knowledge of that type of goods, in which case it was useful. But the shipments always cleared quickly, and if Dave ever did inspect them, he only took a few minutes to do so.

Mike resolved to take a look at the next Maldobourne shipment himself, and when one was due, he tackled Dave.

'I think we'll do a random inspection on this one, Dave. Take a good look at it.'

Dave looked nervous.

'Why d'you want to do that?'

'No particular reason. I like to be unpredictable sometimes.'

'But I've always looked after these. It's my speciality, if you like.'

'Yes, but I've noticed you don't pay them much attention.'

'What are you suggesting?'

'Nothing. Nothing at all. But they could be concealing all sorts of stuff in loads like this, and we've never checked them thoroughly. The ferry's due in tomorrow morning, so we'll take a look as soon as the truck comes off it.'

'I don't think that's a good idea, Mike. I really don't.'

Dave said nothing more. He picked up his hi-vis jacket and left the office, slamming the door behind him, leaving Mike perplexed and even more suspicious.

When Mike arrived for work the following morning, he found an envelope in his pigeon hole. It contained two items: a photograph and a note. The colour photograph clearly showed his locker with the door partly open. Visible inside were a packet of brownish powder, a flick knife and a hand-gun. The note was brief and to the point. 'Back off. Go home sick. No more questions.'

It also featured his address, the addresses of his children at university and the name of his mother's care home. Mike dashed to his locker and wrenched the door open, fearful of what he would find. Instead of the illegal items featured in the photograph it contained a piece of card with one word printed on it. 'Anytime.'

Mike stumbled back to his desk, his legs barely able to support him. He knew he should report his suspicions and hand over the notes and the photo to his senior officer. But he realised that doing so would put his career and family at risk. If they could plant contraband in his locker, in a secure area, what could they do to his relatives out there in the community? Much as he hated himself for doing so, Mike decided to turn a blind eye. Perhaps he could get a transfer to Felixstowe. It would mean a longer journey to work but it would be worth it. And perhaps, in time, he would be able to look at himself in the mirror again.

Chapter Fifteen

Mexton 2019 | Friday 4th October

BY THREE O'CLOCK, the search team had left Ellen's flat with nothing to show for their efforts. Ellen returned half an hour later and spent two hours putting things to rights. She was nervous about being home. What would the villains do next? There was no police presence outside. Should she really go away for a while? And she still didn't know what to do with the gun. Just to be on the safe side, she took the revolver from her handbag and put it in her apron pocket.

She was about to pour herself a sherry when two men in energy company jackets rang her doorbell. Ellen's heart jumped. She opened the door a couple of inches but kept the chain in place.

'Can we come in, love? We've had reports of a gas leak.'

'No, you haven't. I'm not stupid. Piss off. I don't know what you want and I've got nothing of George's.' She slammed the door in their faces and looked for her phone. She should ring Mel or dial 999.

The two thugs were nonplussed. That wasn't how it was supposed to work. Deciding that the subtle approach had failed, they started kicking at the door to no avail until one of them broke it down with a shoulder charge. They found Ellen standing in the lounge with a furious expression on her face, brandishing the revolver.

'That's a dangerous toy for an old lady,' one of them sneered, his shaven head glistening with sweat. 'You'd better give it over, love, before you get hurt.'

'Will you two clowns just sod off? I don't know what you want. I've told you.'

'Well, George left it with you. He said so. We're gonna take you to someone who'll jog your memory. And teach you a lesson for going to the filth.'

'Over my dead body. Get out or I'll shoot you.'

The two men couldn't tell whether Ellen was serious or not. On the one hand, she could barely keep the weapon still and didn't seem to know how to aim it. On the other hand, she was angry and determined. As they approached her, Ellen retreated. She kept the gun pointed at them but out of their reach.

'You wouldn't. You know you wouldn't, you stupid cow,' the shaven man grinned.

His grin turned to shock when Ellen backed into the coffee table and, falling backwards, accidentally pulled the trigger. A .38 bullet slammed into his shoulder, making him stumble. A second later the pain kicked in. He screamed and backed off, his colleague turning white. With Ellen still holding the revolver, and clearly prepared to use it, the two of them fled the house spewing a stream of profanity and threats behind them.

Ellen sat on the sofa trembling. The adrenaline that had kept her going faded away, leaving nausea and fear behind. She knew she would have to call the police. The neighbours might have heard the shot and phoned them already, although there were no blue lights heading up the road. But would she be arrested for having the gun? And she was now in real fear for her life.

She had to find some reason for having the weapon that wouldn't get her sent to prison. If she said she found it in the house, why would they believe her when the search team had been over it only a few hours ago? They were bound to have looked behind the bath panel. And she couldn't claim she'd taken it from her attackers. But what about the sofa she was sitting on? The searchers hadn't actually ripped anything apart, so maybe they hadn't looked there. She turned the sofa on its back and, to her relief, saw that the canvas stretched across the base was intact and covered by a layer of dust. Using a sharp paring knife, she cut a slit in the canvas and shoved the gun and bag of cartridges inside. Then she pulled them out again, ensuring that some of the stuffing was stuck to the weapon.

Within four minutes of her dialling 999 a police car came howling down the road and parked outside.

'Can you tell DC Cotton what's happened?' Ellen asked the uniformed PC who sat with her in the living room. 'She needs to know. And I need to talk to her.'

'Will do,' he replied. 'But, as an offence appears to have been committed, you need to come down to the station.'

Sitting in the interview room, Mel recited the caution, started the recording and asked Ellen to describe the afternoon's events.

'I was cleaning up after your lot searched the place when I found the gun.'

'Where was it? The search team should have found it.'

'In the bottom of the sofa.'

'What made you look there?'

'I heard a thump when I tipped it back to clean underneath. I could feel a lump in there so I got a knife and cut the cloth. I found the gun. There were bullets in a plastic bag, too. George must have come into the flat while I was out and hidden them there. I was so scared.'

Mel wasn't sure she believed that Ellen was scared. She looked as though she could take most things in her stride.

'Go on, Ellen. What happened then?'

'I pulled it out and was about to call you. Then the door crashed open. Two blokes charged in and I backed away. As I fell over the coffee table the thing went off. One bloke screamed and grabbed his shoulder. They both cleared off after that. I didn't mean to shoot him, honest. I didn't even know it was loaded. I didn't get the chance to phone you. Am I in trouble?'

'Well,' said Mel, slowly. 'If it all happened as you said, and you didn't mean to pull the trigger, I'm sure it would be considered an accident rather than deliberate wounding. Technically you were in possession of a prohibited weapon, but as you'd only just found it, I shouldn't think the CPS would consider prosecuting you. But I really think you should find somewhere else to stay until this is sorted out.

'We'll contact the local hospitals to see if anyone's come in to A&E with a gunshot wound. That should help us to track down who attacked you. There's some mug shots to go through in the meantime, and if you can't identify anyone, I'd like you to work with an e-fit artist to draw up pictures of what the offenders looked like.'

Ellen agreed, and Mel brought her a laptop displaying photographs of men convicted of violent crimes. They made grim viewing, but Ellen was able to pick out half a dozen possibles.

'I only saw them for a few seconds,' she said, 'and I was falling over the table as well.'

'Never mind. You've done really well,' Mel reassured her. 'Now, I'll type up your statement for you to sign and we'll drive you back to your daughter's, if that's OK. You can't go back to the flat until forensics have finished, I'm afraid.'

Mel had a niggling feeling that Ellen hadn't given her the full story. But she had obviously had a narrow escape, so Mel didn't feel inclined to pursue the matter.

Chapter Sixteen

Saturday 5th October

FIONA, still haunted by the memory of the failed stakeout, began the morning briefing with a still from CCTV footage provided by the hospital. It showed a thick-set man, with blood on his shoulder and his left arm in a makeshift sling, approaching the A&E department.

'We believe this individual is one of the men who attacked Ellen Wilkins yesterday. He had a gunshot wound to his shoulder. Apparently, he was very lucky. The bullet just grazed the bone – an inch or two lower and he would have been without the use of his arm for months, if not permanently. They treated him and were going to admit him for observation, but when he heard a nurse answering a phone call from Jack he did a runner. He gave his name as Jason Bourne, but we've matched this image up with the faces Ellen picked out, and we know who he is. Michael Ramsey. Armed robber, former pimp and general pain in the neck. Just got out after serving four years of an eight-year sentence for conspiracy to rob a jeweller's. He was convicted of the same offence as Dwight Marlow, who's one of the other faces Ellen chose. So it looks like they're working together.'

'What's the connection with George Wilkins, guv?' asked Mel.

'There's a link through Osbourne. They worked for him as bouncers at his club before they were arrested. There were rumours that he planned a number of robberies that the other two carried out. Nothing was proved, though.'

'Why don't we pull this Osbourne bloke in? Put some pressure on him. That's how we do it in the Met.'

'Well this isn't the Met, DS Jessop,' Fiona snapped. 'We like to have some evidence before we arrest people. Understand?'

'Yes…ma'am,' Jessop replied, leaving the 'ma'am' so late it implied disrespect rather than courtesy.

'George was known for his driving skills. Could he have been the getaway driver?' Mel continued.

'Maybe, but we've no evidence, and the car they used was found burnt out after the raid. None of the jewellery was recovered, so maybe that's what they were looking for. Also, a handgun was used in the raid, and one of them fired it into the ceiling of the shop to frighten the owner. No-one was hurt, but we were able to recover the bullet. The revolver Ellen fired is in the lab at the moment, and they are looking for a match. If it is the same weapon, that's something else they might want back.'

'How about Ellen's account of the shooting? Do we believe her?' asked Martin.

'I don't think she intended to shoot anyone,' replied Mel. 'I'm not so sure about how she came by the gun, though. The story about finding it in the sofa seemed a little odd, but I suppose it's possible. Funny she never noticed it before, though. The search team could have missed it, I guess. I don't see her as being a part of the robbery team, for all her toughness.'

'OK. We'll let that go for the moment,' said Fiona. 'We've circulated Marlow's and Ramsey's descriptions and photos. They've gone to ground, but the Super is considering whether to put out a public appeal for sightings. We've got nothing on George's phone. It was switched off on Sunday night, when Marnie said he was at the Maldon Club. No-one at the club admitted seeing him there. His car wasn't picked up by ANPR cameras after Saturday night. IT found nothing useful on his laptop either, just a load of online betting sites.'

'Opium for the morons,' someone paraphrased, but Fiona couldn't see who.

'For the moment, it might be worth having an informal chat with Osbourne. See how he reacts when we ask him whether he knew the two of them. Find out when he last saw George. One other thing. The white powder in the video cases found at George's place was high-purity cocaine. We could ask for an analysis of George's hair, to find out if he was a regular user, but I'm not sure the budget will stretch to that. If it looks like being relevant, I'll insist.'

'How about me?' Jessop asked.

'I'd like you to review the jewel robbery. See if you can find a link with George or Osbourne. Was anyone else involved? Bring your superior detective skills to bear.'

'Yes, ma'am,' he replied, apparently oblivious to Fiona's sarcasm.

Fiona sent Jack and Mel to interview Osbourne and then wrote up the murder book. She needed to find a more meaningful role for DS Jessop. So far he had been a spare wheel, contributing mainly smirks, scowls and sarcastic remarks. And she didn't like the way he was always staring at Mel. Things were not going the way she had hoped, but there was still time to prove herself. As long as there were no more cock-ups.

Mel and Jack rang the polished brass bell at Osbourne's elegant mock-Georgian detached villa just after lunch time, almost expecting a butler to open the door. Instead, the man himself answered and, on seeing their warrant cards, invited them in. Tall and elegant, wearing expensive casual clothes, he looked every inch the prosperous businessman at leisure. But there was something about his eyes, and his not-quite-right accent, that hinted of a harshness beneath the veneer. Jack, with his smart suit and fiercely polished shoes, looked at home with the décor. Mel, in her off-the-peg and slightly creased trouser-suit, felt somewhat under-dressed.

'To what do I owe the pleasure?' he asked, keeping the detectives standing in the hall and refraining from offering them refreshments.

'Just a quick chat, if we may, Mr Osbourne,' said Jack, switching on the charm.

'Of course. What about?'

'George Wilkins,' replied Mel, her expression neutral but her voice steely.

'George? Well, I haven't seen him for months. He used to look after my cars back in the day, but he gave up mechanics a while ago. Heard he's living over Blackberry Way somewhere.'

'So you wouldn't know why his head turned up on his ex-wife's doorstep, then?'

A fleeting expression, which could have been a grin, flashed over Osbourne's face, almost too quickly to see. He swiftly adopted an expression of concern.

'Poor George. And his poor wife – ex-wife, I mean. No. I've no idea why such a terrible thing should happen. Why ask me?'

'Because you're a known associate. And because two of your goons appear to have been terrorising Mrs Wilkins over something they seem to think she has.'

'Now get this straight, officers.' Osbourne's expression changed to one of anger mixed with contempt. 'I do not employ "goons". I am a respectable businessman. I pay my taxes. I have no criminal record. Who are these people, anyway?'

'Two armed robbers recently released from prison,' said Jack. 'Dwight Marlow and Michael Ramsey. They used to be associates of yours before they were sent down, and they've been seen at your club, the Maldon.'

'I don't know them personally, but I seem to remember the names,' mused Osbourne, pretending to think hard. 'The club manager may have employed them as door staff once, but I would have to check the records. They certainly don't work for me now. If they are using the club I may have to consider banning them – it's a respectable establishment and I don't want criminals there.'

'So you've no idea where they might be?' Mel restrained the urge to either laugh in his face or call him an out-and-out liar.

'None at all. Now if you'll excuse me, I have a golf game booked with your Assistant Chief Constable. I'm sure he won't appreciate hearing that you've made me late. If you want to talk to me again, make an appointment and I'll call my solicitor.'

'One last thing, if I may,' said Jack. 'Do you know if George was involved with illegal drugs at all?'

'No. And if he had been, I would never let him near my cars. I despise drug users.'

Abandoning politeness, Osbourne steered the detectives to the door and slammed it behind them.

'D'you really think he's playing golf with the ACC, Sarge?' asked Mel as they returned to the car.

'No idea. Possibly not. I think they all say that. The ACC may be more politician than policeman but he does have standards.'

Chapter Seventeen

Tom Ferris's eyes lit up when Mel entered the incident room. Working with her was one of the best parts of the job. He rummaged through an untidy pile of papers on his desk, nearly knocking over a cup of coffee, and produced a notepad.

'We've got some more links between George Wilkins and Osbourne. The directors of the company that owns George's house are Osbourne and Kelvin Campbell. We think the firm's involved in money laundering, but we can't prove it. And another thing. George's brief at the MOT certificates trial was Osbourne's solicitor. It could be that Osbourne paid him to defend George, though we've no way of finding out.'

'Thanks, Tom, that's great.' Mel smiled her appreciation, and he grinned. He turned back to his computer as Mel got herself coffee and returned to her desk.

Fiona burst into the incident room, scuppering Mel's plans to get on top of a backlog of paperwork.

'Ellen Wilkins has been kidnapped. They snatched her outside her daughter's flat. Why the hell wasn't someone watching her?'

'But we asked her local nick to roster some bodies to watch her. Didn't they?' replied Tom.

'I'll phone them and give someone a bollocking. Get the troops together for a meeting in half an hour. We have to find Ellen before something really nasty happens to her – if it hasn't already happened.'

Fiona suppressed her feeling of dread, and her fear that things were fast unravelling, as she addressed the meeting.

'The locals weren't watching Ellen Wilkins because there was a burst gas main, an armed robbery and a street protest all at the same time on their patch,' she began. 'They just couldn't spare anyone.'

'Nice of them to tell us.'

'I agree, Jack, but we all know how stretched everyone is. We can have a go at them about poor communication, but that won't help Ellen now. So, we need urgent door-to-door enquiries in the street, ANPR checks on any unusual vehicles in the area and a CCTV trawl. Have we got a photo of Ellen? If not, use the one that was in the paper. Let the blasted rag be useful for a change. Show it to everyone you talk to – and take mug shots of Marlow and Ramsey as well. We know she was taken around three p.m., from a phone call between her and Jenny, so find out who was in the street at that time. Contact Royal Mail, delivery firms, bus companies. Someone must have seen something. Mel – you get round to the daughter's and talk to her. I'll leave it to you, Jack, to organise the rest while I talk to the DCI and the Super about a press appeal.'

DCI Hawkins caught up with Jessop in a corner of the canteen.

'So what do you think of your new team? Are you settling in OK?'

'May I speak frankly, sir?'

'Yes, of course. Go on.'

'I'm not impressed. Ferris is a wimp, a vegetarian for God's sake. Cotton is hot but up herself, Vaughan is past it and Rowse is yawning half the time. As for Gale, she hasn't much of a clue. I was used to much better coppers in the Met.'

Hawkins was taken aback by Jessop's bluntness.

'Well, this isn't London, and all these officers have performed excellently, in their own ways, in the past. I wouldn't be too quick to criticise, if I were you. It won't make you any friends.'

'With respect, sir, I'm here to catch villains, not make friends.'

'That's fine, but try not to rock the boat.'

'Yes, sir.'

As Hawkins got up from the table they had shared, he didn't see Jessop take a surreptitious swig from a water bottle. He walked back to his office, considering whether Jessop would ever fit in. Still, this attachment was only temporary, until the Wilkins case was concluded. He would look for a better role for Jessop afterwards.

Chapter Eighteen

MEL FOUND a tearful Jenny sitting mutely on the sofa while her children played video games on the TV, oblivious to the threat to their grandmother. An untouched cup of tea, obviously made some time ago, sat on a side table.

'Did you see anything at all?' She passed Jenny a clean tissue.

'No, nothing. Mum phoned to say she was by the corner shop and did I want anything. I said to get a pint of milk, and that's the last time we spoke. The shop's only three minutes away, but when she didn't turn up after ten minutes, I got worried. I went to the door and saw a dropped milk bottle and one of her shoes on the pavement. That's when I realised something awful had happened and I phoned the police. Someone came from the local station, made me some tea, and said they would contact you.'

'They did, and I came round as soon as I heard. Have you seen any strange vehicles or people behaving oddly in the street recently?'

'No, not really. There was a silver car I didn't recognise,

parked over the road a few times today. I thought it was a plain clothes police car.' Their conversation was interrupted by squabbling children.

'Mum, Mum, Darren won't give me the controller and it's my turn,' the smaller one whined to Jenny.

'No it isn't, Kayleigh. It's not ten minutes yet.' Darren was just as aggrieved.

'Yes it is. It's my turn.'

'If you two don't shut up I'll switch that thing off and you can go up to your rooms,' Jenny screamed. Sullenly, the children turned back to their game, a temporary truce prevailing.

'You said you'd look after her. You did. You promised.'

Jenny broke down, sobbing. Mel felt awkward, realising that the explanation for the lack of surveillance would not impress her.

'I'm really sorry. We're trying to trace anyone who was in the street at that time. Have you had any post, deliveries or other callers?'

'No. The post comes before lunch, and I've had no parcels. This free newspaper came while I was waiting for Mum. That's all.'

'That could be helpful,' said Mel, picking the paper up from the table. Hoping that someone would still be in the firm's offices, although it was a Saturday, she phoned the publisher and was relieved to find a journalist there. She explained what she wanted, and the writer found her the name of the delivery company.

'By the way,' said the woman on the phone. 'They use residents from a local home for people with learning disabilities for some of the route. Gives them something worthwhile to do, I suppose.'

Mel thanked her and turned to Jenny.

'Have you seen the people delivering the paper before? Was there anything unusual about them?'

Jenny looked confused, but then her expression cleared.

'Now you come to mention it, I did see two people last week. The bloke looked sort of, well, different, and the woman seemed to be helping him.'

Mel broke off the conversation and phoned Tom.

'Tom, can you do me a favour? Contact Easystreet Distribution and find out who delivers the free paper in Jenny's street. If you can't get hold of them, look for a care home of some kind within half a mile or so. Ask if any of their residents deliver papers. Then get back to me. Thanks ever so.'

Mel tried to reassure Jenny that they would do their best to find Ellen and bring her home safely, but deep down, she had serious doubts. She promised to keep Jenny informed and left the house, desperately worried about Ellen.

Chapter Nineteen

As MEL GOT into her car, Tom phoned.

'The delivery company was closed,' he said. 'But there are two care homes in the area. One is for elderly folk, but the other, called Mexton Lifechances, offers supported living for a wide age range of people with learning disabilities. They do deliver papers, and I told the manager you would be round shortly.'

'Terrific, Tom. Maximum brownie points! Text me the address and I'll go straight there.'

Mexton Lifechances, set back from the road behind some ornamental yet functional gates, was brightly painted and had flowers blooming along the path. Mel pressed the intercom and was buzzed into a spacious hall, where she was met by a youngish woman whose kind expression was complemented by an air of efficiency.

'Do come in. I'm Amina Patel, the duty manager. Your colleague explained what this is about. Robbie's waiting for you.'

Once she had signed the visitors' book, Mel was led into a cheerful lounge, where a young man was sitting on a sofa.

'Robbie,' said Amina, 'we have a visitor. This is Mel. She's from the police.' Robbie mumbled a greeting but didn't look Mel in the eye.

'Hello, Robbie.' Mel was unsure how she should pitch her words but was desperate to avoid sounding patronising. 'Amina tells me you deliver papers to people. Where do you deliver?'

Robbie brightened up and recited a list of the streets involved.

'Shakespeare Street, Chaucer Street, Browning Avenue and Milton Road. Millie helps me, but she's not here. She's gone home. I live here but she doesn't.'

Wishing that Millie was available, Mel continued, 'Did you see anything unusual when you were in Chaucer Street today?' She looked up at Amina to see if Robbie would understand, receiving a discreet nod in response.

'There was a new car. I know all the cars in the street. This was new.'

'Excellent. What can you tell me about the car, Robbie?'

'It was a silver Ford Focus. And its number was WX02 HGZ. And two men and a lady were getting into it. It drove off fast.'

'That's great, Robbie. Do you remember anything else about the people?'

'Lady was old. The men had black faces and white eyes.'

'Well, thank you very much, Robbie. You've been really helpful. It was lovely to talk to you, but I must go now. Good bye.'

Mel turned to Amina as she was leaving.

'That's amazing. Is he on the spectrum? How does this paper delivery thing work?'

'Obviously I can't discuss individual service users in detail, but Robbie does love cars, as you've gathered. Here at Mexton Lifechances we believe in involving people in meaningful activities as much as possible. Some places just put them in front of the TV all day and give them little chance to do things for themselves. Millie supports Robbie on his paper round – she'll be in at eight tomorrow if you need to talk to her.'

'Someone will, but Robbie's given me some vital information that I'll need to act on immediately. Thank you so much for your help, Amina.'

Chapter Twenty

MEL PHONED in the car's details as soon as the door closed on her. She drove back to the station, barely keeping to the speed limit. She realised that the men Robbie had described were almost certainly white but wearing balaclavas. When she arrived, the incident room was frenetic, with detectives and civilian staff scanning computer screens, scribbling on notepads and speaking urgently into phones. The tension was palpable as they watched ANPR recordings. No-one wanted to miss the vital sighting that might save Ellen's life. Incoming information was called out to Fiona, who wrote it on white-boards as it arrived.

'Car's registered to Maldobourne Holdings. Insured for any employee to drive.'

'No signal from Ellen's phone – turned off or destroyed.'

'ANPR picked up the car on Cleaver Street, heading west, 15.09.'

'Flagged on Elliott Road, 15.22.'

'Spotted on Mercer Street, 15.30.'

'Clocked coming off the flyover, turning south, 15.45.'

Then nothing.

'Right,' said Fiona. 'They must be somewhere near the flyover. Get a map showing ANPR cameras in the area. Mark up those they were seen on and also those that didn't pick them up. We can use this to find which general area they're in. Get CCTV recordings within that area from 15.45 onwards, if there are any, and see if they've been picked up. Concentrate on the southern area. And work fast.'

Within fifteen minutes Fiona had projected a satellite image of the area south of the flyover on the whiteboard, with the ANPR points shown in red and green – red for sightings, green for blanks.

'Does anyone know this area?' she asked.

'Yes, ma'am,' replied DC Adeyemi.

'So tell us about it.'

'OK. It's mainly residential. Most of the homes are former council houses. There's some light industry, warehouses and the like, near the main road. There's a stream and a small park on the edge of the housing estate, and on the other side there's some larger, posher, houses. The railway runs through the industrial bit on bridges and arches. The station's half a mile away.'

'Thanks. That's really helpful. What do you think, Jack?' They studied the image together. 'Where would you put someone if you'd kidnapped them?'

'I'd say a deserted factory or garage where I wouldn't be noticed. The houses on the estate are too close together, and the big ones probably have private CCTV, a Neighbourhood Watch and alert dog walkers. So it's the area nearer the flyover I'd go for. Unless...' He paused. 'There could be premises in the arches beneath the railway. No-one would hear any noise with trains going by, and I'm guessing torture is involved.'

'Good thinking. We've a firearms unit standing by, and the Chief Super's given the Tactical Firearms Commander the OK to deploy as needed. I want two cars to accompany them, as quick as. We'll follow with a couple of DCs. Mobilise an ambulance. She could be injured. Tom – stay at your desk and phone me with any information coming from the guys scanning the CCTV recordings. Jessop, you're with me. Go, go!'

Chapter Twenty-One

ELLEN BLINKED as a cloth bag was pulled roughly off her head. Her face hurt where someone had hit her to shut her up. She was sick with terror but determined not to show it. Wherever they had taken her, it was cold and damp, the only light coming from the partly open door until someone switched on a couple of strip lights that temporarily dazzled her. She could see a bench with tools spread over its surface, various mechanical junk scattered over a rough concrete floor and a few odd bits of furniture. The two kidnappers shoved her onto a metal chair and fastened her hands behind her with plastic cable ties, which cut painfully into her wrists. One of them winced every time he moved his left arm. Ellen was glad that to see that the gunshot wound still pained him. Small satisfaction.

'You bastards,' she screamed, drowning out the sound of dripping water. 'Why don't you leave me alone? I've nothing for you. I've told you. Are you really that stupid?'

'But we know you have. George told us. He said it was in the flat.'

'What are you talking about?'

'Well, you see, George and a couple of friends were involved in a business enterprise a few years ago, and while his friends were otherwise engaged, George went off with the profits. His friends are very keen to get back what's owed them. Very keen indeed. And there's a piece of equipment missing as well, which we know you have.'

'Stop talking in riddles. It doesn't make you sound clever. You mean a robbery and George nicked the loot. I suppose you morons got caught and George didn't. Well, he never hid it in the flat. The police would've found it when they went through the place. As for the equipment, as you call it, I found it before the police search and hung onto it in case it was useful. I didn't mean to shoot anyone, but I'm not sorry I did. Serves you right. The police have it now.'

'You bitch. That's evidence of something else. The boss is going to be very unhappy about that.'

'Tough shit.'

'Oh it is, darlin'. Tough for you. You see, the boss won't believe you know nothing and he's very persuasive. He's coming to have a chat with you later. George's chat with him lasted four hours before he croaked. How long do you think you'll last? Think about that while we're gone.'

His sneering remark chilled Ellen to the core, but she couldn't reply. She fought the urge to vomit as the two kidnappers turned out the lights, slammed the door and left her in the dark.

Ellen's thoughts were scattered and fearful. What were they going to do to her? She didn't know anything, so how could she give them what they wanted? Would she get out alive? A wave of panic swept over her, and she nearly wet herself. Would anyone come looking for her? How would they find her? She tried to imagine where she was. Some type of industrial premises, perhaps? She was obviously some distance from home, given the length of the drive. Occasional rumblings overhead suggested she was under a railway line, but that didn't help her much. There were railway lines all around Mexton. A little light from the road outside seeped through cracks around the door in front of her, but not enough for her to make out her surroundings. Above the odours of oil and damp there was another smell. A very unpleasant one. A bit like rotten meat. It reminded her of a flat she was called out to as a paramedic. And she really didn't want to remember what she found there.

Trying to suppress her fears, she set her mind to escaping. She needed to free her hands but couldn't move them. The plastic ties around her wrists threatened to cut off the circulation. Could she find a sharp edge to sever the ties with? She looked around desperately but couldn't see one. There might have been something on the bench, but it was too far away and too dark to find. The ropes binding her to the chair were knotted too tightly for her to wriggle out. She began to panic. She considered toppling the chair over, in the hope that she would have more scope to move, but reckoned she would end up banging her head on the floor. She'd seen enough head injuries to know this would be unwise. All she could do was conserve her strength and try and persuade her captors that she knew nothing and was no threat to them. Some chance, a voice inside her head told her. She started to sob.

Ellen sat there for what seemed like an eternity but was, in fact, only a couple of hours. She racked her brains for something she could give them. Something that would buy her time. The gun had gone, but what about the key? Perhaps

George had hidden the stolen jewellery in the garage. She would keep it to herself until she absolutely had to tell them.

Her hands had gone numb, cramp was developing in her legs and she badly needed to pee. Then a door crashed open behind her and the lights were switched on, dazzling her again. As soon as she saw the faces of the three men approaching her, she knew she wouldn't leave alive, whether she told them about the key or not. Two of them were her kidnappers. The other was taller, better dressed and looked vaguely familiar. There was something about his eyes that frightened Ellen, but she couldn't work out what. Perhaps it was the gleam of anticipation they held. Or maybe their icy coldness. Whatever it was, Ellen had never felt so scared in all her life.

Chapter Twenty-Two

'Mrs Wilkins,' said the tall man, his voice silky but with a hint of a chainsaw beneath. 'I am Charles Osbourne, and you and I are going to have a little chat. And,' he continued, as he handed an expensive overcoat to one of the kidnappers and climbed into a boiler suit, 'you are going to tell me everything.'

He was calm and almost reassuring, like a doctor discussing a welcome result from a blood test, although the undertone of menace was unmistakeable. Ellen was far from reassured.

'I've nothing to tell you. I told those two clowns over there.' Her voice trembled as she tried to maintain a semblance of defiance.

'Oh, but you do. I distinctly remember George telling me, between screams, that "it's in the flat". That means you know where it is and moved it before the police searched the place. The fact that the police have the gun is unfortunate, but there are no fingerprints of use to them on it, so I'll let that go. But a cloth bag of jewellery is what I'm after, and you will tell me where it is.'

Ellen's terror mounted. Her guts turned to water. What could she say? She knew nothing. Would they believe her denials?

'I don't know. Honestly.' Her voice began to quaver. 'I've never seen any jewellery.'

'Oh dear,' Osbourne said, his tone of phoney regret failing to cover the excitement in his voice. 'Then it's going to be very painful for you. Get outside and keep watch, Dwight. I know you've no stomach for the entertainment, but at least you can be useful.'

Marlow was glad to leave the room, scrabbling in his pockets for cigarettes as he went.

'Now, where shall we start?' resumed Osbourne, picking up a pair of bolt cutters. 'Fond of your fingers, are you? Or I could do you a facial with the sanding attachment on this power drill. And there's a bottle of battery acid over there. You'd be amazed at the fun I can have with that. Have you seen *Reservoir Dogs*, by the way? I don't have the music, but this pruning saw is sharp enough to take your ear off. Slowly and painfully.'

Ellen wanted to vomit. This man was a psychopath. He was going to hurt her, whatever she said. Could anything stop him? For all her bravado, she dreaded the thought of being tortured. If she knew what he wanted, she would tell him. Then she might get to see her children and grandchildren again. Tears were pouring down her face, and she shook her head from side to side. She would have to tell Osbourne about the key, although the police had it. But could she bluff him? She had no choice but to try.

'Wait...wait a minute,' she yelled, as Osbourne approached her with the pruning saw, its wicked teeth inches from her face. He stopped, almost reluctantly, and lowered the tool.

'Well?'

'I found a key. A garage key. Maybe it's there.' If her fingers had been free she would have crossed them.

'Possibly. George could have meant the key was in the flat. He was rather distressed at the time, as you can imagine. Where is it, and where's the garage?'

'The address was on a tag. I can't remember what it said, but I can get the key for you.'

'No, you won't. Tell me where it is, and I'll send someone to get it.'

'A friend's got it. I don't want her involved. I'll get it for you. You can trust me, I promise.' Ellen hoped she could find a way to escape if they took her to a made-up address.

'No chance. You tell me. And if your friend is helpful, she won't get hurt.'

'I can't. I promised.'

'You don't have a choice. I'm going to put this plastic bag over your head, and you won't be able to breathe. When you're ready to tell me, just nod your head. And if you pass out, I'll wake you up and do it again. It's like waterboarding without the water. If that doesn't persuade you, I'll start on your fingers.'

Just as Osbourne slipped a 'Bag for Life' over Ellen's head and fixed it round her neck with gaffer tape, Marlow crashed through the door.

'It's the filth. They've found us. I told that prick to change the plates on the car, but he said his shoulder hurt and it didn't matter anyway. The cameras must have picked us up. There's cop cars on the flyover, and they're coming our way.'

The sound of sirens drew nearer, and a flickering blue light was visible when the gang opened the door. Leaving

Ellen tied up and suffocating, the men bolted through the lock-up and out the small back door to their car. Osbourne took a second to hit Ellen viciously in the stomach on his way out, sending a bolt of pain through her side as a rib broke.

Ellen groaned at the pain in her belly. At least she was alive. For the moment. But would the police find her in time? She tried to keep her wits about her. The tape around her throat was constricting her airway, but the bag contained a little air, and she realised that, if she didn't panic, she had a bit more time before suffocating. She inhaled painfully through her mouth and managed to trap a section of the bag between her lips. Manoeuvring it with her tongue, she caught it between her teeth and began grinding away, trying to make a breathing hole. But it was a strong bag and the effort was using up oxygen. Her head began spinning and her chest ached. I can't do it. It's not going to work, she wept, thinking she would never see her family again. Slowly the light dimmed, but almost of their own accord, her teeth kept moving. A small hole appeared in the plastic, but it was barely enough, and Ellen's head slipped forward as she lost consciousness.

Chapter Twenty-Three

THE FIRST POLICE car on the scene just missed the gang, who were escaping along the narrow road at the back of the lock-ups. At first it looked as if none of the units was in use, but as the second car drove along the fronts with a similar lack of success, a sharp-eyed PC, Dave Jordan, spotted a narrow strip of light under the door of Ellen's prison.

'Call it in, Joe,' he said, and approached the unit cautiously, fearful of armed villains inside. Listening at the door, he heard nothing from within and risked pushing the door open a crack. As soon as he saw Ellen, head slumped in the chair, he rushed in.

'Get an ambulance, Joe. Now,' he yelled, fumbling with the tape around Ellen's neck. It was taking too long to shift, and he couldn't hear her breathing. He found the hole by Ellen's mouth, shoved his finger in and carefully ripped the plastic. No response. Gently he tipped the chair over so that Ellen's back was on the floor and started CPR. The ropes binding her got in the way, but he managed to inflate her chest. After what seemed like an age, a faint pulse appeared in

Ellen's neck and she started breathing weakly. Jordan carefully unwrapped the tape, easing the pressure on her throat, and a few minutes later paramedics were in the unit, giving her oxygen. He undid the ropes tying Ellen to the chair, and the paramedics slid her onto a stretcher.

'Will she be all right?' he asked.

'Was she breathing when you found her?'

'No, I don't think so. I'm not sure.'

'Well it depends on how long she was without air. You've saved her life, but she could have brain damage. They'll find out when we get her to hospital. But you did good.'

Once Ellen and the paramedics had left in the ambulance, Fiona drew her car up outside the lockup, relieved that Ellen had been found but fearful that she might not recover. Grabbing Jessop's arm to stop him entering, she peered in and assessed the scene.

'No-one's to go in there. We need forensics to give the place a good going-over before we trample about. That smell tells me that something very nasty has happened, and I don't like the look of the stains on those tools. It could be where they killed George. Mel, you go to the hospital and talk to Ellen when she's in a fit state to speak to us – if she ever is. I'll arrange for a guard on her room once the medics have finished. Back to the station for the rest of us.'

She spoke to PC Jordan. 'Well done. You did really well. Could you and your colleague stay here until I can arrange a rota to guard the place?'

'Yes, ma'am. Thanks.'

Two hours later the police officers hadn't been relieved and were bored. Only the passage of the trains and the constant drip of rain on the car windscreen broke the monotony.

'Fancy a pie or something, Dave?' asked Joe. 'Nothing's happening here, and there's a chippy back on the main road.'

'Yeah. Why not? Chicken and mushroom. With chips.'

Joe drove off in the police car leaving Dave to guard the premises, standing damply against the lockup door. He texted his wife to warn her that, yet again, he'd be late home. A particularly long train rumbled overhead. He didn't hear the stealthy figure creeping up behind him. But he felt the small crowbar that struck him at the base of his skull. A searing pain flashed across the back of his neck, and he crashed to the ground, a puppet with slashed strings.

His assailant levered open the lockup door and went in, his torch casting a narrow beam of light. He grabbed Osbourne's overcoat and was starting to pour petrol over the floor when Jordan groaned and looked groggily up at him. Clearly panicking at the thought of being recognised, he was about to hit Jordan again, but before he could finish the officer off, he heard the police car returning. Hastily, he lit a cigarette, hurled it into the pool of petrol and fled through the back door.

A bag of pies and chips in his hand, Joe climbed out of the car and called to his mate. No answer.

'Stop playing hide-and-seek, you twat. Your chips are getting cold.'

Still no answer.

Joe dropped the steaming package of food when he saw Dave's crumpled form on the ground in front of the lockup.

He smelt petrol and saw a pool of liquid spreading slowly from inside the building towards his colleague. He rushed over, the fumes catching in his throat, and knelt beside him, fearful that the petrol would somehow ignite.

'What the fuck's happened, Dave?'

'Can't move, Joe. Can't move. It's fucking agony,' moaned Jordan, panic mounting in his voice. 'Bastard hit me from behind. Did you see him?'

'No, mate. But hang in there and keep still. I'll call for an ambulance and backup.'

Joe found some rags inside the unit to soak up the petrol before it reached Dave, but by the time backup came, there was no point in looking for the would-be arsonist. Two more officers arrived to watch the lockup, with strict instructions not to leave it. The paramedics put a collar round Dave's neck and lifted him onto a stretcher with extreme caution. Joe followed the ambulance to the hospital.

Chapter Twenty-Four

Sunday 6th October

'WELL, THIS IS A BLOODY MESS,' began Fiona, the next morning. 'On the plus side, we have Ellen back, whose life was saved by an alert and courageous PC. We've also found the premises where we think George was killed, and we should get some evidence from the scene. On the minus side, we've no-one in custody and Ellen may be brain-damaged, unable to tell us anything. The hospital sent Mel away last night as she was in intensive care. As well as that, PC Jordan is in hospital and could be paralysed.'

Several detectives swore colourfully.

'We think the villains are after the proceeds of the jewel robbery that Ramsey and Marlow were sent down for, but we don't know for certain,' she continued. 'We have no clue where they are – the jewels or the men. As to who's behind it all, we're pretty sure it's Osbourne, but proving it is difficult, as we have no evidence linking him to the railway arch so far.

We can only hope that Ellen recovers and can tell us what happened to her.

'Forensics are going through the lockup and may discover something – at least what's been going on there, if not who was involved. It will be a long time before they finish, though. It's crawling with biological evidence, and processing it all is a marathon job.

'We can assume that PC Jordan's attacker returned to the scene to remove and destroy evidence – we don't know how successful he was in taking stuff, but he was prevented from torching the place. The cigarette he tried to light the petrol with went out when it landed in the fuel. Apparently, cigarettes are not hot enough and he should have used a burning rag, but luckily for Jordan, he didn't know that.'

The faces of her audience reflected their horror at the prospect of a fellow officer burning to death.

'Jordan's mate said that an overcoat had been taken from the scene – a posh one, he thought. So, we need to find out who rents the lockup. Mel, you get back to the hospital and see if Ellen can talk yet. Check on PC Jordan as well – find out what the doctors have to say about his chances. I'll go to the lockup and see how the SOCOs are getting on.'

When Fiona arrived at the railway arch, SOCOs were loading plastic boxes of collected material into a van for further examination at the lab. She donned the protective clothing the PC logging attendees gave her and walked carefully on the stepping plates into the unit.

'Anything useful, Mark?' she asked the Crime Scene Manager, a doleful man in his forties whose lined face and weary expression testified that he'd seen just about every unpleasant thing people could do to each other.

'Lots, but it'll take time to unravel. It'll be a nightmare sorting out the DNA in this lot. There's plenty of dried blood, urine and traces of faeces on the floor and the chair, as well as fragments of tissue. A few teeth and fingernails as well. Various tools and other implements are covered in blood and tissue, as are a couple of aprons I found on a bench. I think we've found a torture chamber.'

Fiona grimaced.

'Any weapons, valuables, documents?'

'Nothing much yet, but we've still a lot to go through. We did find half a box of .38 cartridges and a bottle of gun oil in a drawer, but no handgun to go with them.'

'I think we've got that already. Any finger marks?'

'Loads, but many are smudged. We've lifted dozens of different ones already and we're still looking.'

'I don't suppose you've found a headless body?'

'Oh, I forgot to mention that,' replied Mark, sarcastically. 'No, but there's an area over there where a lot of blood has pooled. Could be where the head was removed, if it happened shortly after death.'

'Any idea when you'll have something to report?'

'It'll be weeks before we've finished collecting and analysing everything. But I'll ask the lab to prioritise the tissue DNA and see if the blood on the floor matches the head.'

'Thanks, Mark. You're a star.'

When Mel arrived at the hospital she first looked in on Dave Jordan. His head and neck were immobilised, and he was drowsy with painkillers. A machine bleeped steadily by his bed, and an untouched bowl of grapes sat on a cabinet. He managed to speak a few words, the gist of which was that someone had hit him from behind, he hadn't heard them and didn't see them. A vertebra in his neck had been cracked and had pressed on his spinal column, but the doctors were hoping it would heal without leaving any permanent damage. In the meantime, they were keeping him immobile and he was bored out of his mind. Mel offered to bring in an audio book and headphones, but he declined as his neck was too painful at the moment.

She found Ellen much more lively. She was sitting up in bed chatting to the PC who was supposed to be guarding her.

'Well, what have you got to say for yourself?' she said, when she saw Mel. 'So much for police protection. They grabbed me in broad daylight and nobody stopped them.'

'I know, I know. I'm really sorry. The local station was overwhelmed and couldn't spare anyone during the afternoon. They were going to send someone round in the evening, not that it's much consolation. The young man who delivers Jenny's free paper spotted you being snatched but didn't realise what was going on. We found out where he lives, and he remembered the number of the car, which we tracked to the lockup.'

'Well, at least you did something right. I've seen the lad. I'll get him some chocolates when I'm out of here.'

'Well, without him and PC Jordan you probably wouldn't have made it out alive.'

'PC who?'

'He's the officer who spotted a light under the door, ripped the bag on your head open and gave you CPR until the ambulance arrived. He's in the spinal unit because one of the gang hit him on the back of the neck.'

'Oh. Right. I'll go and thank him when they let me out.'

Ellen was clearly thinking a bit more charitably of the police now.

'How are you, anyway?' asked Mel.

'My heart and lungs seem fine, but they're keeping me in for observation because of my age. Load of fuss. I'm not that old. I've got a broken rib, which, luckily, didn't do any damage to my organs. They'll just strap it up and give me painkillers. No surgery needed. They say I'm still in shock, but I don't believe them. It's funny seeing things from the other side. I worked on ambulances for years and never thought I'd be the patient. I've hardly ever been in hospital, except when George broke my wrist once. Makes you aware of your own mortality.'

'Well, I think you're amazingly tough, Ellen. There's plenty more years in you yet. I'm sorry to ask, but do you remember much about what happened?'

At this, Ellen paled and her voice became slightly quavery.

'Not much, and what I do remember is horrible. He was going to cut off my ear and then my fingers, the bastard. I'd rather not guess at what else he'd planned.'

'Of course. I understand. But is there anything else that's not too painful to recall?' Mel realised she was pushing it and knew that Ellen would be quite justified in telling her to piss off.

'Well, it was the same two shits who broke into the flat that took me. They tied me up and left me alone in the dark for ages. Then this other bloke came along. Much posher and really frightening. I was scared of him before he even spoke. It was Charles Osbourne. I saw him with George once, but we weren't introduced and I didn't know who he was. It wasn't pleasant putting a face to the name. George seemed slightly in awe of him and wouldn't talk about what they did together.

He was the one that threatened me with torture and hit me as he left.' She flinched. 'He was clearly the boss.'

'What did he want?'

'A bag of jewellery. And he was annoyed that you lot had the gun. I haven't seen any jewels. And I told him.'

'Anything else?'

'Well he seemed interested in the key I found behind the poster. The one I left for your search team. It might fit a garage George once had in Malvern Row. I said it was with a friend and I'd go with him to get it. I hoped he would take me to some address I made up and I could somehow make a run for it. Fat chance. He wouldn't agree, anyway. I knew he was going to kill me, one way or the other. And the worst thing was knowing I wouldn't see my kids and grandkids again.'

Ellen's voice started to break, and Mel realised she had pushed her enough.

'That's tremendously helpful, Ellen. Thank you. You've been very brave.' She was conscious of sounding a bit patronising, but Ellen didn't seem to notice.

'I'll leave you in peace now, but please let us know when you're well enough to give us a proper statement.'

'Yeah. All right. But you'd better get someone to look out for Jenny, and don't cock it up this time. I don't want her getting hurt as well.'

'I will. I promise,' said Mel, not entirely sure it was a promise she could keep. But the positive ID on Osbourne was a bonus, and she was sure Ellen would give evidence when they caught him. She'd had a lucky escape. She was not meant to get out of that lockup alive.

Chapter Twenty-Five

Mexton 2008

For Campbell, starting operations in Mexton was easy, helped by Marnie's contacts in the local police. The supply of drugs in the town had been haphazard and unreliable, depending on minor players buying moderate quantities in cities and dividing them up amongst a loose group of street dealers, cutting the product with whatever came to hand.

Campbell introduced Marnie to Charles Osbourne, and the three of them set up a much more efficient operation, ensuring that supplies were always available. Kids on bikes, too young to prosecute, were used to deliver customers' requirements. Older youths collected bulk supplies from middlemen and distributed them to the delivery kids. The middlemen never met the next person up the supply chain, collecting supplies and delivering payment at dead drops that changed frequently. Commission was paid at each stage and violence was used to keep everyone in order. The Eastside Estate was the main market for heroin and meth, while high-quality cocaine was supplied to the more affluent customers in the better parts of the town. Ecstasy was used by all social classes. They didn't bother with cannabis, as the profits were too low.

Competing dealers were easily scared off by threats of violence, put into practice on occasions by Osbourne's hired thugs. When Marnie was introduced to Osbourne she quickly realised that here was a ruthless individual who enjoyed hurting people. He didn't get involved in any rough stuff on the streets himself – he had others to do that. But if he considered someone needed serious punishment, they were brought to him and he took great delight in hurting them.

It was Marnie who suggested setting up a company to act as a cover for all their activities. Campbell's transport business was transferred to a new outfit, Maldobourne Holdings, as was Osbourne's Maldon Club. Campbell and Osbourne were the directors, and Marnie kept herself in the background. The company gradually expanded its activities to include a property portfolio, which was ideal for laundering the proceeds of their criminal enterprises. A solicitor who had enjoyed Marnie's services in the past was persuaded to carry out the legal work discreetly, building a facade of complete respectability.

Mexton had a particular advantage, from Marnie's point of view. A police officer who she had known in Glasgow had moved to the town, ostensibly for family reasons but really because his conduct had attracted suspicion. He once arrested Marnie for soliciting and had let her off with a caution in return for a blow job. He didn't realise at the time that she had recorded the encounter on a small voice recorder hidden in her bag. When she moved to Mexton she re-recorded the tape – one of many such recordings of police officers and other useful punters – onto a CD. She sent him a copy and demanded a meeting.

A sweaty, trembling detective met Marnie in a pub on the outskirts of town.

'What do you want from me?' he stammered. 'I don't do that sort of thing any more.'

'It's quite simple,' Marnie replied, after patting him down to check for a wire. 'You're mine. You will keep me informed of any police activity that might affect our business. You will ensure that any investigations are diverted away from me and my associates. You will prevent any of our young dealers being charged with serious offences. And you will not mention this to anyone. If you do, your career and pension will go straight down the toilet once this recording hits the internet, and you will inevitably go to jail. And you know what happens to coppers in jail.'

The police officer nodded his agreement, shivering in terror at the prospect.

'It's not all bad news,' said Marnie. 'We will give you a retainer, to make it easier for you to co-operate. There will be bonuses when you provide us with something really useful. And these will go up, the higher up the ranks you rise. So be a good boy, keep your nose clean and you'll find our arrangement much to your advantage.'

Marnie handed the officer an envelope with a modest sum inside.

'One last thing,' she said, as he stuffed it furtively into his pocket. 'We have someone else in the force who helps us. If you attempt to investigate us, or talk about our arrangement, we will know about it. And you understand the consequences.'

The officer fled the pub faster than he'd ever left licensed premises before. By the time his heartbeat returned almost to normal, it had dawned on him that the situation could benefit him. He was jaded by his police career, and this would certainly make it more interesting. He could work harder for promotion and rise up through the ranks. With a little discreet effort, he could earn a nice supplement to his pension and maybe retire early. 'Yes,' he thought. 'This could work out very nicely. Very nicely indeed.'

Chapter Twenty-Six

Fairwood Waste Management site | Monday 7th October 2019

BILL DANIELS HAD BEEN DRIVING skip lorries to landfills for twenty-three years. He'd seen just about everything tumble out of his skips, especially before environmental regulations were tightened up – drums of toxic waste, tonnes of rotting fruit, a complete Georgian dining table and chairs set, and even a bloated dead sheep. But none of this had prepared him for the sight of a headless body sliding out from under a load of builders' waste when he emptied his skip. Three seconds later, Bill's breakfast was added to the waste on the landfill. He waved frantically at the site supervisor, trying to attract his attention above the roar of machinery and the screeching of gulls. Eventually he caught his eye, and the yellow-jacketed individual walked cautiously across the compacted waste to Bill's lorry.

'What do you want? I was just going off on my tea break. Oh shit.'

The supervisor blanched when he saw the body, and directed a tipper lorry, about to dump its load nearby, away from the scene. He phoned the site office to tell them to close the gates while Bill, still trembling, called the police. Forty minutes later, marked police cars roared up to the site entrance, followed by a forensics van. A cordon of police tape was quickly set up, encircling, as far as possible, Bill's dumped load. A tent was erected over the corpse. Although the landfill site was in a different force area, one of the PCs remembered the appeal for sightings of a headless body and phoned the information in to Mexton CID. The news reached Mel half an hour later.

'Fancy a field trip, Martin? A scenic rubbish dump in the beautiful countryside? Looks like George's body's turned up. We've had a tip-off.' She couldn't resist the pun, a habit she'd picked up from her father.

'OK Mel, since you make it sound so romantic,' he replied, with a cheesy grin.

'Better bring wellies as well as the forensic suit. It could be messy. By the way, what's that new aftershave you're wearing? Eau de babysick?'

She often teased Martin about the stains on his shoulders and the bags under his eyes from sleepless nights, but he didn't seem to mind. He was obviously incredibly proud of his new daughter and was always bringing photos of her into the office.

'The usual. Charlotte was a bit gripey when I said goodbye to her this morning, and I didn't have time to change.'

The two detectives reached the landfill in under an hour.

It was much quieter now operations had ceased, but the avian cacophony still made it hard to hear on occasions. After suiting up and signing in, Mel and Martin peered at the half-naked remains in the tent. Decomposition had started, and the visible flesh was a mottled greenish black, although any smell was masked by the stench from the landfill.

'It's about the right size for George, and the missing head's a clue,' said Mel, gallows humour kicking in. 'You don't need to be a pathologist to see he was hurt before he died. He's clearly been worked over and had some fingers removed. These guys use the same pathologist as we do, so he'll be able to match the head to the body – if it is George. DNA will confirm it.'

'Mr Daniels.' Mel addressed the lorry driver. 'I'm sorry you've had such a nasty shock, but can you tell me when and where you picked up the skip?'

'Yeah, sure. It was about eight o'clock, from Coventry Road in Mexton. A house is being renovated, and it's the second skip they've had from us. Didn't seem anything unusual about it at the time.'

'Did you stop anywhere on the way?'

'No. I came straight here. Can I go now?'

'Yes. Do. Thanks for your help. I'll need your address, and someone will be round to take a formal statement from you later. You'll have to leave the skip here, though, for forensics.'

Mel and Martin thanked the PC who had tipped them off and returned to base, their clothes reeking of decomposing refuse. On the way back, Mel insisted on humming the R.E.M. tune 'Try Not to Breathe', much to Martin's annoyance.

Mel gave Fiona the gist of what had happened while they drank coffee.

'It's almost certainly the rest of George, and it looks like he was tortured. The lorry driver told us where he picked up the skip, and I'll contact the hire firm to find out how long it had been there. It looked like ordinary builders' waste when he collected it – bits of plywood, plasterboard, plastic and so on. The body was well covered up.'

'Thanks, Mel,' said Fiona. 'I'll get some uniforms to go door-to-door in the street, just in case anyone saw anything.'

'Do you want me to go to the PM?' asked Mel, without enthusiasm. She was pretty tough, emotionally, but the smell in the autopsy suite always got to her.

'Not unless you want to. I suppose I'd better go, as SIO. I'll take DS Jessop. That'll be a treat for him.'

Mel smiled gratefully.

'Have we heard anything from forensics on the lockup?'

'There's still loads to do, but we've had a couple of results. Some of the blood on the floor was the same group as George's, but we'll need the DNA for an unequivocal match. And ballistics came back to us about the handgun. It matched the bullet fired into the ceiling during the raid on the jewellers that got Ramsey and Marlow sent down. Of particular interest is a match with a couple of rounds retrieved from the body of a London drug dealer who was found dead in the Mexton canal in 2011. I'll get someone to dig out the details.'

'What about the key Ellen found in her flat?'

'I've asked Martin to take a look at the garages on Malvern Row. See if it fits any of them. If it does, we can check with the council to see who rents it.'

'Are we going to arrest Osbourne?'

'He seems to have gone to ground, along with his nasty playmates. We had someone keeping an eye on his property –

just drive-bys – and there's been no sign of life there all day. He must have a bolt-hole somewhere. Oh, Tom's been on to Network Rail, who own the lockup. It's rented to Maldobourne Holdings, who seem to own just about everything connected with Osbourne, including the Maldon Club. Can you get on to DVLA and see if Maldobourne, or Osbourne, own any more vehicles? We need to get them flagged up for ANPR cameras and mobile patrols. And ask Tom to contact the mobile phone providers to find out if the company, or our suspects, have phones we can track. I'll organise a warrant if they won't co-operate. I'm sure Tom will be happy to do you a favour – I've seen the way he looks at you.'

Fiona grinned, and Mel felt slightly uncomfortable. She did like Tom but knew that romances within the team were frowned on and often led to complications. Still, she thought he was nice and he obviously liked her. Perhaps they could go for a drink after work one evening.

'OK, boss,' she said, and went off in search of a late lunch, although the smell from the landfill lingering on her clothes had all but killed her appetite.

Chapter Twenty-Seven

Mexton 2011

FOR TWO YEARS the arrangement between Marnie and her tame detective proved useful but not vital. The occasional raid failed because of a tip-off, some evidence went missing and low-level dealers tended to receive a caution rather than appearing in court. There was nothing to suggest that significant police corruption was at work, but equally, the detective's assistance didn't have a major effect on the gang's activities. Things changed when an intelligence report, left briefly on the top of a photocopier, fell into his hands.

Marnie's burner phone buzzed early one evening.

'You've got trouble,' the detective said. 'There's a mob from London planning to take over. They call themselves the Hacking Crew. They're tooled up and they're coming to you.'

'You may have earned yourself a nice bonus there. What else do you know?'

'They use black Transit vans to move about and they favour machetes. The occasional shooter. They're responsible for at least seven murders in East London. Five stabbings, one shooting and one battering. The Met's been targeting them, and they're looking for new turf where there's less attention. Mexton looks promising – they have some local connection, I think. A relative or something.'

'How do they operate?'

'They flood an area like the Eastside, grabbing the kids off their bikes, working their way up the food chain until they come across the suppliers. Then they take over. Anyone resisting gets hurt. Badly. It's worked for them on a couple of London estates, and now it's Mexton's turn.'

'Right. Well we'd better set up a welcome for them.'

'Try and avoid a bloodbath. Please.'

'Find out as much as you can about them and get back to me. Fast.' Marnie rang off.

Campbell, Osbourne and Marnie sat in the Maldon Club at eight o'clock, planning their response to the Hacking Crew. Marnie reported what her source had told her, emphasising that he had taken the threat seriously.

'Fucking cheek,' began Osbourne. 'I'm not having our hard work going down the pan because a few scrotes from the Smoke think they can take over.'

'I agree, Charles,' replied Marnie. 'But have we got enough muscle to fight them off?'

'I've several handy blokes work for me at the club. They'll pitch in. And I'd like you to meet someone.' He called to a muscular man in a tight-fitting suit, who was propping up the bar and nursing a pint. 'Come over, George.'

The man joined them at their table.

'This is George Wilkins. He's been doing a few jobs for Kelvin and me. He's pretty useful in a scrap. He's also totally ruthless. George, meet Marnie, our silent partner, as it were.'

George nodded amiably to Marnie, although his eyes remained cold.

'Pleased to meet you,' he said.

'Likewise,' replied Marnie, appraising his physique and recognising someone who could be extremely dangerous. For all her contempt for men, built up through years in the sex trade, she found him strangely attractive – a feeling, she realised, she would have to keep in check.

'There's no point trying to negotiate with these shites, even if we wanted to,' growled Campbell, his accent sounding more Glaswegian by the minute. 'They don't do that. They just do violence.'

George shrugged. 'We can do that, too. And plenty of it.'

'Yes, but we can't afford a prolonged conflict. It attracts too much attention,' said Marnie. 'It's got to be quick and final.'

'I'll see what I can do,' grinned George mirthlessly. 'When do we expect them?'

'My source says they come down in the early hours, in a couple of vans, check out the area and start work in the morning, snatching people off the street and making them talk. They usually have control within a couple of days. It looks like tonight.'

'They'll be gone within a couple of hours, trust me. I'll make a few preparations and post lookouts on the main road. They won't be expecting trouble. But we will.'

Marnie nodded approvingly, reassured by George's confidence.

By three o'clock in the morning a skilfully arranged series of obstructions – derelict cars, oil drums and the odd builder's skip – was in place, so that any vehicles entering the Eastside from the main road were subtly diverted into a semi-enclosed area under a walkway connecting two blocks of flats. Anyone new to the area wouldn't realise it was a dead end, so when two black Transits drove into the estate an hour later they slipped neatly into George's trap.

As soon as the engines in the vans were switched off, head-lights from three vehicles parked in the shadows flared. A tall, Afro-Caribbean man climbed out the front of the first van, swinging a machete, and walked forward. Five others, similarly tooled up, poured out of the back. George stepped into the light, apparently unarmed but with his hands deep in the pockets of his jacket.

'You have thirty seconds to turn your vans around and leave. Permanently.' His voice was icily calm, but a hint of fury burned in his eyes.

'You not understanding, man. You under new management.' The other man twirled his weapon and advanced towards George, a broad grin on his face.

'Twenty seconds.'

The intruder laughed.

'Look like I gonna teach you some respect. We called the Hacking Crew. This's why.'

He raised the machete and sprang forwards. Before the blade could reach his face, George raised his hand, still in his pocket. He pulled the trigger of his snub-nosed revolver twice.

From five feet he could hardly miss, and his assailant staggered, falling to the floor with two .38 bullets in his chest and a look of incredulity on his face.

Immediately, two petrol bombs arced out of the darkness, bracketing the second van and setting it on fire. Six men carrying baseball bats and shields, improvised from the tops of oil drums, swooped on the machete-wielding Londoners facing George, battering them into submission.

The doors of the second van burst open and five more men rushed out, braving the flames. One of them aimed a semi-automatic pistol at George, but the heat and smoke put him off his aim. George shot him in the gut, and the weapon clattered to the ground.

That left five, clearly beginning to think their mission was a mistake. George fired at two of them, hitting one in the shoulder and narrowly missing the head of another. With one round left he was counting on there being no more firearms.

'Put your weapons down and lie on the ground,' he yelled. 'We can keep this up all night.'

Outnumbered and outgunned, the few invaders who were still conscious realised they had no option but to comply. While they discarded their machetes, George reloaded his revolver.

'This is what's going to happen,' he shouted. 'You are going to put your wounded in the back of that van and fuck off back to London. And if you ever come back, you'll never leave.' He fired another couple of rounds over their heads for emphasis.

As the remains of the Hacking Crew sped off in a painfully overcrowded Transit, George's men collected the discarded weapons and bundled the dead leader into the boot of a car, wrapping him in plastic.

When dawn finally touched the Eastside, pools of blood, a

few lost teeth, the stench of burning diesel and a still-smouldering van served as reminders of the night's events beneath the walkway. The police showed little interest. Trouble on the estate was common, and Marnie's contact ensured that no-one looked too closely. Local residents knew better than to take any notice of matters which did not concern them. The corpse was dumped in the canal four miles out of town. There was no great attempt to conceal it, George reasoning that its discovery would serve as a deterrent to anyone else attempting to muscle in on Mexton. It worked.

Chapter Twenty-Eight

'So it went well, then,' said Osbourne, pouring George a large Scotch the following lunchtime.

'Yeah. They won't be back. And nor will anyone else. A couple of the lads got slashed, arms and legs, but they'll be compensated. A good result.'

'You're clearly good at this sort of thing.' Marnie lifted her glass in a mock toast. 'Perhaps we can use you for more jobs like this.'

George smiled and nodded.

'I agree,' said Osbourne. 'George is an excellent mechanic and driver, but we can use more of his other talents as well. We need someone to keep people in order on the estate. We've got a kid called Peel who acts as an enforcer for minor offences – the odd late payment or small theft. But we need somebody who can come down harder when someone really screws us around. Nothing works better than a bit of terror for keeping people in line.'

'Good idea, Charles.' Marnie realised that someone with George's skills could also be useful for her own purposes. She resolved to get closer to him and thought she would probably seduce him when the time was right.

When George was thrown out of the marital home by his aggrieved wife, Marnie saw her chance. She found him one night in the Maldon Club, well gone on whisky, and pulled up a stool beside him. Affecting the sympathetic tone that had served her well with many a client, she commiserated with him.

'What's the matter, George? You look like you won the lottery but burned the ticket.'

'The bitch chucked me out. After all these years. I put food on the table. A roof over her head. And the kids. Now she doesn't want to know. 'Snot fair. Got nowhere to live and I owe the bookies thousands.'

'Of course it isn't fair, George. You don't deserve that. After all those years.'

The conversation continued in that vein for some time, George becoming more maudlin as it went on. Eventually Marnie made her move.

'A handsome man like you should have a woman to look after him,' she oozed, although she had no intention of becoming a housewife or servant. She put her hand on his thigh and leaned forward slightly, favouring him with a view down the front of her blouse.

'Perhaps you'd like to come back to my place and we'll try to sort something out?'

George was not so drunk that he didn't recognise a come-on, and the thought of screwing Marnie was far from unpleasant. Although she was older than the young women he occasionally dallied with, she was still stunning and looked younger than his wife. Her professional experience between the sheets also attracted him. He downed the remains of his drink and walked out of the club unsteadily, leaning on Marnie's shoulder for support.

For half an hour Marnie put up with George's drunken fumblings, until he fell asleep, snoring. She made a mental note to order some of the little blue tablets that had proved so effective when she was in the business. Just in case. She would invite George to stay, but lay down some conditions. She wouldn't mind sex with him – he was reasonably attractive, after all – but she couldn't tolerate a gambler. Gamblers were unreliable. She would talk to him in the morning when his hangover would make him more receptive. If he wasn't inter-ested, she would turn her attentions to Charles Osbourne, although his penchant for torturing his enemies disturbed her.

'So this is how it would work, George.' Marnie set a mug of coffee and a bacon roll on the table in front of him. 'I like you and I think we could work together. You can move in here and share my bed. I'm not seeing anyone else and I don't expect you to. I've a number of personal jobs in mind, which I'll pay you for. But you must stop gambling. No arguments. How much do you owe the bookies?'

'Thousands,' he mumbled. 'Many thousands. I got credit because they know I work for Campbell and Osbourne. But they're getting restless. I've got to pay them back soon.'

'OK. Do you own your house or is it rented?'

'I own it. It's in my name 'cos Ellen wasn't working when we got it and couldn't go on the mortgage.'

'OK. Sell it. Use the money to pay off the mortgage and settle up with the bookies.'

'But what about Ellen?'

Marnie shrugged. 'She'll have to make her own way, unless you want to give her some of the proceeds.'

'No, I can't. There won't be anything left. Houses down our way haven't gone up in value much. She's got a job. She'll be all right. Anyway, it was her threw me out.'

'Do you have any other assets?'

'A car on finance. That's all.'

'So, are we on?'

'Definitely,' grinned George, reaching for the belt that fastened Marnie's dressing gown. She slapped his hand away. 'Later, when you've got your strength back. Now, about a job I want you to do for me. You'll need to be away for a couple of days, but I'll square it with the others. And you'll need a gun.'

Chapter Twenty-Nine

Glasgow 2011

CHARLIE MCKAY HAD RETIRED from the sex trafficking business some years ago, although he still had contacts in the trade and took advantage of new flesh arriving in Glasgow when he felt like it. He was a social worker by profession, and his role in child protection had proved extremely useful to his criminal colleagues. Blind eyes could be turned, records lost and victims' stories dismissed if it was necessary. He had given up the job when a grumbling heart had provided sufficient cause for him to retire on health grounds, with a reasonable pension. He lived alone, his wife having left him in disgust when she discovered illegal material on his computer. She didn't go to the police, partly because she feared some of the shame would rub off on her and also because she needed money from him. She agreed to keep quiet on condition he signed over the house to her, sent her half his pension by direct debit and never made contact with her again.

'They can always find it,' she reminded him. 'You can

never really delete anything, and there's the cloud and your search history. And I've got screen shots I'll send them.'

Charlie had no option but to comply. He could stand the loss of the house – it was more hers than his – and losing half his pension was painful but not crippling. It just meant he had to draw on some of the investments he'd made from his former criminal activities. Nevertheless, he hated her for what she'd done and often pondered on how he could get back at her.

Few people visited him in his modest but comfortable flat on the outskirts of the city. He didn't mind the loneliness, and after all, there were always the internet sites he favoured to provide him with electronic companionship. He was surprised, then, when someone knocked on his door one evening and said he'd been advised to call by a mutual friend.

'Callum Mackintosh said I should look you up,' said the figure through the part-open door. 'He suggested we might be able to help each other.'

'I haven't seen Callum in years,' replied Charlie as he unfastened the chain. 'I heard he moved down south. How's he doing?'

'Very well,' said George Wilkins, shoving the muzzle of a pistol into Charlie's stomach with a force that made him gasp. 'In fact, rather better than you are at the moment.'

George kicked the door shut behind him and propelled McKay along the hall into the living room, where a laptop was set up on a table.

'W-what d-do y-you want?' McKay's terror was palpable. 'I don't have much cash in the house, but you can take it all. And my Rolex.'

'Not interested. I have other business with you. But first a greeting from an old friend.' George hit McKay in the stomach as hard as he could, sending a blaze of pain through his body. 'Martina Baranska sends her regards.'

'W-who's she?' McKay could barely get the words out.

'She was part of a consignment of girls you imported from Poland in the nineties. You promised her a job in a Glasgow hotel. But you locked her up in a knocking shop used by filthy perverts like yourself. When she no longer looked like a teenager, you threw her out on the streets.'

'That wouldn't have been me. That would have been Callum. I only arranged the transport. Please, don't hurt me. I'll get money out of my account. Send it by bank transfer. I've lots. Only please leave me alone.'

George let him sob for a few minutes while he strolled around the room, making sure his gun was always within McKay's sight.

'I don't want your money, you piece of shit. You're going to give me something else. A confession. Pour yourself a drink. We're going to be here for a while.' He put a bottle and a glass on the table.

McKay gulped a tumbler of Scotch and opened up a document on his laptop as George instructed. With continual prompting from George's gun barrel, he described all the trafficking operations he could remember and identified people who were involved. He listed addresses where the girls were taken, officials he had bribed, notables who had used the brothels and corrupt police officers. As George had instructed, he didn't mention Callum Mackintosh.

'That should do nicely,' said George, after reading through the document. 'Now email it to these addresses.' McKay was shaking so much that he could barely type. Ten minutes later, his confession was landing in the inboxes of Police Scotland, the Met, BBC Scotland, STV, the *Scotsman* newspaper and several national dailies. Copies also appeared on social media. Tears were streaming down McKay's face and he had wet himself, terrified at the prospect of imprisonment and violence from other inmates.

'It's a pity you won't be around to see the results of all this,' said George wistfully.

'Why not?'

'Because you're going to commit suicide.'

'Why would I do that?'

'Because I'm going to do it for you.'

McKay's look of bewilderment gave way to horror. He tried to rise from the chair, but George struck him on the back of the head, temporarily stunning him. Before he had time to recover, George placed the semi-automatic dropped by the Hacking Crew in McKay's hand, pushed the barrel into his mouth and pulled the trigger. He angled the weapon so that the exit wound from the 9mm bullet would disguise the damage done by George's blow.

Before leaving he checked that he had left no traces. He had kept his coat and gloves on all the time he was in the flat and he knew the pistol was untraceable. He gathered up the paper towels he had used to wipe away the fine particles of blood and brain tissue that had landed on his head and face when the weapon discharged. He knew there would be gunshot residues on his clothes, but that didn't bother him as he would destroy those when he got back to Mexton. Taking a final look around, he pulled the door shut behind him, climbed into his car and headed for the motorway, confident that the police would treat the case as the suicide of a remorseful old pervert and sex trafficker.

Marnie crossed McKay off her mental list with a feeling of satisfaction. There were other individuals who had contributed to her misery while she was in Scotland, but McKay and Mackintosh were the worst. Most of the others would be caught up in McKay's revelations. She had plans for Mackintosh, but perhaps George's skills could be used elsewhere. He certainly seemed up to the task and clearly enjoyed his work, both for her personally and for the firm. He was enthusiastic in his enforcement role and had quickly become feared on the Eastside Estate. Nobody crossed George.

Chapter Thirty

Mexton 2019 | Monday 7th October

AN UNCHARACTERISTIC BEAM of autumn sunshine picked out the peeling paint and flowering rust on the garage doors as DC Martin Rowse strode along Malvern Row, munching on a sausage roll. He was systematically trying Ellen's key in the locks, and in one about half way along the row, the key seemed to turn slightly. It was clear from the weeds growing at the base of the door that it hadn't been opened for some time. He borrowed some oil spray from a young man who was mending a motorbike in a garage further along the row, and eventually the lock turned completely and Martin heaved the door open.

The last of his sausage roll hit the floor as he stepped back in horror. Three piles of bones, held together in roughly human form by mildewed clothing, were propped up against the back wall of the garage. The skulls lay on the floor in front of each skeleton, their eyeless sockets seeming to stare at him. Stunned by the gruesome sight in front of him, he shut the door, reached for his phone and called it in, warning the curious motorcyclist to keep back. His mind went into overdrive. Was this some kind of ghastly jihadi beheading? Mexton had never suffered a terrorist incident, and such atrocities were normally carried out in the full glare of publicity. A gangland killing, then. But why were the heads removed? Was it to send a message? But that wouldn't work, since the remains had only just been discovered. He would have to wait for the pathologist's report, but once his thoughts had cleared, he was convinced that George Wilkins had been involved.

Within an hour the row of garages had been cordoned off with police tape and the puzzled motorcyclist sent home. Martin had asked him if he'd noticed anything unusual about the garage, and the biker recalled an unpleasant smell a few years ago, which he'd put down to the drains the council were excavating at the end of the row. He confirmed that he knew George but hadn't seen anyone else hanging around. Martin stayed outside, waiting for Fiona and the forensics team to arrive.

'So this is what George was hiding, guv,' he told Fiona as she got out of her car. 'But why would the other gang members be so interested in it?'

'I think this is separate. Nothing to do with the robbery. It may be jumping the gun, but George obviously knew about the bodies. Maybe he killed them. Perhaps he was blackmailing someone? All this is speculation, of course. We have no evidence.'

Martin was about to recite the Sherlock Holmes maxim about the inadvisability of theorising without data but thought better of it. Instead, he put on a forensic suit supplied by the SOCOs and followed the DI into the damp-smelling garage, walking carefully on the stepping plates. The skeletons held a grisly fascination once the initial shock had worn off, and he examined them closely without touching. He'd certainly come across worse corpses in his career, and at least these three didn't smell. He was still staring at them when he heard a voice from outside.

'Hands off my patients, please.' Dr Durbridge, the pathologist, always referred to the bodies he examined as his patients, although they were inevitably long beyond curing. He told people it indicated a degree of respect, although the more cynical officers thought him just weird.

'It's OK, doctor,' Martin replied. 'I've not touched them.'

'I should hope not. And are you expecting a discount for bulk? Three for the price of two?'

Martin grinned at Durbridge's mordant wit. 'I'll leave you to it, then.'

He stepped out of the garage, glad to get back into the sunshine. Of all the sights he had seen during his career in the police, this was the weirdest, reminding him of a Halloween party he had helped organise as a teenager. But this time the skeletons were genuine, instead of plastic, and had been real people. They might have been lowlifes, the type that used to prey on residents of the estate where he grew up. A gross assumption, he realised. But they didn't deserve to end their lives in a dismal garage in the back streets of Mexton.

Dr Durbridge stretched, stepped outside the garage and removed his face mask.

'I can't tell you much at the moment. They've been dead

some years, but I'm sure you knew that. They were tied up, judging by the loops of rope I found behind them, and it looks as though at least one was shot – there's a bullet lodged in a sternum. I might need the opinion of a forensic anthropologist, but they look like young males, judging by the clothing and a first look at the bones. It'll be a while before you get reports, but I can safely say that these were not natural deaths.'

'Can we move the bodies now?' Martin asked.

'Yes. I'll start on them tomorrow morning. At least these three still have their heads.'

'Were they beheaded?'

'Possibly, but I won't know until I get them on the table. The skulls could have fallen off quite naturally as the tissues holding them on decomposed.'

'Thank you, doctor. Much appreciated.'

As Martin made his way back to the station he reflected on the job, something he often did. He loved the work, in the main, but things seemed to be turning nastier. He had new responsibilities, and he was anxious about what life would be like as a police officer with a growing child. Of course, many of his colleagues had families and it didn't seem to bother them, so perhaps he was worrying overmuch. After all, nothing dreadful was likely to happen to him, a detective rather than a front-line uniformed officer. Still, he would have been happier if he had more confidence in Gale. He didn't think there was anything basically wrong with her. She just didn't impress. But working alongside Mel was some compensation. She had spark, that woman, and would go far.

Chapter Thirty-One

JENNY LOCKED the door of her flat and hurried down the path, two reluctant children in tow.

'It's Darren's parents' evening. Why do I have to come?' moaned Kayleigh.

'Because I'm not leaving you alone. You're too young to be left without an adult. Come on. We'll be late.'

Jenny glanced around as she shepherded the children into her Clio, reassured when she saw the police officer over the road. At least her flat would be safe while they were at the school. She would check her mirror constantly to make sure she wasn't being followed.

As soon as Jenny's car disappeared at the end of the road, a bored, plain-clothed PC Roberts climbed out of his unmarked police car, stretched his legs and went in search of a toilet. He was supposed to be watching the flat in case someone tried to attack Ellen's family or searched the place for the missing jewels. But he couldn't ignore the pressure in his bladder and knew he wouldn't be long. He found a supermarket a few hundred yards away and availed himself of its facilities, picking up a can of cola on the way out. As he was paying, he noticed, out of the corner of his eye, a boy in school uniform sneak a couple of chocolate bars into his pocket. He followed the child out of the store and grabbed him, pulling out his warrant card to prevent any misunderstandings.

'You know I could arrest you, don't you?' he said, using his sternest voice. 'We'll see what the store manager has to say about thieves.'

'Sorry. I didn't want to. It was a dare. My mates made me do it. I can pay for them. Honest.'

'I don't think the word honest is the right one, is it?' The PC spent the next ten minutes explaining to the lad the consequences of being arrested, sent to a young offenders' institution and having a criminal record. He laid it on thick in the hope that something would stick, and when he had finished, the boy stood silent and sullen.

'This young man forgot to pay for his chocolate,' he said to the woman serving at the counter. 'But he won't forget again – will you?'

The young thief shook his head and reached into his pocket for the money but didn't meet the officer's eye.

Walking back towards Jenny's flat, and oblivious to the v-sign his recent captive flicked at his departing back, Roberts realised that he had been away from his car for over half an hour. He knew Jenny was at the parents' evening and he wasn't worried about his absence. She would be at least another hour. But when he returned, he noticed a car pulling away from in front of the flat at speed. The number plate was partly obscured by dirt, but he managed to read the last three letters. As he approached the flat he saw that the door had been forced. He pushed it open and entered.

Total chaos greeted him. Every room had been ransacked. Cupboard doors had been pulled off, drawers strewn across the floor, carpets lifted and mattresses ripped. The three-piece suite had been disembowelled, its stuffing spread around the room. Jars and packets in the kitchen had been emptied on the floor, and the bath panel had been kicked in. Someone very angry had turned the place over, extremely quickly, and hadn't bothered with the usual stealables such as mobile phones and an X-Box. Whoever did it must have been watching him and took their chance when he wandered off.

Realising that this was not an ordinary burglary, and knowing that he would get it in the neck for leaving his post, Roberts phoned the station and asked to be put through to DI Gale's team. Jack answered and swore when the PC described the scene.

'You should never have left your post, you fucking idiot. Suppose one of the kids had been left there? It's a good job Ellen's still in hospital.'

'Yeah, sorry,' replied Roberts, aware that he would get a worse bollocking from his own sergeant when she found out. 'What do you want me to do now?'

'Well guard the scene, you numpty, just like you were supposed to. When Jenny and the kids get back, tell them to gather a few essentials, disturbing as little as possible, and move them. We'll put them in a hotel while forensics go over the place, although I doubt that they'll find anything.'

'OK. I got a partial number plate if that's any help. Whisky Hotel Foxtrot. A silver Mondeo.'

'Could be useful, I suppose. We'll see if it matches any

vehicles registered to our suspects. Don't leave your post until forensics and someone from this team's arrived.'

'Yes. Of course. Really sorry, Sergeant. It won't happen again.'

Chapter Thirty-Two

Tuesday 8th October

THE START of the morning briefing was delayed slightly by Tom wheeling his bike into the office.

'Sorry I'm late, guv,' he said, sheepishly. 'Puncture.'

Fiona looked irritated. 'Why can't you leave it in the car park?'

'It's a police station, guv.' Mel interjected. 'It's full of villains.'

Several DCs laughed, but Fiona didn't seem to see the joke.

There was little to report. Two vehicles belonging to Maldobourne Holdings had been identified, but neither of their numbers contained the sequence WHF. ANPR sightings of them were being gathered, but no-one expected them to be particularly useful. Forensics had visited Jenny's flat and found nothing. The searchers had used gloves, and it would have been virtually impossible to separate the DNA of any suspect from all the other DNA in the flat.

'A nice pool of blood would have been useful,' the Crime Scene Manager had grumbled. 'But there wasn't one.'

Jenny and her children would be allowed to return later in the day.

The bullet found in the skeleton in the garage had been sent to ballistics, but it had deformed on impact, and a match with other rounds would be difficult to establish. Five other bullets, some in better condition, had been recovered from the garage, which was leased from the council by George Wilkins. He had paid the rent by direct debit.

The human remains were with the pathologist, who would prioritise them over routine work once he had finished with George, calling in specialist expertise when necessary. Clothing and possessions removed from the skeletons were with forensics, and attempts were underway to date them. Preliminary reports were promised for the afternoon, but full results could take weeks to obtain.

'Let's look at some of the people involved,' said Fiona, trying to inject some enthusiasm into her flagging team, most of whom were gazing morosely into their coffees.

'Osbourne is clearly the torturer, and the two goons, Ramsey and Marlow, are working for him. He doesn't have previous. They do. Maldobourne seems to be a front for Osbourne's enterprises and could be more than just a tax dodge. So I want as much information as we can get on their activities, properties, any other vehicles – everything. Tom, you take the lead on this. And keep on Kelvin Campbell. We know next to nothing about him. He's Osbourne's partner and, like the other three, he's gone to ground. It would be nice to get a search warrant for the Maldon Club, but we've no grounds as yet. Contact the Border Force, see if Campbell or Osbourne have travelled out of the country recently – and if so, where. Is there a pattern? I'm beginning to think there's a lot more to this than a bungled robbery.'

A couple of detectives murmured their agreement.

'Have you got anywhere with the files on the jewel robbery, DS Jessop?'

'Still working on them, ma'am. Nothing yet.'

'OK. Keep at it. Can someone contact the National Crime Agency to see if they've heard any whispers? And also the drug squad – is the Maldon Club known as a place to score? Dig around on social media for any mention of the targets – someone may have let something slip online. And are there any other low-lifes likely to be working for Osbourne, now that we know who Ramsey and Marlow are? Are there any informers we can tap for information? We can make a few quid available if so. OK – get some more coffee and crack on. I've put biscuits by the machine. Divvy up the jobs, Jack. We'll meet up at four to review what we've got.'

Throughout the day detectives and civilian staff began to build up more detailed profiles of Osbourne and Campbell, hampered by the noise of hammering and drilling from builders soundproofing a room for confidential meetings on the floor above. Information came in sporadically, and by five o'clock a slightly clearer picture of the two had emerged. Fiona began the briefing session by introducing a burly figure in a sweatshirt and chinos who was perched on the edge of her desk.

'Guys, this is DS Derek Palmer from the drug squad. He's

got some information to share that could help us. It's all yours, Derek.'

'Thank you, ma'am.' DS Palmer straightened up and spoke, his quiet, Welsh-accented voice hard to hear above the noise from the builders. 'DC Cotton contacted my team about the Maldon Club and its proprietors, Osbourne and Campbell. We've been keeping an eye on the place, when resources permit, and it's a puzzle. It's about the only entertainment place in town where there aren't drugs. The bouncers won't let anyone in if they look under the influence, anybody found using or in possession is thrown out and the staff are required to take random urine tests to check whether they've been indulging. From our point of view, it's the cleanest place this side of the Sally Army. And that makes me suspicious.'

'Why's that?' asked Tom.

'They're too good to be true. Which suggests they're hiding something. If you were a major player on the drugs scene, you wouldn't want your club raided and stuff being discovered, would you? I'm not suggesting that they store kilos of coke on the premises, but there could be incriminating documents or other material. They need to look squeaky clean to avoid our attentions.'

'So, do you have any other suspicions?' asked Fiona. 'How about Campbell and Osbourne?'

'We haven't been able to look into them in depth. We just don't have the time. We've got a major problem in the town with spice and increasing opioid misuse, particularly fentanyl. Cocaine continues to be an issue, and we don't know where it's coming from. And heroin still infests the Eastside. We're really stretched. We have seen both Campbell and Osbourne in the company of a few known dealers, but only casually, at social or sports occasions, with no evidence that they're doing business together. But they are persons of interest.'

'Thank you, Derek, that's been useful,' said Fiona, although privately frustrated at the lack of real information. 'We must keep in touch.'

'Definitely!' Palmer smiled. 'Happy to help.'

Chapter Thirty-Three

AFTER PALMER HAD LEFT, the team members grabbed teas and coffees or wandered off to the toilets. When the hubbub had died down, Fiona reported on forensic results, leafing through a sheaf of email printouts.

'We've had something back from ballistics. I asked them to fast-track the rounds the SOCOs picked up. The bullet in the skeleton could have been fired from the weapon Ellen found, but it was too damaged to give a reliable match. Two others recovered from the garage definitely were. So, we need to ask ourselves what a slightly dodgy mechanic like George was doing with a revolver used in a robbery and three murders. His fingerprints were found on the cartridges, but any that might have been on the weapon were obscured by Ellen's. There's also a partial from Ramsey on one round, but it wouldn't be enough to convict without additional evidence. If we need to, we could ask the lab to look for DNA in skin flakes and other traces in the mechanism, but that would be expensive. Probably not worth it.'

The others nodded while Fiona sipped her coffee and consulted another sheet of paper. Martin yawned, clearly lacking sleep, and Mel dug him in the ribs.

'I phoned Dr Durbridge,' Fiona continued. 'He was unwilling to commit himself to a definite opinion, but he said it looked like the skeletons in the garage were from three youngish males, probably white. They had been dead for years. The clothing looked about five years old, but he's not an expert – it's been sent to the lab for further examination. He's submitted samples for DNA testing and will get the opinion of a forensic anthropologist if there's no match. He found some damage to bones that could have been the result of gunshot wounds but needs to look further. There was no evidence that the victims had been beheaded. He also said that George's head and the body on the landfill matched and he appears to have been tortured. His colleague, Dr Fraser, is carrying out the PM. So, what have the rest of you found?' Fiona turned to Martin.

'I've been looking into George's finances,' he replied, flicking through his notebook. 'He wasn't badly off but hardly rich, on paper at least. His declared income didn't match his lifestyle. He didn't appear to be paying rent on the house or anything to Maldobourne for the use of his car. Marnie Draycott thought he owned them both, but it looks like he was living rent free and had a flash car for nothing. I think he was doing something for Maldobourne; something that they valued highly. Highly enough to reward him handsomely – and off the books. One other thing: a few years ago his bank balances started to drop sharply and he hadn't had much in his accounts for some time. The drops started around the time he began visiting online betting sites. It looks like he had a gambling problem.'

'Interesting, Martin. Thanks. Keep on him. What else have you found about Maldobourne, Tom?'

'Well they file accounts at Companies House, as they should. They're modestly profitable, owning a few properties and a small specialist transport business, moving computers, medical equipment and other delicate items around the EU and elsewhere. They pay their taxes in this country and have half a dozen permanent employees, taking on extra drivers and maintenance people on a casual basis when needed. Given that two of their places are crime scenes, we could get a warrant to search their offices and depot, but I suspect they wouldn't keep anything incriminating on the premises – especially after what's happened. We can't find out whether they rent other places unless we discover some documents – leases, rental agreements, etcetera. But they own a warehouse on the industrial estate, a vehicle repair shop and shop premises that they lease out to an estate agent in town.'

'Hmm. All sounds perfectly legit.' Fiona frowned. 'How about vehicles?'

'Three specialist trucks adapted for moving delicate equipment, a couple of vans and three ordinary cars, two of which we already knew about. I'll put the numbers up on the board and get them on the ANPR list. There's one thing of interest. A silver Ford Mondeo. PC Roberts said he saw a silver Mondeo with a number ending WHF. Maldobourne own one with the number ending in WME. Could be the same one – Roberts said the plate was dirty. And it was reported stolen shortly after the break in at Jenny's place.'

Fiona nodded approvingly.

'Nice work. They must have realised they'd been spotted and are covering their tracks. Check CCTV and ANPR for sightings, but don't hold your breath if the number can't be read.'

'Will do.' Tom looked pleased. 'And by the way,' he said. 'The car used in Ellen's kidnapping was found burnt out on waste ground this morning. The plates were false, but we're trying to trace the owners through the VIN number.'

'Probably nicked,' snorted Jack.

'What about Osbourne and Campbell?' Fiona asked.

'Both have filed tax returns diligently over the past few years. They use the same accountant. They pay themselves salaries from the company and also receive profit shares. They dabble a bit on the stock market but nothing too risky. Osbourne owns that modern place on the edge of town, which cost him a million, and a bungalow in Lymington. Campbell owns a restored Victorian manor house worth about three mill, in large grounds not far from Osbourne's place, as well as a flat in Portsmouth.'

Jessop whistled.

'They're certainly doing well for themselves,' Tom continued. 'Better than I'd expect from Maldobourne's activities. One point perhaps to worry about: both hold shotgun licences and they keep the weapons on their premises. Campbell also owns a rifle, apparently for shooting deer on his estate. Both own Range Rovers, and Campbell has a Merc. They have a couple of speeding tickets between them, but otherwise their licences are clean.'

'They're obviously careful. Don't want to draw attention to themselves. How about associates, friends, family?' She looked around the room.

'Osbourne is unmarried,' reported Martin, 'and Campbell doesn't appear to have been married either. In fact, there's very little on him before he formed Maldobourne Holdings with Osbourne. Social media has turned up a few pictures of Osbourne at business gatherings, and Campbell has attended a few charity galas and the like. We're trying to identify others in the pictures, but they're probably respectable enough. Neither of them seems to use Twitter or Facebook – they generally keep a low profile. They do travel quite a bit, to Europe, mainly. Probably on business, judging by the shortness of the trips. Both have been to the Caribbean on holiday, at separate times. Osbourne has visited Mexico and the States. Campbell has made several trips to Hong Kong and two to Mumbai.'

'Anything on phones?'

Tom lifted his gaze from his laptop.

'There's a few mobiles registered to the company, but they are all inactive at the moment. We're waiting on call histories.'

'OK, thanks. I've had a reply from the National Crime Agency. They were a bit cagey and said they couldn't give us anything useful. That means either they didn't have anything or they had something and weren't prepared to share it. They asked to be kept informed, which suggests they have an interest.'

DS Jessop muttered something about the NCA being 'up themselves' and two others nodded.

'Jack – have we got anything from local intelligence?'

'Not a lot. No-one would talk to us at the Fife and Drum. The neighbourhood officers haven't heard anything about George, Campbell or Osbourne. The usual grasses either knew nothing or would say nothing, apart from the fact that Ramsey and Marlow were none too bright – my words, not theirs. They looked uneasy when Osbourne and Campbell were mentioned, especially Campbell. No-one's been to the Eastside Estate yet – that's a nice job for someone who doesn't mind being spat at.'

A couple of DCs chuckled until Fiona silenced them with a glare.

'Mel and Martin – can you take a look?' she asked. 'See if you can find Billy Peel. He knew George.'

'OK, guv,' replied Mel.

'Shouldn't you send a couple of blokes, guv?' Jessop queried. 'Sounds dangerous, the Eastside.'

Mel gave him a look of pure poison, but before she could say anything Fiona replied.

'Mel is perfectly capable of looking after herself, DS Jessop. In case you hadn't noticed, she's a fully trained and experienced police officer. Surely you came across female officers in the Met?'

'Guv,' muttered Jessop, unrepentantly.

'Go round in the morning, you two. The local inhabitants will still be dozy and easier to talk to. And make sure you wear stab vests. That's all for tonight, guys. Thank you.'

As the team filed out of the incident room, no-one taking up Jessop's suggestion that they should join him in the pub, Jack grabbed Jessop's arm and pulled him into a corner.

'Just what is your problem with Mel?'

'None, mate. But she's tasty and I wouldn't want her to get hurt.'

'Tasty? She's not a fucking ornament, she's an extremely competent detective. If you spent more time listening to her and less time staring at her arse you'd realise this. We're all fed up with your arrogant and patronising attitude. If the Met's so bloody great, why don't you go back there?'

'Are you gonna make me?' Jessop's shoulders stiffened and his hands balled into fists.

'Oh sod off. This isn't a school playground. We're a team here and support each other. You've contributed nothing to this investigation. All you've done is preen and moan. Why do you think no-one wants to go drinking with you?'

Jessop pushed past Jack and strode out of the incident room, muttering. Jack considered raising Jessop's attitude with Gale but thought better of it. She was fully aware of his behaviour, and it was up to her, as their manager, to sort it.

Chapter Thirty-Four

Mexton 2015

By 2015, Maldobourne's business had been prospering for several years, with little or no police attention. An attempt to plant an undercover cop on the estate was foiled, the officer concerned ending up in an alley with two broken legs after George got hold of him.

Marnie, with George, moved into a moderately expensive house owned by Maldobourne and continued to plot her vengeance, all the time gathering evidence, which she stored on memory sticks hidden beneath a concrete sculpture in the front garden. The escort agency was still making her money, but she had little day-to-day involvement. Two long-standing employees now ran it, passing a cut of the proceeds, as well as valuable information, back to Marnie.

Campbell spent less time in Mexton than before, travelling around the UK, Europe and, on a few occasions, to the Far East. He never discussed his travels in front of Marnie, which irritated her. She thought she had won his trust. Although she didn't show it, she was particularly annoyed when she came across Campbell in a restaurant, accompanied by three Chinese businessmen. She approached their table, intending to introduce herself, when Campbell's expression and a slight shake of his head made it clear that she wasn't welcome. She swerved past the table, fuming. Surely he wasn't getting involved with the triads? That was tantamount to suicide. He refused to enlighten her afterwards, and when she broached the matter with George he chuckled.

'Kelvin likes to keep his cards close to his chest. He has a few things going on he doesn't want everyone to know about. I think there's a third major player involved, who we never see. Only Charles knows who he is. Still, if the money keeps coming into the firm, who are we to complain?'

Marnie shrugged outwardly but resolved to find out who the third man was. She was a firm believer in the maxim information is power, and a significant gap in her knowledge worried her.

Despite herself, Marnie had grown to like George and enjoyed his company at home. She kept an eye on his drinking and made sure that he didn't gamble, but otherwise left him to his own devices. She was realistic enough to realise that he would stray. Plenty of unattached younger women came into the Maldon Club, and he could charm their knickers off if he so desired. She would have to deal with that when it happened. But, for now, she was reasonably content.

That contentment was shattered when George admitted to being the driver for an armed robbery. Set up by Charles Osbourne, the raid had netted around thirty thousand pounds worth of jewellery, but two of the gang, former bouncers at the Maldon Club, were arrested and jailed. Marnie was furious with George and with Osbourne. Why they should get involved with such a risky enterprise when they had a substantial income from the thriving import and distribution business was beyond her. Perhaps it was the excitement. Maybe it was just greed. In any event she made George's life uncomfortable for a considerable time. When she asked what had happened to the jewellery he answered vaguely, saying it would all be OK when the others got out.

Chapter Thirty-Five

Mexton 2019

AT THE END of September 2019, it all disintegrated. Marnie had suspected something was wrong. George had been morose and jumpy for some time, but it came to a head when she found him in the lounge one afternoon, halfway through a bottle of whisky.

'Marnie. I'm in trouble.' He was slumped dejectedly on the sofa.

'What exactly have you done?'

'I hung on to the jewellery from the robbery and persuaded Osbourne to wait until Ramsey and Marlow got out before we split the proceeds. He was OK with this, but the others suspected I was double crossing them. Now they all want their cut.'

'So what's the problem?'

'I can't give it to them. I need it for myself. I owe money. I made up a story about it being lost. Someone knocked down a derelict warehouse on the industrial estate a few months ago, and I said I'd put it there. They don't believe me, and now Osbourne is looking for me.'

'So why the hell didn't you fence it after the robbery?'

'It was too hot. Osbourne knows all the fences around here, and they would've told him if I'd tried to get rid of it. I've sold a few bits and pieces but most of it's still stashed.'

'Where is it?'

'I can't tell you. If I do, Osbourne'll come after you as well.'

'Very considerate of you. You fucking moron. Why don't you just give them what's left?'

'I can't afford to.'

'So why do you owe money? Osbourne pays you well enough to look after the Eastside, and you do odd jobs for me. You don't pay rent, and the car's free. What do you need more for? Who do you owe it to?'

George looked shamefaced and couldn't meet Marnie's gaze.

'Online bookies. I need to get rid of the jewels to pay them off.'

Marnie was incandescent. 'You promised me, when I took you on, that you would stop. You said you'd put it all behind you. I was stupid to trust you. Once a gambler, always a gambler. How long have you been doing this?'

'A couple of years. It was fine at first, but then the debts mounted.'

'How could you be so bloody stupid?' Marnie stormed. 'You don't cross a man like Charles Osbourne. Ever'.

'What can I do, Marnie? What can I do? I'm terrified.'

Marnie had never seen George so scared. He had good reason to be. The thought of having a 'chat' with Osbourne would terrify anyone. But she had little sympathy for him, and her feelings had shifted seismically from respect and affection to contempt. She drummed her fingers on the arm of the chair and thought.

'All right, George. This is what you'll do. I still have a flat in London. I'll give you the keys. Leave the car here and get a train.'

She opened a desk drawer and took out a wad of notes. 'Here's a grand to keep you going. Once you get there, phone Osbourne and tell him where the jewels are. Apologise as sincerely as you can and tell him you're handing over your share. He just might let it go, if you're really lucky. Stay in London for a while, until things settle, and I'll be in touch. I'll find you some work. And don't go near any fucking bookies.'

Before George could say anything, she stalked out of the room, slamming the door.

As Marnie watched George's taxi leave, she made up her mind. She picked up her phone and dialled.

'The station. About ten minutes.'

Then she hung up and poured herself a drink.

George Wilkins settled back in the taxi, his head spinning. Could he really make peace with Osbourne, a man for whom forgiveness was an alien concept? Yes, he could tell the others where the jewels were, and where the key was hidden, but would that be enough? He rather doubted it, but at least in London he could keep out of Osbourne's way. He didn't think he would ever come back to Mexton. The threat of retribution would always be there, even if Osbourne agreed to Marnie's suggestion. He would miss Marnie, though. They had a good thing going until his gambling took hold again, and now he would probably never see her again. Still, it was good of her to help him out. Perhaps they could meet up in London, some time.

As he paid off the taxi, George became aware of two figures standing behind him. Marlow and Ramsey. He felt his world collapse.

'Going somewhere nice, George?' Ramsey's mocking tone was suffused with menace.

'Bit of a holiday, is it?' Marlow joined in. 'Before you go, someone would like a chat with you. Get in the car and don't make a fuss.'

George looked around him in panic. As well as Marlow and Ramsey, a third man stood next to the silver Ford that Marlow had indicated. A fourth man sat in the driver's seat, the door open. Tough as he was, George knew he was outnumbered and he had no option but to get in the back. He considered trying to bribe the men with the money Marnie had given him but knew it would be futile. They were bound by fear and wouldn't betray their boss for a few hundred quid each. All he could do was to rehearse his story and hope it would appease the others. And wish, with all his being, that he'd never had a drink with Charles Osbourne.

Chapter Thirty-Six

Mexton 2019 | Wednesday 9th October

BILLY PEEL WOKE UP RELUCTANTLY, dragged himself out of his malodorous bedding and reached for his cigarettes. Cursing the empty packet, he climbed into his trackies, grabbed his hoody and left the flat. He would leave his exercises until he got back. He always liked to keep his impressive muscles toned up, but right now, what he needed most was a ciggie.

Billy lived on the fourth floor of a block on the Eastside estate. He didn't pay rent. The previous tenant had died, and the flat was officially empty. Nobody wanted it. Although there were few furnishings, it was better than living with his mum, whose constant complaining got on his nerves. He didn't mind the boarded-up window either – it made the flat more private. Few people knew where he lived, and he liked it that way. As the enforcer for the Eastside Crew, a role he had inherited when his brother left town, it was useful to be able to come and go unchallenged. And it was somewhere to keep his weights and stash the gear and cash he'd been surreptitiously skimming these past two years.

Returning from the newsagent, he spotted Mel and Martin walking around the estate, talking to the few people awake at the early hour of ten o'clock. He pulled out his phone and made a couple of calls, 'Five-oh on the block,' knowing that the word would spread about the police presence. They wouldn't remain there long.

Five minutes later, the traditional Eastside welcome for the police began. A ten-year old boy scuttled out from behind a row of overflowing bins and sprayed 'Pigs' on the windscreen of the unmarked police car while another levered off the hub caps. Debris was hurled off the upper walkways, including bottles, cans and used nappies. Mel dodged a bottle just in time. As it broke on the concrete, a fountain of urine splashed over her trousers.

'They don't seem to like us,' remarked Martin, brushing the remains of a takeaway curry from his hair. 'Look, there's Billy Peel.'

The two officers pelted across the uneven paving and caught up with Billy as he tried to open a jammed door. He had been enjoying the bombardment and had expected the detectives to retreat, so their pursuit took him by surprise. He struggled as they grabbed him, catching Martin in the ear with his elbow.

'Piss off, filth,' he snarled. 'Leave now if you know what's good for you. You ain't welcome 'ere.'

Mel looked at her colleague. 'What do you think, DC Rowse? Threatening behaviour? Assaulting a police officer?'

'Yep. Billy Peel, you're under arrest. Come with us please.'

Mel and Martin scanned their surroundings for further attacks as they dragged Billy to the car. The shower of rubbish had ceased once Billy was in the firing line, but six or seven youths, some carrying baseball bats, poured out of a doorway and charged towards them. Martin shoved Billy in the back of the car, and Mel fired up the engine, screeching away from the scene before the gang could reach them. A belated blow from a baseball bat shattered a wing mirror while Mel desperately worked the windscreen wipers in an attempt to remove the graffiti. She could hardly see, as all the wipers did was smear the paint, but managed to negotiate the labyrinth of narrow roads around the estate without hitting anything. Once clear, she radioed for another vehicle, as the current car was effectively undriveable. She wasn't looking forward to seeing Jack. He was bound to have a go at her again. But it was Fiona who had sent them in without backup. Was she losing it?

Chapter Thirty-Seven

Back at the station, Billy was searched and put in an interview room while Mel and Martin showered and changed into clean clothes. A faint aroma of curry still persisted around Martin, but Mel no longer smelt like a public toilet. Billy, however, smelt sour and much in need of a wash. At twenty-three, he was well-known to the police and his lack of personal hygiene was legendary. Martin wondered if he used it to terrify people on the estate.

'Now then, Billy,' began Martin, after reciting the caution, switching on the recording equipment and offering him the services of the duty solicitor, which he declined. 'We want to talk to you about George Wilkins.'

Billy sneered.

'Never 'eard of 'im.'

'But you have. You were stopped in a car with him a few years ago. Surely your memory isn't that bad.'

'Oh. Yeah. Haven't seen 'im for years. Sorry, officer.'

Regret was conspicuously absent from Billy's voice.

'You see, Billy, George and his head were separated the other day. We know who did it but we want to know why.'

Billy's arrogance vanished and fear flickered across his face.

'Nothin' to do with me.'

'We don't think it is. But we think you know what George was up to. We've got you on a couple of charges here, so it's in your interest to help us.'

'Look, I don't talk to the filth. Two charges – even if I didn't get off it's a fine I can earn back in a day or two. Or community service, which no-one checks up on. So piss off.'

Some of Billy's bravado had returned, but he still looked worried. Martin tried another tack.

'Have you heard of Charles Osbourne or Kelvin Campbell?'

Billy's denial came a little too quickly.

'And like I said, I don't talk to you bastards.'

'Well, suppose we let it be known you did. We could drop you back at the estate, shake your hand and perhaps pass you a brown envelope in full view of your mates. How would that play for you?'

All the colour drained from Billy's face. 'You wouldn't. They'd kill me. That's entrapment or somefing.' His finger traced the outline of a skull tattooed in his forearm.

'Well, help us, then.'

Mel looked shocked at Martin's ruthlessness.

'I ain't naming names. And you can't say anyfing came from me. But George was known on the estate. He worked for some serious people. Nobody messed with George. 'E was hard.'

'How about drugs. Was he involved?'

'No comment. And that's all you're getting. So charge me or let me go.'

Mel and Martin conferred outside the interview room. It looked like they'd wasted their time – they wouldn't get anything more from Billy. Charging him wasn't worth the paperwork and certainly wouldn't get him off the streets. So they let him go, leaving him to find his own way home.

'Was there any point in that?' sniffed Fiona. 'We already knew he'd met George, but he did seem to know of Osbourne and Campbell. It's not a lot, considering there was substantial damage done to the car and you two could have been badly hurt. It's high time that cesspit was demolished. We can't have no-go areas for police officers.' She wondered whether she should have made them take some uniformed backup.

'Well, it does support our belief that George was more than a dodgy mechanic,' Mel replied. 'Billy wouldn't say who he was working for, but it's clear he was feared, as were his bosses. Sorry about the car and Martin's jalfrezi hair conditioner.' Mel grinned and Martin chuckled.

Fiona's phone rang and she turned away from the detectives, asking them to stay. 'Yes? Oh, hello David. What have you got?'

After a brief conversation she turned back. 'That was forensics. They've got a match from the DNA in the skeletons. Three members of the Eastside crew who fell off the radar five years ago. And one of them is Billy Peel's brother. Can you get after him before he reaches home? Call for backup if he gets back to the Eastside before you.'

Mel and Martin dashed to the garage and picked up a pool car. They caught up with Billy just before he reached the estate.

'What do you want? This is harassment. I ain't talking. I told you.'

'Sorry, Billy, I'm afraid we've some bad news. Would you like to get in the car?' said Mel.

Billy looked uneasy.

'What sort of news?'

'It's about your brother, Dean.'

'What about 'im? 'E pissed off years ago. Got into some bother and left town for 'is health. Never got in touch again.' Billy got into the car nervously, checking around to make sure he wasn't seen. 'So what's all this?'

'A couple of days ago,' began Mel, gently, 'We found the remains of three people in a garage that George used to rent. They'd been murdered. We've just had DNA results back, and I'm afraid one of them was Dean. I'm really sorry.'

Billy's face crumpled as he took in the news. Close to tears, he pressed the detectives.

'Dean? You sure? 'E was going up north for a bit until the bother died down. Can I see the body? I'm sure it can't be 'im.'

'I'm afraid there's no doubt. And he died so long ago that you wouldn't be able to identify his remains. We had his DNA on file, and it's a perfect match. But we do need to know what he was involved in and why he was killed.'

Billy sat in the car, trembling. It was unclear whether fear or grief had the upper hand, but eventually he spoke.

'Get me away from 'ere. I can't be seen with you. I can tell you somefing, but no-one must know it came from me or I'm dead. And I ain't testifying in court. No way.'

They entered the police station by the car park entrance

to reduce the chance of Billy being spotted. Billy refused to be recorded, but once seated in the room furnished for interviewing children and vulnerable witnesses, he began to talk, fiddling with his tattoo all the time.

'Dean always wanted to be the big man. 'E threw his weight around on the estate, and when the dealers needed a body to give someone a slap, 'e was the obvious one to do it. He got himself trusted and became a middle man. Word is 'e got a bit cocky. 'Im and a couple of mates, Danny Collins and Jason Burke, began to cut the product and skim some of the cash. No proof, but the dealers suspected. Then all three of 'em disappeared.'

'So you thought Dean had just left town?'

'Yeah. 'E looked scared the last time I saw 'im. Said 'e'd be going away for a bit. Didn't realise I'd never see the stupid sod again.'

'Well, I'm sorry he died, Billy. The DNA in the other bodies matches Danny and Jason. They were killed by the same person or people.'

Billy shrugged. 'They were always stupid, those two. An' I don't know who the main dealers were. I wouldn't tell you if I did. They'd kill me.'

'I understand, Billy,' Mel said. 'We don't want to get you hurt. But I'm sure you'd like us to find out who killed Dean.'

'Yeah – but I wanna find 'im first.'

'Best leave it to us. Tell us a bit more about George Wilkins.'

''E was a driver. One of the best. Didn't 'ave anything to do with drugs. Liked his drink though. Funny, drunk 'e was everyone's friend. Sober 'e was a hard bastard and nobody crossed him.'

'Did you see him around the estate much?'

'A bit. Not so much since Dean went.' Billy started as the penny dropped. 'Did 'e kill Dean, the bastard?'

'I'm afraid we can't comment,' replied Mel, 'but anything linking him to Dean's disappearance would be useful.'

'I dunno anyfing more. But if George did it and 'e's dead, 'e got what he deserved.'

'Can you think of anyone who would want to kill him?'

'Apart from me, you mean? Nah. 'E slapped a few people around, but they knew they deserved it. No-one would fight back or go after George. 'E must have pissed off somebody serious.'

'And who might that be?'

'No comment.'

'Word is that you're now doing Dean's job. Slapping people about when they deserve it. Enforcing for the Eastside Crew.'

'No comment. I ain't saying nothin' more. Can I go now?'

'I suppose so,' said Mel. 'But we may need to talk to you again.'

'Not if I see you first.'

As Billy left the police station, misery and fury fighting for pole position in his mind, he didn't notice the white van keeping pace behind him. When he turned into a side road leading to the Eastside Estate the van accelerated, pulled across the pavement in front of him and stopped with a mechanical clatter. Two men in ski masks leapt out of the back doors. In under three seconds they had scooped Billy up, thrown him in the back and jumped in beside him.

''Allo, Billy,' said Michael Ramsey as the van roared off.

'Looks like you've been talking to the filth. Someone wants to 'ave a little chat with you about that.'

'No. No. I never,' whined Billy, nursing a twisted ankle. 'They just told me they'd found Dean's body. He's been killed. I never said nothin'. Honest. Please. You've gotta let me go. Don't take me to 'im.'

'It's not us you've got to convince, is it? Now shut up before I shut you up.'

The only sound audible above the van's engine was Billy sobbing as a pool of urine formed around his trainers.

Chapter Thirty-Eight

Malvern Row 2014

'WHAT DOES 'e want with us down 'ere?' Dean Peel looked nervously around the garage where George had told them to meet.

'D'you think 'e knows?' Danny Collins couldn't keep still, twitching and shifting from one foot to the other.

'Nah,' Jason Burke replied. 'We were careful. No-one knew.'

'Knew about what?' A voice behind them petrified the three young men.

'Nothin', George, nothin'. We was just talkin'. It's a surprise for Danny's dad's birthday. We nicked 'im a bottle of Scotch. That's all.' Jason's voice trembled.

George Wilkins stepped into the garage, switched on a lamp hanging from the ceiling and closed the door.

'So it's nothing to do with the product you've been skimming, then. Or the cash you've been stealing from your employer?'

'Dunno what you mean, George. Honest.' Danny's fear made him twitch all the more.

'And what about you, Dean? What have you got to say? You're supposed to keep these two in order.'

'I'm sorry, George, I didn't know what they was up to. I'd've told you if I 'ad. Course I would've.'

George said nothing but drew a small revolver from his pocket, pointing it at the trio.

'Dean. There's some bits of rope on that bench. Tie these two little shits up, hands behind their backs, and sit them on the floor by that wall.'

Dean complied, Danny sobbed and Jason shivered with fear. When the two were secured, George walked casually up to Dean, smiling slightly.

'That's better. Now for you.' Before Dean could react, George slammed the revolver into his stomach and hit him on the side of the neck as he doubled over in agony. Dean slumped to the floor, semi-conscious, and George tied his hands together, pushing him against the wall beside the others.

'You must be fucking stupid to think you could get away with this. Your only chance is to tell me where you've hid the gear and the money. So start talking.' He kicked each of them in the guts to emphasise his point.

'It's nothing to do wiv me, George, honest.' Dean pleaded desperately while the others simply sobbed. 'I'd no idea.'

'Even if I believed you, you'd still be in the shit for not knowing about it. But I don't. So where is it?'

Dean continued with his denials, so George switched his attention to Jason. Cocking the revolver, he placed the muzzle against Jason's right knee.

'This one or the other one?' he asked calmly. Jason cringed and pleaded with George.

'Don't do it. I'll tell you. It's all in Dean's mum's flat. We cut a hole in the floor of a wardrobe. It's safe. She was too out of it on smack to know what we did, and the wardrobe was full of junk anyway. We'll get it back. Promise.'

'That's all right. I'll pay her a visit myself. After I've finished with you three.'

Stepping back, he shot Jason twice in the chest and did the same to the other two. He reloaded the revolver, checked that all three were dead, and collected their mobile phones and any identifying documents. His ears still ringing from the gunshots, he slipped out of the garage, locked the door and pocketed the key. As he returned to his car, he dialled a number on his mobile phone.

'All cleaned up. I'll recover the missing items tonight.'

'Thank you, George,' said Charles Osbourne.

Chapter Thirty-Nine

Mexton 2019 Thursday 10th October

'WE'VE GOT the pathologist's report on the body from the landfill. It was George's,' announced Fiona at the morning briefing. 'He was badly tortured before he died. The pathologist said he must have been in agony.'

Some of the civilian staff looked pale.

'How about cause of death?' asked Jack.

'His femoral artery was nicked, slightly. He would have taken several minutes to die. He would have known what was happening until he passed out from loss of blood. Guys, we're dealing with a total sadist here. Tom, can you get onto HOLMES 2 and see if there are any other cases like this?'

'Yes, guv. Any news on the skeletons?'

'The pathologist is still looking at them. We should have something from him later today. As you know, the victims have been identified from DNA. Dean Peel, Danny Collins and Jason Burke – they all had previous. Billy Peel has been told, and we're trying to trace next of kin for the other two. No luck so far.'

'Probably inside or dead,' murmured Jack.

As Mel was leaving the incident room a text from an unknown number appeared on her phone. 'DC Mel Cotton. Meadowgrove playground. The swings.' She dashed back into the room.

'A message, guv.' She showed Fiona her phone.

'Better follow it up. And take a couple of uniforms as backup this time. Oh, and give the phone number to IT. It's probably a burner, but you never know.'

Meadowgrove playground abutted the Eastside Estate, and the same rules applied as in the flats. You see nothing, you hear nothing and you say nothing, especially to the police. Periodically, the council would clear up the needles and used condoms from the bushes surrounding it, but it was not a place most people would want their children to visit. As the police entered the playground, the gate long-since wrenched off its supports, they found it deserted – apart from a figure draped over one of the swings. A dark pool was visible beneath the swing, which moved slowly in the chill wind that scoured the site.

'Stop!' shouted Mel to the uniforms. 'Keep away from the crime scene.' She phoned Fiona, asking for a doctor and forensics, and told the uniforms to ensure that no-one else entered the playground.

'Judging by the clothing, that's Billy Peel. And he looks dead. I'll go and check, but no-one else should go near him. Film me on your phone, Martin – that'll help establish a common approach path.'

It was clear that Billy was dead. His throat had been cut and his feet were bare, with bloody stumps where several toes should have been. Mel didn't touch the body but could see massive blood stains on the front of his shirt.

The SOCOs couldn't get a tent up over the swings but set up screens to hide the grim tableau. Half an hour later Dr Durbridge arrived and confirmed death. He conducted a preliminary examination before Billy's body was removed to the mortuary.

'He's not been dead long, but I can give you a better idea when I get him on the table. You noticed the missing toes, I'm sure. Oh, and someone carved the word 'Grass' into his chest – while he was still alive, judging by the blood flow. I'll look for vital reactions and confirm later.'

'Thank you, doctor,' said Jack, who had arrived with the forensic unit.

'Looks like someone saw him leaving the nick,' said Mel. 'We smuggled him in and out the back way, but someone must have been watching or knew he was there. Ironic. He didn't really grass anyone up. He wouldn't say who the big players are.'

'Pity. Sounds like he couldn't convince them. But it's also worrying that someone knows who you are and has your number. Better be careful – you don't want to fall into the hands of whoever's doing this.'

Mel shuddered and tried not to look scared.

'Don't worry, Sarge. I'll keep on my toes. I'll see if Billy was picked up by CCTV when he left the station. We might get an idea of who took him. But they're clever and wouldn't do it where they could be seen.'

'They snatched Ellen in broad daylight, don't forget.'

'True. But they know we're after them now and wouldn't

be so reckless again. I'll ask Tom to track down his next of kin. I think his mother's still alive. She'll need to be told that Dean's not coming back either.'

Chapter Forty

Dr Durbridge emailed his report on the garage skeletons to Fiona as she was finishing a sandwich at her desk. Brushing crumbs from her blouse, she called the team together and summarised its findings.

'The three skeletons belonged to young men between eighteen and twenty-five years old, which is what we knew given that we have DNA matches. There was no soft tissue to go on; decomposition, insects and rats saw to that, so there were no gunshot wounds visible, although two of them had chips out of their ribs consistent with being grazed by bullets. The three victims were tied up, and it appears they were executed.'

'Were they beheaded?' Martin asked.

'Dr Durbridge didn't think so. The skulls probably fell off of their own accord some time after death. And they don't seem to have been tortured in the same way as George – all their toes were in their trainers and their fingers were on the floor where the pathologist would have expected to find them if they'd just fallen off. But they could have been beaten without any bones breaking. With no evidence of bruising, Dr Durbridge couldn't tell. As we know, some of the bullets came from George's revolver, and it's reasonable to assume they all did. They're certainly all the same calibre, .38s.'

'Why didn't he shoot them in the head like a traditional gangland execution?' asked Martin.

'Possibly he was on his own and they wouldn't keep still,' Jack suggested. 'It's a short-barrelled revolver, not very accurate. Hard to hit a moving head unless you're standing pretty close and risking getting kicked or spattered with blood. A couple of rounds in the chest from six feet is easier but less efficient.'

'Well, thanks for that, Jack,' said Fiona. 'I'll know who to ask when I want someone executed.'

A ripple of grim laughter went around the room.

'Clearly the victims have been dead a long time,' she continued. 'A receipt from a supermarket found in Dean Peel's trousers had a barely legible date from five years ago, and this is consistent with the style of clothing found on the bodies. The hoodies and trainers were discontinued shortly before that, so we have an idea of the year they died.'

'That ties in with what Billy Peel told us,' said Mel. 'It was that summer when he last saw his brother.'

'OK. So it looks like we've solved this part of the case. George killed them, or was told to kill them. We can't be absolutely certain why, but according to Billy they'd been skimming cash or product. Why don't these idiots ever learn? But we've still no proof of who was behind George's death. We suspect Osbourne because of the torture marks on his body, but there's no actual evidence.'

'I think we should focus on the drugs angle,' said Jessop. 'If George was also skimming and Osbourne found out, he'd want to make an example of him. Can we get Derek the Drugs back?'

Fiona smiled at the reference.

'OK. I'll call him.'

Mel looked unconvinced that it was just about drugs.

'It's the attacks on Ellen that started this off, and they're all about the robbery. The gun is incidental. Suppose George convinced Osbourne that the other two had hidden the jewellery but, in fact, he kept it himself? When they came out, they went after him for their share. And Osbourne would want his cut if he organised the raid, which we think is possible. Ramsey and Marlow convinced Osbourne that they didn't have the jewels and that George was holding out, hence the torture. They could have accused him of skimming as well, I suppose – prison rumours and so on.'

'George must have been bloody stupid, or desperate,' said Martin.

'I agree,' Mel continued. 'So a valuable associate became a traitor to Osbourne. Not to be trusted. He had to get rid of George – but not before he extracted the whereabouts of the jewels from him. Once they'd got that information, George got it in the neck.'

Two people groaned and hurled empty paper cups at Mel, while Fiona looked sceptical. Jessop sneered at Mel's theory but said nothing.

'Your thinking is a bit muddled and speculative, Mel, but full marks for trying,' Fiona replied. 'Our priority now is to track down Osbourne. We're sure he killed George, and the motive doesn't matter for the moment. And we do need to talk to Campbell. We've nothing on him, but his name keeps coming up. Let's TIE him, please.'

Mel felt slightly put down by Fiona's lack of enthusiasm for her theory. Speculation it might have been, but so was Jessop's suggestion that George had been skimming. She got on with the job nonetheless, her mind on the elusive Kelvin Campbell. She wondered how someone could be traced, interviewed and eliminated if they didn't want to be found. According to the Border Force he hadn't left the country by any conventional route, but he could well have slipped away on a private plane or boat. Britain's coastline was nothing if not porous, and Campbell had the money to make his own clandestine travel arrangements. She felt mentally sluggish and realised she needed some exercise, so she persuaded Fiona to let her leave after lunch, promising to come in early the following morning.

'You know that garage door key,' said Jack to Fiona as they queued for sandwiches at the machine in the canteen. Hot food was only available three days a week, following austerity measures, and this wasn't one of them.

'Yes. What about it?'

'Well, why would George hide it in Ellen's flat? Surely he would get rid of it? He'd killed the Eastside lads and wouldn't need to use the place again. It wasn't a regular execution site, as far as we could see.'

'So, he had a reason to go back there. Let's take another look.'

Jack signed the key out from the evidence store and joined Fiona in an unmarked car. Arriving at the garage they saw that the crime scene tape had been removed and there was nothing to distinguish the scene of carnage from the other units in the row.

'We'd better get one of our own padlocks on this,' said

Fiona as Jack opened the door. 'We don't want anyone forcing the door open to take photos or souvenirs. There are too many ghouls about.'

'I'll get on to it. Now what possible reason could George have for coming back here?'

'Perhaps he hid the jewels from the robbery somewhere.'

'Yes, but the SOCOs searched the place thoroughly and found nothing.'

'Apart from three skeletons and a number of bullets, you mean.'

'Very funny. They even used ground-penetrating radar to check there were no more bodies buried under the floor.'

'Well, if the jewels are here, they obviously missed them. Perhaps some fresh eyes will have better luck. I'll take this side, you take the other.'

The garage was littered with car parts and other mechanical debris. Tools hung in an orderly manner on wall racks, and a solid wooden workbench was fitted with a vice and a drill on a stand. The two detectives poked around in a couple of steel cupboards, examined the floor for anomalous patches of concrete and looked behind the racks of tools. They found nothing.

Just as they were giving up, a shadow fell across the floor and a tall figure stood in the doorway. It was the motorcyclist from further down the row.

'I'm afraid you can't come in here, sir.' Jack moved to block him.

'No, that's all right. Just curious. That's odd, though.'

'What is?'

'That crankcase on the bench. It looks like one I lost a few years ago. Someone pinched it. Can I take a look?'

'Crankcase?'

'Yes. That large lump of aluminium. It's the base of a motorbike engine.'

'All right, but please don't touch anything.'

The motorcyclist walked up to the bench, his curiosity overcoming his nervousness at being in a place of such horror, and examined the chunk of metal.

'Yes, that's mine. I recognise the engine number, BA10 2302. It's from a BSA Gold Flash, 1951. The bike was scrapped, but I was saving bits of the engine for parts. I don't understand why George should have it. He hated bikes and was always taking the piss – in a friendly way, though. Can I have it back?'

'In good time,' replied Fiona. 'We need to examine it. We'll let you know when we've finished. Thanks for your help. We'll be in touch.'

'We should really wait for forensics,' said Fiona when the motorcyclist had left. 'The search team should have done a more thorough job, but I guess they were focussed on murders rather than jewellery. I'm inclined to take a quick look ourselves.'

Jack agreed. The detectives donned nitrile gloves and examined the engine part closely. Shining a torch into the opening at the top, they could see nothing of note, but there were two external metal panels on opposite sides that appeared to be removable, one roughly Y-shaped and one oval. It didn't take long to find tools suitable for taking the panels off, and they took one side each.

'Will you look at this!' exclaimed Jack, as he removed the oval plate. Around two cogs, where, presumably, a chain would normally be, a couple of necklaces were draped. Cloth bags, full of small items of jewellery, were stuffed into the remaining space. More jewellery was found behind the other panel.

'This is what George was tortured for,' said Fiona. 'When he said "It was in the flat" he meant the key, not the jewels. Call for a couple of uniforms to guard the scene until we can get this back to the station. It's worth getting any finger marks off the jewellery and the engine, for completeness.'

Fiona was relieved to have solved part of the puzzle, but they were still no closer to catching George's killer – and she was well aware that Hawkins would be watching her and expecting progress. The thought of screwing up the investigation made her shiver.

Chapter Forty-One

MEL SLUNG her bag over her shoulder as she left the gym and headed back to the station, where she'd left her car. Refreshed by her workout, and the shower that followed, she was still thinking about Kelvin Campbell and how to track him. Lost in her musings, she didn't notice the white van parked on double yellow lines a few yards ahead of her. As she reached it, the back doors crashed open, two men jumped out and a jet of liquid hit her in the face. Pepper spray. Burning pain seared her eyes and she started wheezing, her face on fire. Too disorientated to fight back, she was bundled into the van and kicked in the ribs by one of her attackers.

'We've caught ourselves a lady piggie,' he sneered, grabbing her tied-back hair and leering in her face. 'We'll have some fun with her when he's finished.'

'If there's anything left,' said the other man.

Mel shuddered. Despite the pain in her eyes she was sufficiently aware to realise she was being taken to Osbourne. The prospect terrified her. She had seen what he had done to Billy Peel. She had no way of summoning help. Her phone was in her bag, which had been snatched from her. She wasn't expected back at the station until the following morning. No-one would miss her until it was too late. Although she couldn't see them, she assumed her captors were Marlow and Ramsey. Both were physically powerful, and she had no hope of subduing the pair of them, even if her eyes weren't still agonisingly painful. It would be some time before she could see properly, so all she could do was wait and hope for an opportunity to escape.

The van finally stopped, with a cough and a rattle. Mel, nauseous from exhaust fumes and the jerky ride, was grabbed roughly, bundled through a doorway and dragged up some stairs. The bag placed over her head was superfluous; she could still barely see because of the spray in her eyes. She had no idea where she was and strongly suspected she wouldn't leave the place alive. The two men pushed her into a musty-smelling room and jerked the bag off her head. She could just about make out a desk and filing cabinet. It was clearly an office of some kind. A tall man was leaning against the desk.

'Detective Constable Cotton,' he said. 'I am Charles Osbourne. You and your colleagues have been taking too close an interest in my affairs. We are going to have a chat. And you will tell me everything you've found out.'

'Not a chance. And you can't go around kidnapping police officers. This isn't some cheap thriller.' Mel tried to radiate defiance, but inside she was terrified.

'I can guarantee you won't find any of this thrilling. I can also guarantee you will talk. Unfortunately, my equipment and premises are in the hands of your colleagues, so I'm going to have to improvise.

'Michael.' He addressed the taller of the two men. 'Go down to the builders' merchants. Get me a couple of heavy-duty plastic sheets, some bolt cutters, a pair of pliers, a saw, a hammer and some acid cement remover. Dwight, go round to Sutherland Place and get my overalls, face mask and gloves. And a bottle of Scotch – I may need refreshments during the process. Tie her up first.'

'Yes, boss,' replied Marlow. He tied Mel's hands together behind her back with nylon rope and sat her in an adjustable office chair, forcing her arms over the back and fixing them to the chair with parcel tape. Her ankles were similarly fixed to the wheeled base, and more tape was plastered across her mouth.

'Miss Cotton,' continued Osbourne, 'I am going out for a while. I have a business meeting. We will chat when I and my colleagues return and the premises downstairs are empty. You might care to marshal your thoughts to avoid as much pain as possible.' His calm, matter-of-fact tone was more chilling than hate-filled rage.

Before Mel could think of a suitable retort he left the room, taking his lackeys with him. She realised that letting her stew was a psychological ploy. She was expected to dwell on what might happen to her, but she refused to do so.

Left alone, Mel's only thought was escape. She realised that no-one would come to the rescue and she would have to draw on her own resources. Her bonds prevented her from stamping on the floor or making other noises to attract the attention of the people in the office below, and the tape over her mouth prevented her from calling out. She didn't know how much time she had but knew she couldn't wait for her eyes to clear. The rope was too tight for her to free her wrists and threatened to cut off the circulation in her hands, making them useless. There was some give in the parcel tape, and as she worked at it she detected movement in the chair back. Praying it was similar to those used in the police station, she groped around with her fingers until she found what she was looking for. The knob that adjusted the chair back. Clamping it between her bound wrists she managed to turn it a few degrees, chafing her skin as she did so. By repeating the manoeuvre over and over again, she unscrewed the knob and was able to lift the chair back up and out of its socket. It fell clear of the tape and left Mel's hands secured only by the rope.

By now her eyes were clearer, although extremely sore, and she could see that the filing cabinet next to the desk was unlocked. It was a cheap and battered steel object. One that, perhaps, had a sharp edge somewhere? She propelled the chair across the room by jerking her upper body. Turning her back to the filing cabinet, she hunted for a drawer handle. After an age she found one approximately level with her wrists and pulled it, her fingers bending as the rusty drawer screeched out. As she hoped, the corner of the drawer was sharp. She reckoned she could use it to wear away the rope around her wrists. If there was time.

It had been dark outside for over an hour, and the noises coming from the ground floor had ceased some time ago. Osbourne, or his goons, could be back any minute. The edge of the drawer was some distance above her wrists, so she had to raise her body half out of the chair while she rubbed the rope against the sharp corner. Holding the position was painful. The nylon was slippery and it kept sliding off the edge. The metal ripped into Mel's skin, flowing blood making the nylon even harder to cut. Gradually the steel made an impression on the rope, and she could feel it fraying. Acid burned in her muscles as she struggled to maintain her half-standing position. Her hands were going numb.

Then she heard a van pull up outside. Its distinctive rattling exhaust identified it as the one her kidnappers had used. She couldn't spend any more time sawing at the rope. She had to break it. Straining with all her might, and ignoring the fire in her wrists, she flexed her gym-toned muscles and tried to force her arms apart. The sound of the door opening below added extra urgency. The rope snapped. Her wrists came free, spraying blood across the wall. She reached down to free her feet. She heard footsteps on the stairs. Someone fumbled with a key in the lock. Only a few seconds left.

She had just managed to pull the tape from her ankles when the door opened. An astonished Dwight Marlow stood there, a bottle and a plastic bag in his hands. Now was not the time for official police restraint techniques. Mel picked up the base of the chair and threw it with all her strength at Marlow's face. It bounced off, leaving him dazed and with a broken nose. She picked up the back of the chair, hobbled over to the swearing scrote and smashed it into his groin. Howling with pain, Marlow crumpled to the floor. Mel pushed past him, locked the door behind her and stumbled downstairs into the street, her legs barely able to move.

The van was unlocked and the keys were still in the ignition. Mel started it up and slammed it into gear, swerving across the street and only just missing an oncoming bus. She didn't know where she was but kept on driving until she had left her prison miles behind. She pulled in to a side road, retrieved her phone from her bag in the back of the van and phoned the station. Then she threw up.

Chapter Forty-Two

IT TOOK LESS than half an hour for Jack, following a patrol car with blues-and-twos going, to find Mel. A low-loader arrived shortly after to take the van away for forensic examination.

'Don't say a word, Sarge. Just don't.'

Jack held up his hands as if in surrender.

'I wasn't going to. I only want to know you're OK.'

'I think so. A few cuts, and my eyes are sore. I just need to get home.'

'Not a chance. You're going to A&E. Come on, get in the car.' His tone was sympathetic but insistent. 'You have to get checked out. And we need to find out where you've been. Do you think you can remember?'

Jack interviewed her informally in the car and while she was waiting to be seen in A&E. She couldn't remember the route she had taken when she escaped but was able to tell him that she was held in an upstairs room above some kind of office.

'It was Marlow and Ramsey who grabbed me. Osbourne

was waiting and said he was going to torture me, to find out what we know.'

Mel started to panic as she recalled the scene, but she was damned if she would break down in front of her DS. Breathing deeply, she continued.

'They left me alone while Osbourne went to a meeting and the others were sent off to get tools. I managed to free myself just as Marlow came back. I decked him and found my way to the van. The twat had left it open with the keys in the ignition. I just got the fuck out of there. I don't know where it was, but I'd been driving for about five minutes when I called in.'

'You did great, Mel. Really. We'll need a detailed statement in the morning, but that'll do for now.'

At that point a nurse took Mel into a cubicle, dressed the cuts on her wrists and rinsed out her eyes. Eventually a doctor appeared, prescribed some pain killers and sent her home, advising her to take a couple of days off.

Jack took Mel home and reiterated the doctor's advice, which she fully intended to ignore.

The combined effects of the painkillers given to her in A&E and a large glass of wine had just about overcome the ghastly thoughts swirling round her head, but there was one more thing she had to do. She rang her dad.

'Hi, Dad. How are you doing?'

'Heard you've been in the wars, love,' her father said. 'I got a bit worried.'

'Yes. I didn't want to bother you but I thought you might have heard. I'm fine. Well, a few scratches but I'll mend, no problem.'

Mel knew that her father, now retired, had his ear to the ground and had friends still serving who kept him up to date with Mel's career. Sometimes she felt as though he was watching her to see if she was shaping up, something she knew he would deny. But she also felt comforted that he cared and supported her, despite his initial efforts to dissuade her from continuing when her mother died.

'I don't want to lose the only two women who have mattered to me,' he had said, and Mel had been quick to reassure him that she would take great care to come home safely at the end of her shifts. She knew he was pleased when she moved to CID, partly because he had been a detective himself but also because it was safer than some uniformed jobs.

She ran through the events of the evening, omitting some of the threats Osbourne had made, and described how she had escaped. Her father laughed when she told him how she'd disabled Marlow, and praised her ingenuity in escaping. She was just about to ring off, pleading exhaustion and the effects of the medication, when he said something that brought a lump to her throat.

'You did great, love. Your mum would have been proud of you.'

Chapter Forty-Three

Friday 11th October

THE TEAM CHEERED when Mel entered the incident room the following morning. Her wrists were bandaged, her back ached and there was still some redness around her eyes.

'You had a lucky escape. But well done,' said Fiona, smiling.

'Invincible, me,' grinned Mel, displaying more confidence than she felt. Despite the conversation with her father, the night had been full of ghastly dreams, and coming into work was better than sitting at home and reliving her ordeal. She was running on coffee and orange juice, unable to face a solid breakfast.

'Ssshh. That's almost as bad as using the Q word,' joked Martin. 'You're tempting fate.'

Mel knew that police officers on duty never say 'It's quiet' in case all hell breaks loose.

'I know. I'm all right really. Have we made any arrests?'

'Not yet,' replied Jack. 'We tracked the van back to the

Leyford area using CCTV and ANPR cameras. Tom remembered that Maldobourne own a property on the High Street, which they let out to an estate agents. That fitted your description, and we went in earlier this morning. There was no-one there, but there was blood spray on the walls, a broken office chair and a length of rope as you described. Forensics are there now, and hopefully they'll find something useful. Osbourne and Co. may have been sloppy. They clearly didn't intend you to get out alive.'

Mel gave Tom an appreciative smile, which made him fidget. His haggard appearance suggested he had been up all night.

'At least we're sure it's Osbourne,' she said, 'and we'll have some actual evidence as well as Ellen's statement.'

Fiona grimaced. 'OK. The good news is that Detective Superintendent Shah has agreed to put out an appeal for sightings of Osbourne. The bad news is that I have to do the press conference. I hate those things.'

A few grins were quickly suppressed when Fiona glared at the culprits.

'It's scheduled for noon, and I'm working with media liaison to decide exactly what I can say. DSup Shah will be there, but I'm leading.'

The press briefing room was packed with journalists, eager for the latest bloody revelations. Reporters from the local papers and radio station were joined by freelancers and representatives of some of the national media outlets. They hadn't had a story as juicy as this in Mexton for decades. Already nervous, Fiona found the packed rows of hacks extremely daunting and hoped her ordeal would be over quickly.

'Thank you all for coming. I am Detective Inspector Fiona Gale from Mexton Major Incident Team. We would like your help in tracing an individual who is of particular interest to us. His name is Charles Osbourne and his photograph has been distributed to you.'

An image of Osbourne appeared on the screen behind Fiona's head as the assembled reporters flicked through their press packs.

'Is he the Head-in-a-box Killer?' asked Jenny Pike, from the *Mexton Messenger*.

'We aren't making any accusations at the moment, but our interest is part of that enquiry. We would urge anyone who sees Mr Osbourne to contact us immediately. On no account should they approach him.'

'So he is the killer.' A murmur went around the room.

'I'm not saying that, Ms Pike. I am saying we need to speak to him and that the public should not approach him. I would be very careful what you write, if I were you.'

Fiona was already nettled. Jenny Pike was a notorious shit-stirrer with no love for the police since she had been pulled over for drink-driving a few months ago and now had to do her job by public transport and bicycle. Fiona realised the importance of keeping the press on side, but hated the sensa-tionalist approach of the tabloids and their cavalier attitude to the facts. Pike, in particular, held to the old saying 'Never let the facts get in the way of a good story'.

'We would also be grateful for any sightings of this white van – there is a picture and the registration number in your packs – which was involved in the kidnapping of a police officer yesterday.'

'Is this connected with the body found in the Meadowvale playground?' asked a stringer for one of the national papers.

'We cannot comment at this stage, but sightings, dashcam

footage and any other information on the van's movements during the past three days would be very helpful.'

'We've had two ghastly murders and the discovery of three long-dead bodies in the past week, DI Gale. Is there some kind of gang war going on? Are we safe on the streets?' Jenny Pike, again. Other reporters echoed the sentiments, and Fiona was bombarded with questions challenging the competence of the police.

'I can assure the public that there is no need to panic,' snapped Fiona, fuelling speculation all the more. 'We have no reason to believe that anyone else is at risk. There is no serial killer at large in Mexton.'

'Brave words, Inspector. But what if someone else is killed? And why are you in charge instead of a more senior officer?'

At this point DSup Shah intervened, sensing that Fiona was losing control.

'Detective Inspector Gale and her team are doing an excellent job and have a number of leads to follow up. I have every confidence in them. Please help us to do our jobs by doing yours responsibly. That is all. Thank you.'

Fiona stalked out of the room, angry at Jenny Pike and slightly humiliated by Shah's intervention. At least Osbourne's face would be all over TV and social media, she conceded, so something good might come of the unpleasant exercise.

Chapter Forty-Four

Saturday 12th October

THE FRONT PAGE of the *Mexton Messenger* was even worse than Fiona had expected. The headline was 'Hunt for Playground Killer', and a picture of Charles Osbourne appeared half way down the page. The main text ran:

Police in Mexton are floundering as a murderer stalks the town. Last week's horrific discovery of her husband's head on Ellen Wilkins's doorstep was followed by the brutal murder of a young man from the Eastside Estate, found disembowelled in a children's playground. Police have also disclosed that the skeletons of three young men have been discovered in a garage in town, victims of a gangland execution. Detective Inspector Freda Gale, the relatively junior officer in charge of the case, yesterday denied that a serial killer was at work in Mexton. She asked for the public's help in finding Mr Charles Osbourne (picture below) but refused to confirm that he was a suspect.

'Are we safe in our beds? The Messenger *wants to know. Shouldn't the local police bring in someone competent to handle the investigation? Why are they bothering pursuing trivial offences while citizens are in danger of being murdered? To keep our readers safe, the* Messenger *is prepared to pay for the services of a forensic profiler to help stop the terror threatening the town. (More details on pages 3 and 4.)*

Fiona was incandescent. She knew Jenny Pike was behind the piece and was riding her own hobby horse. It would be hard to think of a less helpful way of reporting the press conference. Fiona was grateful that DSup Shah had been there and would realise how she'd been misrepresented.

'And what the fuck would a profiler do for us?' she said to Jack, swearing uncharacteristically, when he poked his head round her office door. 'We're not looking for a cat-hater who wet the bed until he was fifteen. We're looking for professional criminals. We need a profiler like we need a hedgehog suppository.'

Jack grinned at her graphic simile and tried to reassure her.

'Don't worry, guv. Everyone round here knows it's shit. And the paper will find something else to sensationalise in a few days' time. A politician shagging a sheep or a reality TV star dealing coke or something.'

Fiona was mollified a little, but still dreaded meeting Hawkins for his daily update. The whole case was turning into a shower of shit, and she couldn't see her way out of it.

Charles Osbourne poured himself a large measure of his best malt whisky. He had just finished telling Dwight Marlow and Michael Ramsey what he thought of them, making it absolutely clear what would happen if they screwed up again. He had other people he could use. Perhaps it was time to dump those two and bring some new faces into play. But what about the long-term? He didn't normally drink before lunchtime, but now that his identity was known, and his face splashed all over electronic and print media, he needed something to steady his nerves while he planned his next move. Perhaps he should withdraw from the Maldobourne operation, leave the country and find something else to do. He did have resources, and plenty of money, but it would depend on whether the others would agree. Then his phone rang. The phone he only used for special, private conversations. He knew who it was although the number was not displayed. The man he feared more than anything.

'Yes,' he replied, a hint of a tremor in his voice.

'Charles. We need to talk. Meet me in an hour. You know where.' The caller's voice was calm but the undertone of menace was unmistakeable.

Osbourne shivered and poured himself another whisky. He pulled out the central drawer of his ornate writing desk and removed the small pistol taped to its back, checking that it was loaded and there was a round in the chamber. He put it in his pocket. Just in case.

Before he left the house, he made a point of using the toilet. He had a suspicion about what the caller planned and wanted to preserve at least some of his dignity. Looking round the flat, furnished impeccably with antique furniture and modern technology, he wondered if he would ever see it again.

PC Reg Dawnay peered through the rain that sluiced across his windscreen, looking for the caller who had reported a body. 'What kind of idiot goes walking in this weather?' he mused. 'Of course, a dog owner.' Dawnay had a dog himself, but the creature was lazy and usually preferred a warm kitchen to a soggy ramble. Just ahead, a figure in a yellow jacket waved at him to pull in. An agitated woman of about sixty ran up to the car.

'He's hanging from a tree in a clearing. I'm sure he's dead.'

'OK, madam, let's take a look,' PC Dawnay replied, attempting to calm the woman. She retrieved a small white dog that was tied to a signpost and guided the officer through the woods. A hundred metres or so from the road, hidden from sight by the trees, the body of a well-dressed man was visible, hanging from a branch. Blue nylon rope encircled the man's neck and a chair was lying on its back beneath the corpse's feet. Dawnay gulped. It was the first body he'd seen, apart from road accident casualties during a spell in Traffic, and the banality of it unsettled him. He called it in, put the woman and her dog in the back of his car and waited by the body until CID and forensics turned up.

Two hours later, Fiona called the team together.

'We can stop looking for Osbourne,' she said. 'He's been found dead in Darley Woods. Looks like suicide but I've asked for a quick PM. A car with false number plates was found nearby, which looks as though it could have been his. It's been recovered for examination. The tech guys are going through the satnav to find out where it's been. We may get some idea of where Osbourne's been living and who he's been visiting.'

'Told you we should have pulled him in,' said Jessop, just loud enough for Fiona to hear. She ignored him.

'So, with Osbourne dead, where do we go from here?' asked Jack.

'I haven't a bloody clue. I don't see why he should kill himself. Although his face was everywhere, he's been off the radar completely. He could have left the country if he'd needed to. There's so much we don't know about his dealings. Clearly, we must find Marlow and Ramsey. With Osbourne gone they may be prepared to give us something, though I don't hold out much hope.'

At that point her phone rang.

'Dr Durbridge, hello. May I put you on speaker?'

The whole team listened as the doctor reported his findings.

'I've not done the PM yet but I thought you'd like to know it's not a simple case of hanging. There's a horizontal bruise appearing across the front of his throat, and the tissue behind it is damaged. I'm not committing myself, you understand, but a possible scenario is that he was incapacitated or killed with a blow to the throat and then strung up. The marks from the rope are in the correct place for a hanging but fainter than I would have expected if he had struggled to breathe while dying. I'll know more when I've opened him up.'

'Thank you very much, doctor.' Fiona ended the call and turned to address the others. 'I think we can be sure that this was murder. Check that the scene is still cordoned off and get forensics back there. Tell them to look at the branch he was hanging from – see if it tells us whether the body could have been hauled up after death. DS Jessop – can you retrieve the rope from the pathologist, for the lab to examine?'

'Yes, guv,' he replied, muttering 'I'm not a fucking messenger boy' under his breath.

'I may be jumping the gun, but it looks to me as though Osbourne was an embarrassment, with his face all over the media. Someone couldn't afford to have him arrested so they killed him. Someone very powerful and with a lot to lose. And that person, ladies and gentlemen, is our prime target.

Chapter Forty-Five

Tuesday 1st October–Saturday 12th October

MARNIE HAD NEVER FELT it necessary to be attached to a man. In general, she despised the gender. She had serviced, and been abused by, too many of its members to have much respect for dick-led morons. George's lapse into gambling again had only reinforced this view. But she had found it convenient to have a relationship of some kind, with someone powerful. In return for sex she could gain information and influence, useful commodities in a world where trust was not a prominent feature.

She had long thought that it would be worth getting closer to Charles Osbourne. True, he had a reputation as a torturing sadist. But, as far as she knew, this only applied to people who had crossed him. On the plus side, he always looked clean and well turned out, and was powerful and wealthy – not that she needed extra money. Handing him George was not a malicious action. She just knew that George was useless and it was dangerous to shelter him. But it gave her an in to Osbourne that she exploited.

The day after George's departure, and probable demise, Osbourne invited her to dinner, 'to thank her for her help,' he said. He had a look of feverish excitement in his eyes when she joined him at the restaurant, which Marnie knew was nothing to do with her presence. She preferred not to speculate about how he'd been occupying his afternoon. With a little manoeuvring from Marnie they ended up at Osbourne's flat. She was somewhat nervous about what his sexual preferences might be but chuckled inside at the irony when she found he was a torturer who liked to be spanked. Still, she'd come across stranger things in her previous career.

'Charles,' Marnie began, one sleepy morning when they were lying in bed. 'George said something about a third man. Someone important. What was he on about?'

Osbourne stiffened.

'What did he tell you?'

'Nothing much, only that he was someone powerful. He didn't give a name.'

'I suppose you've been around long enough to be told. Yes, we have a third partner. He's involved with some highly profitable imports, the nature of which I won't go into. He keeps well in the background, and only Kelvin meets him, usually in a hotel a long distance away. George would never have met him, but there have always been rumours about his existence. He certainly wouldn't know his name. Only two people do.'

'Well, are you going to tell me?' Marnie reached down and he stiffened again, only this time differently.

'If you tell anyone else, he'll kill you. And me, probably.' Osbourne whispered a name in Marnie's ear and then gave his full attention to what she was doing with her hands.

Marnie's involvement with Osbourne was brief. As soon as his picture was splashed over the newspapers and social media, she realised he was a liability. She phoned Campbell, who quickly agreed. She waited in her car outside Osbourne's flat, and when he answered the final summons from Campbell, she let herself in with the key she had copied. Her target was the gun cupboard in the spare room, and it didn't take her long to find the key at the back of a desk drawer. Opening it, she removed an expensive shotgun and a handful of cartridges. The weapon and ammunition went into a bag of golf clubs, which she hoisted over her shoulder and carried to her car.

'It's a shame about Charles. But he had to go. Were you fond of him?'

'Not really,' replied Marnie. 'He was good enough company. When he wasn't torturing people, that is.'

Campbell chuckled and poured her another whisky. 'So what did your source find out about the polis? Who are they and what's the risk?'

'It's a team of about twenty, police and civilians. Most of them are just working in the background. The key figures are DS Jack Vaughan and three DCs, Melanie Cotton, Tom Ferris and Martin Rowse. There's a new DS, Paul Jessop, just moved down from the Met. He doesn't seem to do much, but there's an outside chance he might know of me. DI Gale is in charge. DCI Hawkins delegated the job to her, and we were hoping she'd screw up. She's not much of a detective – she got where she is on the strength of her admin and budget management skills. She talks a good talk, but there's not so much there. Likes a drink but not an alkie. The others are more of a danger, especially Cotton and Ferris. They're dogged and intelligent. They've found out stuff we didn't think they would. I'm not saying they'll take us down, but you're certainly their prime suspect, so keep lying low. They're not looking at me – they just think I was George's squeeze.'

'So have we got anything on them?'

'No. They're all squeaky clean.'

'Things are getting a bit messy. It would be handy if we could put a block on the investigation until things have quietened down a bit. They won't stop, of course, but we could do with some breathing space.'

'I know a few useful people. I'll see what I can do.'

'I'm sure you will.' Campbell smiled.

With Osbourne out of the way it was time for Marnie to finalise her plans for Campbell. Should she blow open his criminal career with the evidence she had gathered over the years and let him serve time? Should she maim or kill him? She would have to give her options some serious thought.

Chapter Forty-Six

Sunday 13th October

'MEL,' called Tom, 'I've got an address for Billy Peel's mother if you still want it.'

'Yes please. I'd better go over and tell her what's happened to her sons, and I'd like to take a look at where Billy's been living.'

'Shall I come with you?'

'Why not? If you feel like an afternoon out of the office.'

Tom grabbed his jacket and followed Mel to the car park. His forte was desktop detection, but he liked to get out into the real world occasionally. And, as a bonus, he would be riding with Mel.

The Eastside was much quieter today, the stark outlines of the tower blocks blurred by misty rain. The two detectives, wearing stab vests and backed up by a couple of uniforms, pulled up outside Rutherford House. Mrs Peel lived on the ground floor. This was just as well, as the woman who opened the door to them clearly had problems breathing. The cigarette dangling from her mouth wasn't helping her condition, and Mel spotted an oxygen cylinder beside a rancid-looking armchair.

'Mrs Peel? I'm Detective Constable Cotton and this is DC Ferris. Can we talk to you about Dean and Billy?'

'I ain't seen Dean for years. And what's Billy s'posed to 'ave done now? Can't you leave 'im alone? You're always trying to fit 'im up.'

'It's nothing like that, Mrs Peel. Can we come in?'

The woman let the detectives in, pulling her threadbare cardigan closer around her skinny frame. Her hair, perhaps blonde once, was a dirty grey tangle, and her arms were scabbed and scarred. Her face looked a hundred years old, but she was probably no more than forty-five.

Mel and Tom picked their way through the debris that littered the floor, their feet occasionally sticking to the purulent carpet, and waited until Mrs Peel had slumped back into the chair. They diplomatically ignored the dish containing a syringe, spoon and lighter on the floor beside it. The flat was filthy and reeked of stale cigarette smoke. Mel and Tom remained standing as there was nowhere to sit. What passed for a sofa was heaped with dirty crockery and the remains of takeaway meals.

'Go on then. What's happened?' the woman rasped.

'I'm afraid we've bad news, Mrs Peel. Dean and Billy have been murdered.'

Billy's mother sniffed. Either the information didn't register with her, or she didn't much care. Eventually she spoke.

'I knew it would 'appen one day, the bastards they hung

around with. Still, they're all like that round 'ere. Serves 'em right for pissing off and leaving me on me own.'

'We know that Dean was killed about five years ago. But you haven't seen Billy for a while?'

'Nah. Two years or more. And I'm still s'posed to pay rent on a two-bedroomed flat. The social thinks he's still living here and caring for me, but he ain't.'

'Could we have a look at his room, please? We need to find out everything we can about what he's been involved with. Tom will make you a cup of tea if you like.'

'S'pose so. He'll have to magic up the tea 'cos I've got none.'

Nonplussed, the detectives searched Billy's room while his mother finished her cigarette and reached for her oxygen mask. Predictably, they found nothing of interest in the stale-smelling room, whose only furnishings were an unmade bed, a chair and a smashed X-Box.

'Have you any idea where Billy was living?' asked Tom as they prepared to leave.

'Still on the Estate. Dalton House. I heard he was squatting in a flat on the fourth floor.'

'Thank you, Mrs Peel. I'm sorry about your sons. Would you like us to ask Social Care to get in touch about arranging funerals?'

'S'pose you'd better. I'm not paying to bury 'em. Billy was meant to be my carer. Got an allowance for it, too. Never did nothing.'

'Well that's the fifth time I've had to deliver a death message,' mused Mel as they left. 'And it's never been received with such total indifference before.'

'A mother's love, eh? But she clearly needs help.'

'She's not going to get it from the neighbours, is she? They'll sell her smack but do nothing to make her life bearable.'

'Perhaps that's what the smack does.'

'Yeah, you're right. Let's take a look at Dalton House.'

Dalton House was much the same as the rest of the East-side Estate. The lifts were broken and might as well have had 'WC' painted on the doors. Rubbish, burned out bins and the odd half-dismantled car were strewn across the tarmac in front of the building. The flats were barely accessible, as the walkways that connected them served as dumping grounds and buggy parks. Over half the windows had steel grilles fixed across them, and the piles of dogshit on the walkways outside many doors suggested that something large, and probably ferocious, lived within.

The detectives and the two uniformed PCs knocked on the doors in pairs. Few were opened, and when someone did respond, it was usually to swear or spit at them. No-one admitted to knowing Billy Peel or where he lived. Mel and Tom, coming to the end of the row and also their patience, knocked on a door next to a flat that had clearly been broken into. The door opened and the smell of skunk wafted out. A rangy individual with long hair and a straggly beard, in a T-shirt and jeans, appeared in the doorway, a large spliff in his hand. He tried to shut the door as Mel introduced herself, but she managed to get her boot in the way.

'We're looking for Billy Peel's flat. And you're going to help us.'

'Piss off,' came the reply.

'Well you're obviously breaking the law with that cannabis, and I bet you've got more inside. How about we wait here until a search warrant arrives and we can turn over your premises? We might even find enough to charge you with intent to supply. Or you can help us and we'll leave you in peace.'

'Next door. It was trashed this morning. Billy's not been back. Now sod off.'

'Thank you for your assistance, sir.' Mel squeezed as much sarcasm into her voice as she could manage. 'Enjoy the rest of your day.'

The flat next door had been turned over thoroughly. What little furniture there was had been hurled around the room and broken. The stained and smelly mattress had been slashed open, its contents covering the floor with mounds of foam. It took Mel and Tom only five minutes to realise there was nothing of use to them in the flat.

'Not worth bothering with sniffer dogs here,' said Tom. 'Any drugs are long gone. What's that written on the wall?'

'Looks like a phone number. And the word "Twitch". Someone's name, perhaps?' Mel dug out her phone and dialled the number. Faintly, through the flimsy wall dividing the flats, they heard it ringing next door. Mel killed the call before anyone answered.

'I think we need another chat with Billy's helpful neighbour.' Mel loosened her baton in its holster. 'Get the uniform lads to give us a hand.'

When they knocked on the neighbour's door there was no answer, but Tom's repeated banging eventually provoked a stream of abuse. Still the door didn't open.

'Police. Open up or we'll break the door down.'

By now an audience had gathered along the walkway, looking menacingly at the police officers and muttering obscenities. Mel felt uneasy and was glad they'd brought backup.

'Mr Twitch?' she asked, when the door finally opened.

'We'd like to talk to you. Down at the station. You can come with us voluntarily or we can arrest you. Your choice.'

'Fuck off. I've got nothing to say to the filth.'

'Really? The word "twitch" seemed to ring a bell with you. You look nervous. And your phone number was on Billy's wall. A now-deceased drug dealer's.'

Without warning, the suspect lunged at the two detectives, knocking Mel backwards and elbowing Tom in the face, setting off a prolific nose bleed. The two uniformed officers wrestled him briskly to the ground and Mel handcuffed him.

Mel shut the flat door, noticing that a high-security lock was fitted, and stuck some 'Police Do Not Enter' tape across it. Despite his struggles, and the hostile onlookers, they managed to manhandle Twitch down four sets of stairs and into a police car while Tom attempted to staunch the blood pouring from his nose and down his neck. Mel handed him a paper tissue.

'You'll need a new sweatshirt,' she smiled, sympathetically.

'I need a new nose, more like,' came Tom's muffled reply. 'An afternoon out of the office. A bit of fresh air, you said.'

'Yeah. Work's a bitch.' Mel chuckled. 'Better make sure your tetanus shots are up to date. I hate to think what diseases Mr Twitch is carrying.'

'Thanks a bunch.'

'Still, at least we've got grounds for arrest and we won't need a search warrant to go over his flat. Every cloud, eh?'

Tom seemed unimpressed.

Tom sat in the station canteen, an ice pack clamped to his nose. He wasn't really hurt, just a bit embarrassed. He hoped he hadn't made a complete idiot of himself in front of Mel, but she hadn't said anything. He knew she appreciated his research skills, but could she like him for himself?

He certainly wasn't looking his best in a bloodstained shirt, so he headed off to the custody suite in search of a clean one. There was always a store of clothing for people arrested or rescued, whose own clothes were unwearable or had to be removed for forensic testing. He just hoped there would be something there to fit his lanky frame.

Chapter Forty-Seven

MEL AND MARTIN had just got the suspect settled in the interview room when the door opened and Fiona entered, followed by Derek Palmer, the drugs squad sergeant.

'Could you turn off the tape, please?' Fiona looked annoyed. 'Derek here has something to tell you.'

'Hi. I'm afraid you've just nicked an undercover detective,' Derek informed them. 'He's been deep in the Eastside Estate for over a year now. I couldn't tell you any more about our operations when we spoke before. It's all on a need-to-know. Anyway, this is David Parry, known as Twitch.'

Parry stood up and proffered his hand to Mel.

'Sorry about your mate's nose. I had to make it look convincing or my cover was blown. You'd better charge me with assaulting a police officer and let me out on bail. It's vital that I stay embedded for at least the next six months, so make sure the trial date is a long way off.'

'Yeah, we can do that,' said Fiona. 'But what can you tell us in return?'

Parry looked at Derek, who nodded.

'I think you already know that Billy Peel was an enforcer and middle man for the Eastside Crew. I've managed to listen in to a few of his calls, and it was clear that he was skimming product and, possibly, cash as well. He had aspirations. If he hadn't been suspected as a grass, he would have been killed for that eventually. He was obviously scared of someone who phoned him frequently.'

'Do you know who?' asked Martin.

'I'm not sure, but I think it was Charles Osbourne. The voice seemed a bit posh. We believe he was the main source for the heroin and methamphetamine feeding into the estate and probably the rest of the town. We also think he was running county lines operations into the villages. He didn't handle the drugs himself. People like Billy and George Wilkins were middle men. They would pick the stuff up from a dead drop somewhere – an empty factory or derelict house – and get it onto the market.'

'What about Kelvin Campbell?'

'His name doesn't crop up very often, but when it does people seem scared of him. Even more than of Osbourne. We think he's a senior partner who keeps himself well in the background. There's a third person at the top, too.'

'Oh?'

'Yeah. Wilkins referred to the "Three Wise Men" on a couple of occasions.'

'So you knew George?'

'I met him a few times. I started some low-level dealing to maintain my cover. Cannabis. He dropped in to explain what's what and collected tax from me. His lot weren't inter-ested in weed, but they took a cut of everything sold on the estate. He was feared.'

'I thought Billy was the enforcer,' interjected Mel.

'Yes, for small transgressions. But if you'd really pissed

someone off you had to deal with George. I know of at least three hospitalisations for which he was responsible, and there were rumours that he'd killed people. Not just the three kids you found in the garage but other players who tried to move in to the Eastside.'

'So that explains why he was living rent-free and had a flash car registered to Maldobourne,' said Fiona. 'He was doing their seriously dirty work for them and expected to be rewarded. A bit of a step-up from handling dodgy MOT certificates. Do we know where the drugs are coming from?'

'Now that's what I'm there to find out. We think the coke is coming in from Mexico but we're not sure of the route. The heroin seems to start from Afghanistan and come in via Turkey or Albania, the meth from Amsterdam. We've got no hard evidence, though. Now Billy's gone I might be able to get in deeper. Find out more. The National Crime Agency's dealing with that side but they're not giving much away.'

'Anything else you can tell us?'

'I don't think so. I'll pass on a message if anything comes up. You'd better charge me and release me. Oh, you need to rough me up a bit. They'll expect that if I've hit a copper.'

'I'm sure we can arrange that. Why "Twitch", by the way?'

'I affected a mannerism as part of my cover. Part of my face twitches on and off. It helps me to conceal lies.'

With David Parry charged and released with the beginnings of a black eye, Fiona, Mel and Martin were joined by Tom. His bloodstained shirt had been replaced with a faded Grateful Dead T-shirt, which barely reached past his midriff.

'Peace, man,' joked Martin, in slurred hippy tones.

'It's all they had in the custody suite that fitted me,' Tom explained apologetically, pulling the T-shirt down to cover his firm belly.

Over coffee they concluded that they weren't much further forward.

'With both Billy Peel and Osbourne dead, and the East-side Estate off limits because of the undercover cop, we have to find another way in,' said Fiona, gloomily. 'Any ideas?'

'I could have a word with a few old mates in the Met drug squad if you like,' suggested Jessop. 'See if they've heard anything.'

'Good idea. Thanks,' replied Fiona.

'Surprised he's got any mates,' Mel whispered to Tom, who suppressed a grin.

Jack joined them and reminded them that they still needed to find Campbell.

'I was looking over the notes from conversations with the Border Force,' he reported. 'There have been a couple of instances where Campbell has left the country but not been seen re-entering. So either he's getting back in through unofficial channels or using an alias.'

'Why would he do that? Use an alias, I mean,' asked Martin.

'Could be he was meeting someone who only knew him under an assumed name. He wouldn't risk his real identity coming out. He must have duplicate – or multiple – passports. Or he just didn't want his movements monitored.'

'Well spotted, Jack,' said Fiona. 'Let's take a look at his credit card transactions around those times. That's your speciality, Tom – and you can even do it in your fashionable T-shirt.'

The others laughed, and Tom grinned ruefully.

'In the meantime, can we look more closely at

Maldobourne's operations? Frequent trips to and from the EU could be a cover for drug smuggling. And any thoughts on the third man would be most welcome.' Fiona turned to Jessop. 'When did the lab say they'd look at the rope, Paul?'

'Oh shit. It's still in my car. I got diverted. Sorry, guv.'

'Well you'd better get it round there now before they shut, hadn't you?'

'Yes. Right away. Sorry, again.'

After Jessop had left, Jack let rip.

'Is he really that useless or is he trying to screw things up? He's as much use as a concrete lifejacket, and he pisses everyone off royally. How the fuck did he ever make sergeant?'

'I don't think he's being deliberately obstructive,' said Fiona, 'but I agree he puts people's backs up. DCI Hawkins thought he'd be an asset, but I've yet to see it.'

She looked at the clock.

'That's enough for today. Join me in the pub. You've all earned a drink.'

Jack declined. 'I'm booked for a pub quiz with Sarah tonight. But thanks anyway.'

The others knew that Jack and his wife made a formidable team, but they wondered whether there was another reason why he wouldn't join them for a quick one.

The White Hart was a traditional pub, without fruit machines or a giant screen showing sports games. It stayed in business because it offered decent beer, simple food and a place to relax. Sitting round a table in the corner, the detectives agreed not to talk about the case as they could be overheard.

'So how are you enjoying CID, Mel?' asked Fiona, as the DCs sipped their beer. 'You've been here, what, five months?'

'Great, ma'am. Great.'

'Drop the ma'am, please. We're off duty.'

'OK,' replied Mel, still unsure how to address her senior officer. Surely she shouldn't call her Fiona?

'You've certainly had a lively time, what with Wilkins, Osbourne and Peel. Sound like a firm of solicitors, don't they?'

The others grinned dutifully.

'It's not always this exciting,' said Martin. 'I've been in CID for five years and only once before has it been like this. A bloke was going around attacking sex workers, sometimes fatally. Turned out to have been a defrocked vicar who'd taken to crack and believed they were agents of the devil sent to steal his stash.'

'What happened?'

'Jack caught him on Bowyer's Row, about to stab another victim. Hung on to him till backup arrived. Lost nearly two pints of blood in the process. That's how he got the scar. He's a good man to have in your corner, is Jack.'

Mel looked thoughtful.

'So why did we all join, anyway?' Tom asked, his jacket concealing the logo on the T-shirt. 'I went to university to study IT but didn't complete the course. Too much debt was building up. I wanted to use my brain for something worthwhile and didn't fancy working for some mammoth American software corporation. Computers are vital in policing these days, so I thought it would be a good career. My parents were horrified, as they wanted me to work in a nice safe office for an inflated salary. My old schoolmates laughed themselves silly at the thought of the class computer geek joining the police and mixing it with criminals. But I love it. I may apply to join the NCA when I've had a bit more experience.'

'My mum and dad were both in the job,' contributed Mel. 'So I guess it runs in the family. They tried to dissuade me at first, but once they recognised I was serious they supported me. I was always fascinated by their war stories, although I realise now they omitted a lot of detail. Dad was a DCI when he retired. My mum was killed while I was still in training. Dad wanted me to give up then, but I felt I owed it to her to finish, so I explained how I felt and he backed my decision to continue. I'm glad I did. I feel I've got a lot to live up to.' The others nodded approvingly. 'How about you, Martin?'

'It's a bit of a cliché, but I wanted to make things better. I grew up on a rough estate, like the Eastside, and it would have been easy to slip into crime. Several of my mates did. When my mum was mugged on the way to the shops, I could have gone vigilante but figured I would be better off doing things officially. Three years later, as a probationer, I had the plea-sure of helping to nick the bastard who did it. I lost a few friends from the estate but gained some great colleagues.'

Fiona's explanation was rather more prosaic. 'I was bored working in retail, managing a shop. I was still in my twenties and wanted something a bit more exciting. A recruiting poster for the Specials caught my eye, but I thought why not join the regular police? The career structure and pension appealed, so I went for it and got in. Best decision I ever made. I love the job, and it's much more interesting than managing teenagers selling make-up and clothes.'

'OK,' said Martin. 'Best and worst. What's the best thing about the job and what's the worst?'

The detectives thought for a minute before Tom, hesi-tantly, spoke.

'Finding stuff out, putting it together and completing the puzzle that sends a villain down, I suppose.'

'Proper little Inspector Morse, aren't you, Tom?' Mel said, affectionately.

Tom blushed and continued, 'The worst bit is seeing how vile people can be to each other.'

The others nodded in agreement, and Fiona spoke up.

'Feeling you're doing something to protect people and right wrongs is the best bit. And the worst is trying to patch up the holes in the fabric of society with decreasing resources.' She finished on an unusually angry note, which made the others sit up. 'You asked, Martin,' she said. 'How about you?'

'Putting away the scum who prey on the poor and vulnerable, like the scrote who robbed OAPs outside post offices on pension day. It took us four months to catch him, but he went down for a lot longer than that. The worst bit is knowing there are plenty more out there.'

'I've not been in CID as long as you three, but I guess it's seeing a tricky case to its conclusion and getting the crim into court,' contributed Mel. 'My worst experience was delivering the death message to the parents of a seventeen-year-old whose body was found decomposing in a squat after she'd OD'd. Sorry. A bit of a conversation-stopper.'

They continued chatting for another half an hour, with Mel trying to lighten things by telling a series of jokes and Martin relating anecdotes, until Fiona offered to buy another round. The others declined, explaining that they were driving. Thanking her, they drifted back to their cars while she decided on another gin and tonic. Just the one, for now.

Chapter Forty-Eight

Monday 14th October

FIONA SAT DISCONSOLATELY in her office and shuffled paper-work half-heartedly. Yet again she felt that things were slipping away from her. She had no complaints about her team. They worked well together and seemed to have accepted her as the boss. They were as eager to crack the case as she was. But she knew that Hawkins was breathing down her neck, and if she screwed up she could say goodbye to promotion, at least for a good few years.

She wished she had someone to talk to, but without her husband, and with no siblings or close colleagues in the job, she was pretty much alone.

After the team had spent a moderately productive day trawling through databases and witness statements, she called them together in the briefing room.

'OK, people. We have a warrant to search Kelvin Campbell's home. A drone flight early this morning showed some activity on the site, and we're going in, with firearms support.

We know he keeps a rifle and a shotgun on the premises, so I'm taking no chances. We'll strike at dawn, so go home and get some sleep. Meet here at five a.m. please.'

Tuesday 15th October, early

Kelvin Campbell's country house was a large Victorian building in substantial grounds, surrounded by a tall stone wall and protected by sturdy, electrically powered, iron gates. It loomed out of the dawn's autumn mist like the set for a 1960s horror film. Mature trees hid most of the house from the road and cast ominous shadows across an unmown lawn, adding to the spookiness.

There was no sign of life within, and the intercom fixed to the gatepost remained silent when Mel pressed it. The gates were unlikely to respond to the Big Red Key, the battering ram used to gain entry to normal premises, but after walking half way round the perimeter, Martin discovered a small wooden door set in the wall. This quickly succumbed to blows from a burly constable wielding the ram, and the firearms unit approached the house through a disused vegetable garden.

The impressive main door to the house was unlocked, and the lead firearms officer pushed it open with his foot, keeping his body to the side of the opening.

'Armed police. Come out with your hands on your heads. Now.' His shouts echoed through the building, but no-one answered. 'OK, guys. In we go.'

Four Authorised Firearms Officers stormed into the house, carbines at the ready, shouting warnings and commands. It only took them three minutes to declare the building empty. They then turned their attention to a couple of outbuildings, with a similar result. Nothing.

Fiona mused over the unlocked door.

'D'you think we're expected, Jack? Or does Campbell just rely on the gates for his security?'

'Anyone who knows Campbell's reputation wouldn't risk breaking in. But surely he'd be at risk from casual burglars unfamiliar with the area?'

'But someone just passing by wouldn't see the building through the trees. They certainly wouldn't know the door was unlocked.'

'Perhaps he knew we were coming and didn't want his nicely painted door smashed in,' Jack joked, giving Fiona pause for thought.

'Hmm. OK, let's get on with the search. The AFOs have finished.'

Looking around, Fiona recognised wealth. The house was comfortably furnished in an old-fashioned style. The furniture was mainly reproduction antique pieces, and the wallpaper was printed with William Morris designs. Ornaments and oil paintings reflected the late Victorian era, and Campbell obviously had a fondness for antlers in his decorating, judging by the glassy-eyed animal heads adorning the hall. A polished turtle shell was fixed to the wall above a doorway, and an ivory chess set sat untouched on an occasional table. Modern audio equipment, and flat-screen televisions in several rooms, seemed out of place. As to evidence linking Campbell with any crimes or suspicious behaviour, there was none. His gun cupboard, opened with keys found by Martin in a desk drawer, contained a shotgun and a few cartridges, but no rifle.

'Look at this, ma'am,' called Mel from the kitchen. Fiona followed her voice and found the DC brandishing a half-eaten sandwich, yellow mayonnaise clashing with her blue nitrile gloves. 'This is still fresh. The bread is soft and the lettuce has only just started to wilt. It can't have been here more than a couple of hours. It was in the bin next to an empty milk bottle with a use by date two days away.'

'Well spotted. I'm getting the feeling something spooked Campbell and he cleared out in a hurry.'

'Such as?'

'Jack joked about him expecting us. Suppose he was? Suppose he had a tip-off? He would have made himself scarce and taken anything incriminating with him. We've not found a computer or a phone here, and there are no documents to speak of.'

'That means someone's bent. Someone on the team?'

'Not necessarily. Dozens of people knew the raid was going to happen, from civilian support staff to the JP who signed the search warrant. I should have been more discreet, and I think we'd better be a bit more careful about telling people what we're up to in future.' Fiona wondered whether she had screwed up again.

'Need-to-know?' said Jack.

'Yes. Need-to-know.'

The detectives returned to the station after a fruitless two hours. Fiona bought bacon rolls from a nearby café and a fried egg sandwich for Tom. They washed the food down with coffee from the coffee maker in the office, a donation from a grateful restauranteur. Mexton CID had put away a couple of young thugs who were demanding protection money from him. While gifts to individual officers were strictly forbidden, the powers-that-be decided that providing an alternative to canteen dishwater for anyone serving as a detective was acceptable and good for morale.

Brushing crumbs from her jumper and wiping grease from her fingers, Fiona voiced the thoughts of the other team members.

'Campbell is as slippery as Lord bloody Lucan. He seems to have arrived from nowhere, and no-one can find him. Tom, you're our database whizzkid. I want you to make Campbell your priority. Drop everything else. Find out where he came from, where he's been and what he's done. So, let's go to work.'

Chapter Forty-Nine

'GOT HIM!' shouted Tom, after several hours sifting through databases and social media. Martin and Mel gathered round while Jack looked on from his desk across the room.

'I figured from his name that there could be a Scottish connection, so I started digging around in records of births, deaths, marriages and name changes up there. I wrote an algorithm myself and came up with gold!

'Kelvin Campbell was born Callum Mackintosh, in Glasgow in 1963. He changed his name in Scotland by declaration but didn't take out an enrolled deed poll in England. It meant he could get a birth certificate in his new name and hence a fresh set of official documents.

'I've run a search on Scottish media, and it seems he operated as an investment broker in Glasgow for a while, staying just this side of the law. When things went pear-shaped and the police started looking at him he disappeared, changed his name and moved to London. He had a wife, Eleanor, who seems to have dropped out of sight. His business partner apparently committed suicide just before he left and took the blame for various frauds. The Met's vice squad had their suspicions about his London activities, but couldn't find anything that would stick. Then he moved to Mexton and set up Maldobourne Holdings with Osbourne.'

'Brilliant!' said Jack, his face animated for the first time in days. 'So he could still be travelling, driving and owning property as Mackintosh?'

'Yep. And I've checked with the Passport Office. There's a current passport in his original name, which was renewed a couple of years ago. He could have made dozens of journeys we've missed because we were looking for Kelvin Campbell.'

'Nice work, Tom.' Fiona had joined them when she heard his exclamation. 'Can you build up a profile of him under the Mackintosh name? Vehicles, property, PNC etc. You know the ropes.'

'I'm on it.'

'Something else, guv,' said Mel. 'Osbourne mentioned Sutherland Place when he was trying to frighten me.'

'Sutherland Place?' interjected Tom. 'The satnav in his car showed journeys starting and finishing in that area. The last journey was deleted, though. But we don't have any record of him owning property in that part of town. He must have used an alias to rent or buy.'

'It's worth taking a look,' Mel continued. 'There was a set of keys on his body. I'll take them along.'

'Good idea,' said Fiona. 'Take Martin with you. But be careful in case Marlow and Ramsey are lurking there.'

Sutherland Place turned out to be a block of luxury flats in an affluent part of the town. Half an hour's knocking on doors and trying the keys identified Osbourne's flat. Before they could enter, his immediate neighbour, disturbed by the activity, poked her head round her door and was happy to talk to the detectives.

'Oh, Mr Cameron, you mean. Such a nice gentleman,' she gushed. 'Always courteous and smartly dressed. Never made any noise.'

Martin and Mel thanked her politely. They explained that Mr Cameron was deceased, without saying how, and that they were looking into his affairs.

Putting on nitrile gloves, they turned Osbourne's key in the door. It opened silently, and they were surprised that it wasn't alarmed. The flat was expensively furnished, with a masculine touch. Antique furniture was complemented by hunting prints on the walls and some old oil paintings, although none of the artists' names rang a bell with the detectives. A collection of expensive malt whiskies graced a sideboard, and a grandfather clock stood silently in the corner. A sleek OLED TV was fixed to the wall above a top-of-the-range music system.

'Look at this, Mel.' Martin was examining an open steel cupboard bolted to the wall in a spare room. 'It's a gun cupboard. There's nothing in it apart from a half-empty box of cartridges. So, where's the shotgun?'

'The guys didn't find it when they searched his house. Hampshire police looked over his Lymington place and would've said so if they'd found a firearm.'

'I'm not happy about an unaccounted-for weapon.' Martin frowned. 'Either it's on premises we don't know about or someone else has it.'

'We'll have a quick shufti at the other rooms and then get forensics to look for finger marks. Any documents we find, we'll take back to the station.'

The detectives found little of interest elsewhere in the flat.

A bedside cabinet contained a half-used packet of condoms and a plastic bag with traces of a white powder.

'Looks like he's had company.' Mel held up a pair of abbreviated lacy knickers. 'I'll bag these for DNA.'

'Not his size, then.' Martin grinned.

'Funny. I'll send the powder to the lab – I doubt very much that it's for indigestion.'

'True. Here's a car key fob. A Jaguar. He must own another vehicle we don't know about. We'll check out the underground car park as we leave.'

A lift took them down to the car park. In the corner, a gleaming red Jaguar flashed its lights when Martin pressed the key fob. The car was spotless, inside and out, with no documents apart from the manual, a wallet of Osbourne's business cards and a form from the DVLA notifying the owner that the tax was due. According to the document the car was registered to a Mr Clement Atkins, who, no doubt, did not exist.

Chapter Fifty

Glasgow 1998

CALLUM MACKINTOSH PUT down the phone and drummed his fingers on his desk. The news was bad, but he paid his informants for accurate information, not just the information they thought he would wish to hear. Time to move on, then. Start afresh. Use the new identity he had been crafting. And get rid of some loose ends that could come back and strangle him if he wasn't careful.

Peter McAvoy was the first. He knew all about the investment schemes that had proved so profitable for the partnership but, sadly, far from profitable for the investors. He suffered from an affliction that made him quite unsuitable to continue as Mackintosh's partner: he was honest. Honesty had made him an ideal front man. He had a sound reputation and people trusted him. But his honesty would be the downfall of the partnership when the fraud squad came calling. Mackintosh hadn't found it difficult to deceive him into believing the whole project was above board, but he realised that McAvoy would be horrified at the truth once the imminent investigation started. He would tell the authorities everything. So Peter McAvoy had to go.

Mackintosh called on McAvoy that evening, bearing whisky. He found him in his study, working at his computer. That suited Mackintosh perfectly. He collected a couple of glasses from McAvoy's kitchen.

'I'm off on a wee trip, Peter. Thought we could have one for the road.'

'That's decent of you, Callum. Where are you off to?'

'Down south for a while. Looking for new business. Here, get this down you.'

Mackintosh poured McAvoy a large measure and a smaller one for himself.

'Sláinte!' The two men toasted each other.

Mackintosh watched as McAvoy enjoyed the whisky, chatting generally about business, the weather and Rangers' prospects for the weekend. He wasn't drinking much himself, just a few sips now and again, while McAvoy drained his glass and accepted a refill. After half an hour McAvoy's speech began to slur and he had trouble remaining upright in his chair. Five minutes later he was asleep. Mackintosh prodded him in the ribs to make sure, slipped on a pair of thin leather gloves and pulled a plastic bag from his pocket. He put the bag over McAvoy's head and held it tight while his partner suffocated, too drugged to offer any resistance.

Calmly and efficiently, the murderer manipulated the scene to make it look as though McAvoy had killed himself. He replaced the drugged bottle of whisky with a half-empty one, free of fingerprints, and rolled McAvoy's fingers around it a few times. He rinsed out McAvoy's glass and splashed some whisky into it. His own, he washed and replaced in the cupboard.

The next step was to make it look as though McAvoy had put the bag over his own head. Mackintosh lifted up the dead man's arms and dragged his fingers over the plastic, tearing it slightly so that a sliver of material lodged under his victim's fingernails. He then used the man's hands to type out a short message on the computer. 'I committed the frauds. They were all down to me. I'm so sorry.' Finally, he placed a half-empty bottle of diazepam tablets, the label removed, on McAvoy's desk, spilling a few on the surface.

Mackintosh let himself out of McAvoy's flat and crept noiselessly down the stairs to the front door. Five minutes later he had walked the three blocks to where his car was parked and was on his way home. One loose end disposed of and one to go. But he wasn't really looking forward to the next one.

***

From the moment Eleanor had thrown the Polaroids onto the table in front of him, Mackintosh had realised he would need to take action. Blurred as they were, they clearly showed him in bed with a girl who looked about fourteen. He couldn't understand why he hadn't seen the flash from the camera, but he supposed he must have been too involved with what the girl was doing to him to notice.

'What do you want?' he had snarled.

'The flat, your car and half your cash will do for a start. Obviously a divorce. I want you gone for good, you filthy fucking pervert. That girl's no older than your nieces, for God's sake. How could you?'

Eleanor's slight frame had vibrated with fury, and the look of loathing on her face could have stunned a charging bull.

'It's a business enterprise I'm involved in. It's nothing to do with you. I just got carried away with one of the staff. That's all. It doesn't affect us.'

'Staff? So you're a brothel keeper as well as a paedophile? And you think it doesn't affect us? What fucking planet are you on, Callum? There is no "us" any more. I'm going to my mum's until you've moved out. Don't worry, I won't tell her why. Yet. But if I don't get what I want, those pictures will go to the papers and Strathclyde Police. You can keep those. I've made copies. Now get out of my life.'

Mackintosh had been on the verge of strangling her there and then but held himself in check, realising that unplanned murders were usually detected.

'OK. OK. I'm sorry. I was weak. I couldn't help it. But the business has provided us with much of our wealth, so you'd be found guilty of living on immoral earnings too, if it came to court. Tell you what I'll do. I'll get the firm's solicitor to draw up the documents transferring the flat to you. I'm moving down south anyway so I might as well. I'll put together some cash. I can find a couple of hundred grand within a week. You can have the car when I go. I'll buy a new one. I'll agree to a divorce and transfer half the remaining joint assets to you. Then we're quits. OK?'

Eleanor narrowed her eyes and thought for a few moments.

'OK. But if you try to screw me over you know what'll happen. Be out of here by the end of the week.'

The door slammed behind her.

Mackintosh had played a role. His demeanour had been that of a broken man, desperate to save his skin. But underneath he had been seething, determined to hand over nothing to that bitch. He'd only married her because she looked much younger than her real age and he could pretend she was a schoolgirl. When she grew older, the pretence stopped working, so he'd had to slake his desires in the brothel. He would string her along for a while, appearing to comply with her demands, until he could find a more permanent solution.

With McAvoy out of the way, Mackintosh phoned Eleanor, his tone as contrite and unthreatening as he could manage, and arranged to meet her in the bar of his golf club. At nine o'clock on a Tuesday it would be quiet and they would have no trouble finding a table. He promised to bring the necessary documents for her to sign and a holdall with the cash, which he would give her as they left.

Mackintosh walked into the central station and took a taxi to the club, his face partly obscured by a baseball cap and scarf. Arriving at a quarter to nine, he picked up a rock from an ornamental flower bed and hurled it at the CCTV camera covering the car park, ensuring that his face was covered. The rock bounced off the metal casing but did little damage. So he tried again. This time there was a satisfying crunch as the lens disintegrated. The club secretary would put it down to mindless vandalism, he was sure, and wouldn't link it to the rest of Mackintosh's plan.

Two minutes before nine he saw Eleanor's car coming up the drive. He waved at her and held up the holdall, indicating that he had brought the money as agreed. He pointed to an empty space at the back of the car park, and Eleanor drew the car to a halt beside a clump of trees. Mackintosh walked casually towards her and she got out, unsuspecting. He struck her across the throat, the lethal karate blow crushing her windpipe and starting to suffocate her. Just to make sure, he hit her again on the side of the neck with a knife hand blow, knocking her unconscious. He bundled her limp body into the back of her car and drove out the car park cautiously, so as not to draw attention to himself.

Two hours later, Eleanor's weighted body was at the bottom of a loch and Mackintosh was on his way back to Glasgow.

Before he could leave he had some arrangements to make. He checked there was nothing incriminating in Eleanor's car and took her mobile phone. He retrieved the car registration document from the flat and sold the vehicle to a dealer who would ask no questions. Taking Eleanor's passport, he visited the house where his girls were working and compared their faces with Eleanor's photo. One of them, slightly older than the rest, looked a reasonably close match.

'Do you want to go home, Katya?' he asked. 'I'll cancel your debt and give you some money if you do a favour for me.'

'What kind of favour?' The girl looked fearful, as if she was expecting some new form of depravity.

'I want you to fly to Croatia using my wife's passport. You will be Eleanor Mackintosh until you get there. Then you can travel home using your own name. I'll give you your passport back and plane tickets.'

'Why you want this? Have you done something to your wife?' Her eyes narrowed with suspicion.

'Eleanor is perfectly fine,' he reassured her. 'She just needs to hide away for a while. She's in a bit of trouble. Will you do this for me?'

'OK. OK.'

'That's a good girl.' His gentle tone hardened. 'One more

thing. You say nothing to anyone about this. Remember, I know where you came from and where your family lives.'

Mackintosh arranged for Katya to be cleaned up, provided with new clothes and given an envelope full of dollars and Croatian kuna. Three days later, her hair cut and dyed to resemble Eleanor's passport photo, she was on a flight to Zagreb.

Mackintosh could now relax. He had a project in London to set up, and no-one would link Kelvin Campbell with Callum Mackintosh, whose wife had suddenly run out on him to set up a new life in Eastern Europe. Life was looking good.

Chapter Fifty-One

Mexton 15th October 2019

'HAVE you got anything more on Mackintosh, Tom?' asked Mel when she and Martin returned to the station.

'He's not on social media as Mackintosh. It wasn't around when he was in Glasgow. There are a few press articles online that mention him, though, especially when his investment schemes started to go wrong. He's been photographed at sports events and on a deer-stalking weekend. There's also a picture of him as a teenager in the *Glasgow Herald*, collecting a trophy at a karate competition.'

'Interesting. Perhaps the blow to the throat we think killed Osbourne was inflicted by Campbell.'

'Maybe. With karate skills, a hunting rifle and a shotgun he's dangerous,' Martin said. 'No wonder people are scared of him.'

'He looks a bit different in these images,' continued Tom, comparing old press photos with new pictures on social media. 'Obviously he's grown a beard, but his nose may have been altered and his cheeks filled out a bit. He must have thought it worthwhile to pay for plastic surgery when he became Kelvin Campbell.'

'Hiding from someone, you think?'

'Perhaps. Certainly, the people who lost money in his investment schemes would want to get it back, but small investors aren't normally violent. It's more likely that he upset some local villains who would bear a serious grudge.'

'Vehicles? Property?'

'Still working on property, but there's a Land Rover and a Mercedes registered to him. We'll look for them on ANPR, though these guys seem to make a habit of using false plates.'

'Anything more on his time in Glasgow?'

'He's not on the PNC, so he must have managed to avoid getting arrested. I've asked someone in Police Scotland if he's crossed their radar. He'll check around and get back to me. It was Strathclyde Police when he was up there, before Police Scotland was set up, so they could have a few problems finding records.'

'Nice work, Tom. Better let the DI know. I'll chase up forensics in the morning. See if they got anything useful from Sutherland Place.'

———

Fiona knocked on Hawkins's door, her palms sweating and a flush developing on her neck.

'You wanted to see me, sir?'

'I'm really not happy with your team's performance, Fiona.' Hawkins scowled and told her to close the door. He didn't invite her to sit. 'This was supposed to be your big chance, but you've not made much of it so far.'

Fiona's flush deepened.

'You've spent a fortune on forensics, wasted a massive amount of overtime on a stakeout that yielded nothing, a young DC was nearly killed, and persons of interest keep winding up dead. And we still have no-one to charge with an offence.'

His aggressive manner made Fiona step back a pace, but she kept her response civil, with some effort.

'I realise that, sir, and no-one's more frustrated than I am. But we seem to be up against a sophisticated operation. And our prime suspect – not that we have any real evidence against him – is extremely elusive. Believe me, my team is working all out on it. Despite the setbacks, morale is good and they work well together.'

'Look, I'm more interested in results than morale at the moment. Detective Superintendent Shah is on my back, demanding a case review, and the Assistant Chief Constable is on his. The press are still asking embarrassing questions about why we haven't arrested anyone for Osbourne and Peel's murders, accusing us of letting Mexton turn into Sicily. If you can't make any progress, I'll have to request help from outside. And that will be extremely humiliating.'

'I'm sure that won't be necessary, sir. We do have new leads that we're pursuing. It just takes time.'

'Well, we don't have time. You'd better get on with it. Review tomorrow. And continue to keep me informed on a day-to-day basis.'

'Yes, sir,' Fiona replied, neutrally, but wishing she could stuff Hawkins's words back down his throat. She closed the DCI's door gently and stalked out of the building for an emergency cigarette. She didn't really smoke, but a cigarette at work was more acceptable than the G&T she would have preferred. She was furious at the prospect of an outside officer getting involved. That would be the ultimate insult.

When Fiona got back to the incident room the team was flagging. The early morning start and lack of results had left them exhausted and dispirited. Before she sent them home, she recounted the interview with her boss.

'DCI Hawkins has just given me earache about the lack of progress, and the Super's holding a case review tomorrow at eleven thirty. Hawkins will be there as well – he's been keeping a close eye on us and he's bound to stick the knife in. The Super has to provide an update for the ACC, so I need you all participating. Show them we're doing a decent job. Which you all are. They're threatening to bring in an outside SIO if we don't make progress, and we really don't want that.'

'Yeah, that really would be bad for your career,' whispered Jack to Martin. Fiona didn't hear him.

'Now go home and get some sleep. I need you all fresh and bright, first thing tomorrow.'

Chapter Fifty-Two

Wednesday 16th October

By MID-MORNING NEXT DAY, Tom had identified a flat in Glasgow and a modest house outside Mexton as belonging to Campbell, both under the name Mackintosh. He asked Police Scotland to check on the flat and offered to visit the Mexton house with Mel, later that afternoon.

'Any luck with forensics at Sutherland Place?' he asked.

Mel grimaced. 'Only one thing of interest. They've matched some finger marks in the bathroom and bedroom to a woman's prints on file. Martina Baranska. She had a few convictions for soliciting in Glasgow back in the nineties, the last one in 1999. She seems to have given up the game since then.'

'So what was she doing with Osbourne? He's hardly the sort to use the services of a sex worker, who, let's face it, must be getting on a bit for that profession.'

'Who knows? Perhaps it's love.' Martin sniggered.

'Don't be such a cynic, Martin,' mocked Mel. 'It's a beautiful thing.'

'Yeah. And I'm sure he treats his flying pigs humanely as well.'

'That's enough, guys. We do have a killer to catch,' chided Fiona. The review's in half an hour and I hope you're all ready for it.'

'Yes, guv,' they chorused.

As the team trooped into the conference room, Jessop was just leaving, a satisfied smile on his face. He didn't join them. The case review was a miserable experience. Fiona went through the events in detail and explained why they had made no arrests. DSup Shah didn't give the other team members a chance to speak in support of Fiona, and they were forced to sit there in mute fury. Hawkins reiterated his criticisms from the day before, and Shah, normally restrained in his comments, was angry.

'It's a shambles. A total bloody shambles! You have a poor woman terrorised by thugs; you know who they are but you've no idea where they are. It's not good enough.'

'They obviously have a hiding place somewhere, sir,' argued Fiona.

'Yes, Detective Inspector, obviously. And it's your job to find it. How difficult can it be? Mexton is a medium-sized town. It's not London or Birmingham. And one of them was shot – he shouldn't be difficult to spot. Meanwhile, Campbell is a ghost – you've had no success tracking him down and he seems to have murdered your prime suspect for the Wilkins killing. DC Cotton was nearly tortured to death, your stakeout was a farce and this Peel character was also murdered. And what about this so-called "third man"? You've no idea who he is, have you? They're running rings around you and making you look like a bunch of bloody amateurs. They really are.'

Fiona flushed and strove to contain her temper. 'I know, sir. But we're working as hard as we can and are still pursuing a number of leads on Campbell, aka Mackintosh.'

She hoped that the DSup wouldn't ask for more details, as they were scanty to say the least. 'Also, we're looking at Martina Baranska. A sex worker from Campbell's old patch turning up in Mexton and associating with Osbourne is too much of a coincidence. I've an excellent team working on this, and we do have some useful material. But we're up against some very clever people.'

'The fact is, you don't have much to go on.' Shah just about refrained from sneering. 'The press are making Mexton look like the Wild West, and our credibility is crumbling. I need to see progress, quickly, and the ACC is of the same view.'

He glared at the assembled detectives as he stood up to leave. 'If you can't make significant process in the next week, I'll be bringing in a senior officer from another force to identify where you're going wrong. DS Jessop, who I have to say is far from impressed, has suggested a former colleague from the Met who may be willing to help. It won't look good for any of you – and particularly not for you, DI Gale.'

He stalked out of the room, followed by Hawkins, whose expression was equally grim. The team waited a few seconds until they were sure the senior officers were out of earshot before bursting in to an indignant uproar.

'Who does he think he is?'

'Has he ever done any real detective work?'

'He's trying to get blood out of a stone!'

'Total pillock.'

'And what's that shit Jessop up to?'

'That's enough.' Fiona's voice cut through the clamour. 'I'm as gutted as you are. But I wouldn't criticise senior officers so openly, if I were you. I think we need a change of atmosphere. The pub, twenty minutes.'

Smarting from the criticism from Hawkins and Shah, Fiona took Mel, Martin and Tom for lunch at the Queen's Head. Jack made excuses and declined to join them, leaving the station on an unspecified errand.

'He seems a bit off these days,' ventured Martin.

'Maybe. Could be problems at home,' replied Fiona. 'He's on his private phone a lot, but I've not said anything. Right, what are you having?'

The pub was nearly empty, and they found a quiet corner away from potential eavesdroppers. All four ordered sausages and chips, although Tom's were the vegetarian version. The temptation to wash the food down with beer was almost irresistible, but the DI insisted on soft drinks only. Over coffees they threw around ideas on how to proceed with the case, a fruitless exercise that arrived at the same conclusion they had reached two days previously. They needed to track down Campbell and find out more about the third man. Mel suggested talking to David Parry again, but Martin pointed out that this could compromise his cover. Fiona asked Mel and Tom to check out Campbell's Mexton house and promised to sort out a search warrant. As they were preparing to leave, Fiona had a thought.

'When we contacted the National Crime Agency they said they couldn't give us anything useful. I got the impression they knew something but were unwilling to share. We've had two more deaths since then, and Martin's found the bodies in the garage. It might be worth going back to them to see if they feel able to help us now.'

'Good point, boss. And thanks for lunch,' replied Martin.

Chapter Fifty-Three

Thursday 17th October

NEXT MORNING the team was joined by Derek Palmer and two sharply dressed detectives from the National Crime Agency, DS Moore and DI Slade.

'I'm sorry we couldn't tell you more when you first contacted us,' said Slade, 'but we were keeping information strictly on a need-to-know basis. Things are hotting up down here, and we need your help with something, so we can tell you a bit more.'

Fiona was unimpressed about being kept in the dark until needed, but said nothing.

'We believe that Kelvin Campbell, through Maldobourne Holdings, is involved in something much bigger than supplying drugs to a sink estate in a medium-sized town. We're convinced that their specialist transport operations are a cover for drug smuggling. The equipment they shift is very delicate and wrapped so thoroughly that any drugs inside wouldn't be picked up by sniffer dogs or electronic detectors.

Some shipments are on behalf of government agencies and get special clearance. And we believe they have someone in the customs office at Harwich who smooths things along as well.

'Drugs are not the only commodity. We also think they're bringing in firearms, another profitable line. For instance, a clean Beretta 9mm semi-automatic and a few rounds of ammo can fetch five grand in some quarters, an AK47 much more. It would be easy to conceal a few in a dummy server cabinet. Also, Campbell was suspected of sex trafficking in Scotland, before he changed his name from Mackintosh and moved south. We're not sure how that fits with Maldobourne, but he may still have an interest in importing women for brothels. There's something else, too, but we're not sure what. The operation is clearly big enough to warrant murder.'

'Do you know anything about the jewel robbery?' asked Jack.

'We think that was probably just a sideline – Osbourne getting greedy and setting up the job. Campbell wouldn't touch something like that. Too much risk of things going wrong. He likes to keep a very low profile.'

'Do your guys have any idea where Campbell is?' asked Martin.

'We've had a few possible sightings but nothing confirmed. He may be using another alias as well. And we haven't got enough evidence to put him away.'

Fiona was annoyed but managed to hide it.

'You said you needed our help. What did you have in mind?'

'There's a shipment of computers coming from Hamburg via Harwich tonight. We've had a tipoff that it will also contain twenty kilos of uncut heroin. We believe it will go to Maldobourne's warehouse on the outskirts of Mexton in the early hours of the morning, where the drugs will be removed. We want to raid it and we'd like your guys to help. Derek here has offered us a couple of bodies, but we'd also like some AFOs – there's a strong likelihood the bad guys will be armed.'

'Happy to assist. Give me the details and I'll brief the team. I'll ask the Chief Super to authorise firearms and we'll meet you there.'

'I'm pretty pissed off with those buggers,' said Fiona, after the NCA officers had left. 'We were chasing around looking for Campbell, but they knew he was Mackintosh all the time. It wouldn't have hurt them to tell us. Anyone would think we were the enemy, but now they need us, we're all friends. Still, at least we'll be in at the collar. It doesn't get us any closer to proving who killed George – or Osbourne, for that matter.'

The others murmured agreement and wandered back to their desks, intending to clear some paperwork before lunch.

Chapter Fifty-Four

MEXTON'S RUNDOWN warehousing centre was a gloomy place at the best of times, but at four in the morning, in the freezing cold, it was particularly bleak. The constant drizzle didn't help, either. A stray cat prowled along the pavement, while a couple of rats scurried along the gutters, dodging the streaming rainwater and looking for anything remotely edible. Many buildings were disused and derelict, companies having gone out of business and left them to rot and rust.

Occasionally, a private security van would crawl around the estate, its occupants no doubt as bored as the police officers waiting for their target. The police had been there for several hours in five unmarked vehicles dotted around the various parking areas, with lights out and radio silence in force. Initial excitement had given way to desultory chat, and even that had died as officers began to wonder if the consignment would ever appear. One or two dozed off, while the others played games on their phones or simply brooded.

Finally, a message came through from the vehicles tracking the Maldobourne truck.

'Target vehicle on road into Mexton. ETA twelve minutes.'

The police vans came alive with excitement. The AFOs, adrenaline flowing, checked their carbines once again, while the other officers adjusted their stab vests and stretched their legs as far as the cramped conditions allowed.

DI Slade reiterated the instructions he'd previously given.

'When the van pulls up in front of the warehouse, firearms vehicles will deploy before anyone else gets out. Victor One will approach from the left, Victor Two will approach from the right and Victor Three will pull up behind. I repeat, no-one else is to leave the vans until the scene is secure.'

'That includes you, DC Cotton,' said Jack, snarkily.

'Yes, Sarge,' she replied meekly, flicking him a v-sign, which he couldn't see in the darkness of the CID van.

Eleven minutes later the Maldobourne truck came into view and pulled up in front of the warehouse. Three armed response vehicles raced out of the darkness, blue lights flashing. They boxed in the Maldobourne truck, and armed officers swarmed towards it, shouting.

'Armed police. On the ground. Now.'

Nothing happened for a minute, and the tension mounted. Were the van's occupants preparing to shoot at the police or planning to make a break for it? The off-side door of the truck opened, and the driver climbed slowly out of the cab, arms raised. He lowered himself to the ground. His mate got out of the other door and unhurriedly sank to his knees, prostrating himself as instructed. After cuffing and searching the suspects the AFOs retired to their van and waited, in case they were needed to deal with any recovered weapons.

'Doesn't look like we were needed after all,' said Fiona,

irritated at another cold stakeout with no action at the end of it.

'Nice to see a result, though,' replied Jack.

'Yes, but it's not our result.'

The Mexton contingent joined the NCA officers as they opened the back of the van. It was completely empty apart from a cardboard box with biohazard labels on it and a sticker stating that it should only be opened under laboratory conditions.

'What the hell is that?' a furious DI Slade demanded. 'Get the dog over here. Now.' DS Palmer and a dog handler approached cautiously, but the animal showed no interest in the package whatsoever.

'Well, it's not drugs,' he said. 'But maybe your forensic lab could open it and see what's inside.'

'We could ask them,' replied Fiona. 'But they won't want to put themselves at risk. If it looks like anything really nasty it will have to go to Porton Down for examination. We'll take it back, though, and see what they can do with it.'

With the grinning driver and mate released, and the van double checked for contraband, the police vehicles left the scene. As they cleared the site the driver sent a one-word text.

'Confirmed.'

'This is getting to be a habit,' moaned Martin as they drove away. 'Sitting on our arses in freezing vans for hours with nothing to show for it. I'm getting too old for this shit.'

'That's police work for you. Ninety-eight percent boredom, two percent terror,' observed Jack. 'Anyway, you're only twenty-nine.'

Martin, who rarely felt bored at work, and hadn't felt terrified since he stopped working a beat in uniform, sniffed at the old saw.

'Have a lie-in tomorrow, guys,' said Fiona. 'Be in the office at ten. I'll drop this off at the station and get it couriered to the lab first thing.' She hefted the package suspiciously, feeling a slight movement of something inside as she tilted it.

An hour after the failed raid two figures crept along the fourth-floor walkway of Dalton House. They knocked on a door, and a bleary-eyed Twitch opened it.

'What's up, guys?' he asked. Ramsey and Marlow grinned.

'You've been talking. To the filth.' Marlow cracked his knuckles in anticipation.

'Bollocks. They arrested me, worked me over and charged me with assaulting a cop. You know that.'

'Yeah. But the boss set a trap. A rat trap. The bait was a dummy shipment. And you took it. You were the only one who thought there was gear on board. You're dead.'

'No, no, it wasn't me. I must've told someone else on the estate by mistake. I've been on skunk a lot. Don't know what I'm saying. But I'd never grass. You know me. I've been here over a year, working with Billy Peel. I'm sound.' Twitch's voice faltered as he realised they didn't believe him. He started to make a run for it, but two pairs of hands gripped his arms and lifted him off his feet.

'One other thing,' sneered Marlow. 'Rats can't fly.'

Twitch felt his knees scrape the parapet as they hurled him off the walkway. It took him less than two seconds to fall, but they were the longest two seconds of his life. He just about registered the cold night air rushing past his face. Then he hit the ground with his back, his head snapping onto the concrete and smashing his skull into half a dozen pieces.

Chapter Fifty-Five

Friday 18th October

THE DETECTIVES ASSEMBLED at ten o'clock as instructed, clutching coffee to combat their lack of sleep.

'First off, I've some bad news.' Fiona's tone was sombre. 'DS Palmer has just informed me that his undercover officer, who we know as Twitch, was murdered last night. They must have identified him. He was thrown off his balcony, by persons unknown, and died instantly. He had a partner but, fortunately, no children.'

The others were stunned by the news.

'Did Derek Palmer say how he was found out?' asked Jack.

'There's no way of knowing. He reported back to Derek after we released him. No-one had queried his arrest and the assault charge. He still felt safe.'

At that point Fiona's phone rang. Seeing that it was the lab, she answered it and put it on speaker.

'That package you sent,' began Dr Nigel Mordaunt,

Director of the forensic lab. 'We were expecting viruses or scorpions or something nasty so we opened it in a biological containment cabinet.'

'Yes, go on,' snapped Fiona, impatiently.

'It was grass seed. Not cannabis. Ordinary lawn grass. And there was a photo of a rat in with it. Nothing dangerous at all.'

'Oh. Thank you, Dr Mordaunt. Sorry I was abrupt. An officer lost his life last night and I think this tells us why.'

She turned to the others, eyes blazing.

'The bastards played us. They used the raid to flush out Twitch. They killed him last night and put the hazard labels on the box, knowing we wouldn't open it 'til this morning. So we wouldn't have time to pull him out. They must have suspected him and fed him the phoney information about the shipment. I'd better get back to Derek and explain.'

Mel and Tom went off to search Campbell's Mexton house. After talking to Derek, Fiona spent the rest of the day on admin, dealing with a heavy backlog. She realised that her colleagues would find it hard to concentrate. The death of a fellow officer hit everyone hard, and the atmosphere of shared grief was hardly conducive to serious work. Fiona sent the rest of the team home at five and reported the lack of progress to Hawkins, as he had demanded.

'Another cock-up, I see. Still, I suppose it's not your fault this time,' he said, grudgingly. 'But I want to see some real results soon. And so does DSup Shah.' He reached into his desk for a bottle of whisky but didn't offer Fiona a drink. She left with a curt 'sir', relieved that she wasn't getting the blame this time.

Chapter Fifty-Six

IT WAS FIONA'S CUSTOM, after work on a Friday, to nip into the Queen's Head for a single gin and tonic before going back to her empty flat, putting something in the microwave and opening a bottle of wine in front of a historical drama box set. She had no interest in cooking and subsisted on ready meals and takeaways, a diet that accounted for her increasing girth. She lived alone, and the busy atmosphere of the pub cheered her up, at least temporarily. As she moved away from the bar a woman in a hijab and glasses bumped into her, apologising profusely and just catching Fiona's glass before her drink spilled.

'I'm so sorry,' the woman said, in a Birmingham accent. 'Can I get you another of those?'

'No, it's all right. Nothing much spilled. And I'm driving.'

Idly wondering what a Muslim woman was doing in a pub, let alone offering to buy gin, Fiona sipped her drink slowly. It seemed a little more bitter than usual. Too much tonic, she thought. She had almost finished it when a group of noisy young lads on the lash came into the pub, so she decided to leave. She knocked back the rest of her G&T and headed for her car.

Fiona walked unsteadily, as if she'd had four gins rather than the one, and couldn't understand why she was feeling rough. She wished she had gone straight home. She got into her car and turned the radio on, hoping the music would wake her up. A couple of hundred yards from the pub she felt dizzy and pulled in to a layby, winding down the window to let in some fresh air. Less than a minute later a traffic patrol, blue lights flashing, pulled up behind her.

'Would you mind getting out of the car, madam?' asked the officer. 'I must ask you to take a breath test.'

'What on earth for? I've had one gin. I'm nowhere near the limit. And I'm a detective inspector.'

'A member of the public saw you in the pub car park and said you looked drunk. She phoned us as she was concerned. And, as you know, ma'am, we're none of us above the law. Breath test. Please.'

Fiona blew into the machine and was relieved to see that she was clear. The officer seemed satisfied and asked her if she felt OK.

'Yes, thank you. A busy week. I must be more tired than I thought.'

'Well, mind how you drive, ma'am. Enjoy the rest of your evening.'

Fiona sat in her car for a while longer, reviewing what had happened. The woman who knocked into her. She must have put something in her drink to make her look drunk. She probably made the call to the police as well.

She drove slowly back to the police station, alerting the police forensic physician that she was on her way. Technically she could have been committing the offence of driving under the influence of drugs, but she was more alert now and confident that her judgement was not impaired. On arrival she asked the doctor to take blood and urine samples, for immediate dispatch to the lab for analysis with a summary of her symptoms attached. She asked for them to be fast tracked, emphasising that she believed an offence against a police officer had been committed, and hoped desperately that someone would be able to analyse them before any traces of drugs disappeared.

Saturday 19th October

Martin folded up his cricket clothes and put them in his sports bag. His broad shoulders ached a little, and he was pleasantly tired after an afternoon's practice in the nets, made possible by a lull in the rain. He was looking forward to getting home, seeing his daughter and sharing a curry with his wife. Unusually for a housing estate kid, cricket, rather than football, had become something of an obsession with him, despite the fact that a fast-moving cricket ball had broken his nose when he was twelve and it had never really healed properly. He was once teased for turning up at a crime scene in his whites, having had no time to change when the call to attend came through.

He dropped the bag into the boot of his vintage sports car and drove out of the car park, heading down the hill towards home. He pressed the footbrake as he approached the speed camera near the bottom of the hill. Nothing happened. His speed increased and the camera flashed as he passed it. Realising that his brakes weren't working, Martin slammed the car into first, wincing as the gearbox screamed in protest. The car juddered and slowed to walking pace, just in time to avoid hitting a bus pulling out from a layby. Martin steered into the vacant space and stopped the car by switching off the engine and putting it into reverse.

His hands shook and sweat beaded on his brow as he contemplated what could have happened if he had been driving faster. He couldn't understand why the brakes had failed. He was always tinkering with his pride and joy and knew he'd adjusted them correctly. Although the car was too old to require an MOT he had asked the garage to test it anyway, and the machine had passed the relevant sections easily. Perhaps his wife was right when she urged him to replace it with a more sensible family car. When he crouched down and looked underneath he could see why he had nearly died. Brake fluid had spattered the underside of the car and, by the light from his phone, a small hole was visible in one of the brake pipes.

This was no accident or mechanical failure. This was attempted murder.

Chapter Fifty-Seven

Sunday 20th October

TOM RETURNED from Sunday morning Tae Kwan Do practice and climbed the stairs to his flat, damp from the misty rain. As he put his key in the lock he noticed faint scratches in the paintwork on the jamb. He froze. Someone had used a credit card, or something similar, to break in. Tom berated himself for not fitting a proper mortice lock, which he had intended to do ever since he joined CID.

Several scenarios flashed through his mind. He could have been burgled. Or someone had tried to get in but failed. Worst of all, an intruder could be waiting inside with a weapon. Tom pushed open the letter box and peered in. He saw nothing untoward in his dark hallway, but a strong smell of gas seeped from the flat. Easing open the door, he was about to switch on the hall light as he always did, when he stopped himself. He felt sick when he realised that the spark in the switch would have ignited the gas and blown the flat, and him, to smithereens.

Taking a deep breath, Tom rushed into the kitchen and turned off the four unlit burners on the hob. He opened all the windows in the flat and stood with his head outside, breathing fresh air until the gas dissipated. He then phoned Fiona's mobile and left a message, explaining what had happened and asking her to arrange for forensics to attend. He had no expectations that the SOCOs would find anything, but this was clearly an attempt to kill him. Perhaps the attackers had been careless, expecting any evidence to be destroyed in the explosion. He wasn't one to worry, as a rule, but the thought of his own death, and the undoubted loss of life amongst the other dozen or so people living in the building, horrified him. Being attacked during a riot or at a football match was one thing, part of the job, really, but a murder attempt in his own home, with many other potential casualties, chilled him to the core.

Chapter Fifty-Eight

Monday 21st October

At eight o'clock on Monday morning, Mel walked into the police station, her bag slung over her shoulder and a smile on her face. She had come straight from the gym, and a morning workout had set her up for the day. She nodded to the uniformed dog handler in reception, puzzled why he was there. As she passed him, the dog started to bark.

'Could you come over here, please?' asked the dog handler.

'Sure. But she doesn't seem to like me.'

The officer remained impassive.

'Would you open your bag, please?'

Mel shrugged and complied, opening her gym bag and placing it on the floor. The dog grew more excited until the handler told her to sit. The officer put on a pair of latex gloves and searched the bag. As he rummaged through it, Mel realised she knew him. She had trained alongside him at police college. After a night in the pub he had grabbed her breasts and she'd decked him with a knee in the balls. I bet he's enjoying every second of this, she thought. Opening a side pocket, he pulled out a small plastic bag containing plant material.

'What's this, detective constable?' he asked.

A chill gripped Mel's stomach.

'I've never seen it before. I didn't put it there and it's nothing to do with me.'

'That's what they all say, isn't it? I believe that this material is cannabis and that you are unlawfully in possession of it. I am placing it in this evidence bag, and it will be sent for analysis. If the tests prove positive you may be charged with an offence and will face disciplinary action.'

'Oh, come on. It's obviously planted. I wouldn't touch that rubbish.'

'That's for you to argue should the tests confirm my suspicions. We were told that someone in this station was using drugs, which is why PD Popeye is checking everyone coming in.'

Mel was stunned and made her way to Fiona's office. She explained what had happened and vehemently denied owning the drug.

'Someone must have put it in my gym bag, probably while I was in the shower. I've never used drugs. You know I come from a police family. It's inconceivable.'

'I believe you. Not only do I trust you, but someone tried to fit me up on a drink-driving charge on Friday evening. They put something in my drink and tipped off Traffic. I'm waiting for the lab results. Somebody tampered with Martin's brake pipes on Saturday and he almost crashed his car at the bottom of a hill. Tom came home to his flat after his Sunday morning martial arts session and found it full of gas. Fortunately, he smelt it and didn't turn the lights on, or he would have been blown to bits. This looks like a concerted attack on the team. The only person who hasn't said anything is Jack.'

———

For the first time in her career, Fiona was scared. She had been in dangerous situations before, when on patrol or dealing with riots, but she always had someone with her to watch her back. The attacks on her and her team were something different. They were personal, coming out of the blue from an unseen hand. They relied on detailed knowledge of the team's movements, and the thought that they were being watched all the time made her shiver. The attackers had failed this time, partly through luck. Next time they could be more successful.

Chapter Fifty-Nine

MEL FELT SICK AND ANGRY. All police officers knew they could be in danger when out on the streets, but being attacked off duty and at home was terrifying. She'd had a narrow escape at Osbourne's hands, but it was no comfort to know that her colleagues had been targeted as well. She was particularly concerned about Tom. She occasionally teased him about his IT talents, but she did like him and he had proved himself able to work on the streets when they arrested Twitch. She really didn't want anything to happen to him, she realised.

'When the others get in, we'll go somewhere private to discuss this,' said Fiona. 'I've been reviewing everything that's happened, from the stakeout at the supermarket to these attacks. Somehow the villains know who's working the case and what's going on. They must have someone on the inside. I don't feel comfortable talking about it at the station. Did you find anything at Campbell's place?'

'No, nothing. It was tidy but unoccupied,' Mel replied. 'There was no food on the premises, the heating was off and there was loads of junk mail on the doormat. I could hardly open the door. The place smelt slightly of sewage, so I guessed the u-bends in the sinks had dried out. They can't have been used for months.'

'OK. Thanks. Looks like it was just there as a bolt hole. Or an investment.'

Mel concurred, and typed up reports on her computer until the others arrived and they could go out for coffee. The four officers affected wandered out of the incident room separately and met up in a nearby café, which was relatively quiet at that time of the morning.

'Where's Jack, guv?' asked Tom.

'I didn't invite him. He doesn't seem to have been targeted. I think it's best we keep this among ourselves for the moment.'

'I suppose he has been a bit odd recently,' mused Martin. 'But surely you don't think he's bent?'

'I'm not accusing him of anything. I've worked with him for nine years, and he's always seemed completely honest and diligent. But someone seems to be leaking information, either deliberately or accidentally. They – whoever "they" are – know who's on the case and our personal habits. Mel's gym, Martin's cricket and my Friday night G&T. They also knew when Tom would be out so they could switch on his gas cooker.'

Tom shivered at the memory of his narrow escape.

'Of course,' she continued, 'there are others working on this, including civilian support staff. But we four, plus Jack, are leading, so we're the biggest threat to their operation. If they put us out of action it wouldn't stop the investigation, but it would hamper it severely, giving them time to reorganise, cover their tracks or whatever.'

'Could it be Jessop?' asked Martin. He's never tried to fit in and has been pretty hostile at times.'

'No, I don't think so,' replied Fiona. 'He hasn't been here long enough to learn our routines, and he didn't know about the raid on Campbell's place. He went home sick before I announced it. It's someone else.'

'So, where do we go from here?' asked Mel.

'Well if they can set up a sting to flush out an informant, so can we. I'll concoct a false lead, lure the bastards into a trap and scoop up the informant afterwards. In the meantime, I'll have a quiet word with Jack. Try to find out why he's been a bit odd. Act as if I'm concerned for his welfare – which I am, of course. How does that sound?'

The others murmured their assent and they drifted back to the station separately.

'Jack, can I have a word?' Fiona called the sergeant into her office, and when he had sat down, she studied him closely. His normally smart suit was creased, his tie was slightly askew and his face bore patches of stubble, missed by his morning shave. Sitting at an angle to him, rather than across her desk, Fiona explained that she wanted to raise a couple of issues with him but this was in no way a disciplinary matter. He seemed to relax but still looked slightly nervous.

'Mel,' she said. 'How do you think she's getting on?'

'OK,' he replied. 'She's bright, diligent, keeps her paperwork up to date. She'll do well.'

'I'm glad you think so. Only I've noticed you tend to put her down a lot. You're a bit more critical than you were of Martin when he first joined. Is it because she's female?'

Jack looked indignant.

'Of course not, boss. I've nothing against female officers. If you must know I think she's a bit too desperate to prove herself. To be as good as her parents, especially her mum. She's rather headstrong and has taken risks when she shouldn't have. And I think she gets an easy ride because of her background.'

'You're wrong about that, Jack. She's not been treated any differently because she comes from a police family, certainly not by me. I agree she has a lot to live up to, and she's doing her best. But she's still young and needs supportive guidance, not excessive criticism. You're supposed to be her mentor, and I'm looking to you to provide it, OK?'

'Yes, guv.'

'There's something else. You seem a bit preoccupied these days. You're on your personal phone a lot – which is OK if you have a good reason. Is there something wrong at home? Or something else I should know about?'

Jack fiddled with his tie and averted his gaze. He remained silent for some time then took a deep breath.

'Someone's trying to get at me,' he said, his face pale and drawn. 'It started a few days ago. I've been sent videos of my kids at their universities, taken without their knowledge. My wife has been getting anonymous silent calls at her pottery studio and my car's been scratched. Small things by themselves, but they add up to some kind of campaign. I'm not sure what to do, whether to quit the job or transfer. But I can't have my family put at risk.'

'Oh shit. You should have come to me earlier, you idiot.' Fiona was both concerned and relieved at Jack's account. 'If it's any consolation, which it probably isn't, you're not alone. Someone tried to kill Martin and Tom. Both Mel and I were fitted up for offences that could have got us dismissed at the very least. Someone's targeting the whole team. And someone with inside knowledge is helping them do it.'

Jack looked aghast.

'So what do we do about it?'

'I'm working on something, but in the meantime I'd like you to take a discreet look at all the other officers working on the case as well as the support staff. Anyone who would know about our habits, families and other personal details. Don't worry about the forensics guys, just concentrate on people in the office. Now, what do you want me to do about your situation? Do you want to take some leave until the case is over?'

'No. Definitely not. I want to nail these bastards. I suppose you could get our personal phones monitored – my wife's and mine, that is. We may get something from that. I don't want to tell the kids yet, but I'd better let Sarah know. I'll keep you informed of anything else that happens.'

'You do that, Jack. Don't leave it too late. And if you need some time off, please let me know.'

'I will do. Thanks, guv.'

Chapter Sixty

JACK LEFT THE OFFICE, looking slightly more cheerful, leaving Fiona to ponder. She felt that she had made a mistake in suspecting Jack – but could he have given away information inadvertently? He was an experienced officer and knew the importance of discretion, of not discussing the job outside work, so that seemed highly unlikely. But if it wasn't Jack, who was it? Who else had access to day-to-day information about the investigation as well as details of the officers involved?

Only one name came to mind, and she had to be sure that she wasn't letting prejudice against someone she disliked influence her thoughts. Hawkins. He had been demanding more and more information about the case as the days went on. Much more than she would expect, in the normal course of events, from a DCI who had a host of other cases and officers to supervise. She had thought he was keeping an eye on her because he doubted her abilities. And he'd inflicted the useless Jessop on her. Could he be a plant? But surely Hawkins couldn't be bent? A long-serving officer coming to the end of a moderately distinguished career? He might be irritable and controlling, but that didn't mean he was corrupt. She would have to give this idea further thought and tread very carefully indeed.

———

Later that afternoon, Fiona knocked on Hawkins's door, contempt and doubt fighting for control of her emotions.

'I think we may be on the verge of a breakthrough, sir. Someone from Maldobourne's trucking operation is prepared to talk. It looks like the armed raid scared him and he wants to get out.'

'That's excellent news, Fiona. Thanks for telling me. When are you interviewing this person?'

'He won't come to the station, at least not at first. Martin Rowse is meeting him at eleven o'clock tonight at the gazebo in the ornamental gardens. He's nervous and is only prepared to speak to one officer initially, so Martin will have to go on his own. He's happy with that and we'll only be a few dozen yards away.'

'Are you sure? Have you done a proper risk assessment?'

'Yes, of course. You can't get a car into the gardens after dark, but there's a small gate that's broken. Kids nip in there to smoke weed occasionally, but we'll chuck them out well before the meet. We can see the gazebo clearly from outside, so Martin should be OK. We'll fit him up with recording equipment. Are you happy with this?'

'Yes of course. Carry on.'

———

A light drizzle fell on the grass as Martin paced around the gazebo, faint light from a streetlamp outside the gardens casting moving shadows as he walked. His feet made squelching sounds on the sodden ground. Once a pinnacle of civic pride, the ornamental gardens had fallen into disarray, being maintained principally by volunteers. Shrubs behind the gazebo had grown to an unruly height, which perfectly suited Fiona and Mel, who lurked behind them.

Just before eleven a figure in overalls and a hoodie, with a scarf concealing his face, walked tentatively towards Martin. The detectives heard a swishing sound and a metallic whirring coming in their direction. Turning to look at the gate, they saw a figure on a mountain bike hurtling across the wet grass. The bike slowed as it approached the man in the overalls. A blade glinted, and the rider shoved a knife into the would-be informant's back.

Before the bike could pick up speed again, Martin stuck his extendable baton into the spokes of its front wheel. Cursing, the rider tumbled to the ground, giving Martin and Mel the chance to jump on him. Despite the pepper spray that Mel squirted into his face, the assailant continued kicking and yelling. The knife, still in his flailing hand, caught Martin on the bridge of the nose, spraying blood into his eyes.

Mel grabbed for the knife hand, but blood on the man's wrist made it hard to grip. She felt it slipping away from her. It was an inch from her throat when Fiona's baton struck the man's arm with a sharp crack and made it go limp. Mel pulled off the moaning attacker's balaclava.

'Michael Ramsey,' she said. 'What a surprise. We've been looking for you. I'm arresting you for attempted murder and kidnapping. Other charges will follow, but that will do for now. Get up.'

Ramsey was handcuffed and frogmarched to the unmarked police car parked near the gate, struggling and swearing.

'Good job he didn't go for my throat,' said Tom nervously, as he unwrapped the scarf around his neck and peeled off the hoodie and stab vest, examining them for damage. 'That was exciting, but on balance, I think I prefer databases to knives.'

'Well done, mate,' said Martin. 'We owe you several large drinks for this. It took guts to volunteer for this one. It was probably crazy, but we got a result.'

Mel said nothing, feeling both admiration and relief at Tom's narrow escape. Fiona smiled but shuddered inside at the thought of Tom lying on the ground with his throat cut. It was a high-risk strategy, improvised in something of a hurry, but the stakes were also high. It could have failed catastrophically if a firearm had been used. Tom would have been a sitting target for anyone with a rifle. Perhaps she should have had some AFOs on standby, but she had thought it unlikely that guns would be involved. She did wonder whether her judgement was sound. This time it had paid off, but she didn't think she would be doing anything similar again.

Tuesday 22nd October

'Good morning, sir,' said Fiona to Hawkins. She had emailed him a preliminary report on the night's events, omitting to mention that the stabbing victim was Tom. She was joined in his office by Jack, who she had kept out the loop, just in case he was inadvertently involved. She felt she owed him the privilege of making the arrest.

'Just what the hell were you playing at, Fiona?' The DCI's voice was audible far beyond his office. 'Another bloody shambles. We've had one officer wounded, a potentially valuable informant stabbed to death, and all we have to show for it is a minor thug in custody. You had no firearms backup and barely enough officers to make an arrest. You must have been out of your mind. I thought an officer of your experience would have better judgement. I'm removing you from the case as of now.'

'Well, I'm afraid you don't have the full picture, sir. Firstly, while I said in my initial report that someone was stabbed, I didn't say fatally. He survived. Secondly, there was no informant. It was DC Ferris, in overalls and a stab vest, who was meeting DC Rowse. He has a slight bruise on his back but is otherwise unharmed. Martin's OK, too. He'll have a small scar on the bridge of his nose, but first aid and antiseptic sorted him out.'

Hawkins looked worried.

'What are you talking about? You said you had an informant.'

'Yes, I did. And you were the only person I told. We suspected that someone at the station was leaking information, and you've been taking an unusually close interest in this investigation. You know all about us and our habits, and you knew where we would be at certain times, making it easy for the gang to target us. Two of us could have been killed and two dismissed, to say nothing of the threats to Jack's family. You're a disgusting individual and a disgrace to the uniform.' Fiona could barely control her temper. 'There are two people from the Independent Office for Police Conduct waiting to talk to you once you've been processed. In the meantime, Jack – do the honours.'

Jack stepped forward holding handcuffs.

'Robert Hawkins, I am arresting you on suspicion of

corruption and misconduct in public office. You do not have to say anything but it may harm your defence…'

The caution completed, a handcuffed Hawkins was escorted to the custody suite, taking the longest possible route through the station to maximise his humiliation. He sobbed as officers looked at him with revulsion.

'They made me do it,' he tried to explain. But no-one was interested.

Chapter Sixty-One

Thursday 24th October

Two DAYS LATER, Hawkins was out. There was no safe place for him to be remanded, so the magistrate agreed to bail, on condition he surrendered his passport, stayed at home during the hours of darkness and didn't communicate with his colleagues in any way. He was glad not to be in jail, but his empty house, full of the bitter memories of a failed marriage, felt like a prison in its own right, albeit without the violence meted out to imprisoned cops. But when a black Mercedes pulled up outside his house late one afternoon, he knew he would have to go for a ride. The prospect terrified him.

'Get in, Bob. It's good to see you.' The passenger held open the car door, inviting Hawkins to sit in the back with him. 'Long time, no see.'

'Er...yes, Kelvin. Good to see you too.' Hawkins could barely speak. His mouth was dry but his guts had turned to water. He had never experienced such fear, not even when confronted by rioters hurling petrol bombs.

'You've been extremely useful to us over the years, Bob.' Campbell's tone was affable, and, to a bystander, would not have seemed the least bit threatening. 'A bit of a slip-up recently, of course, and it's a pity you're blown. Bound to happen sometime, I suppose. Still, I hope you'll have a drink with me. You do still like Scotch, don't you?'

'Yes, er, thanks. Please.'

Campbell produced a bottle of one of the peatier single malts and poured both of them a generous measure.

'Sláinte,' he toasted, taking a sip. Reassured that there was nothing wrong with the whisky, Hawkins did the same. It tasted a little bitter, but he put it down to the peat. He wasn't a connoisseur of malts, anyway.

'I think it's time to review our arrangement,' Campbell continued. 'I believe your retirement is in order, don't you?'

'No. No. I'm going to fight the case. It was clearly entrapment. I'll clear my name, I promise you. Even if I lose my job, I've still got contacts on the force.' Hawkins trembled and took several more swallows of the whisky.

'I don't think you can beat it, Bob. I've talked to my tame barrister, and you stand very little chance. Unless you make a deal.'

'I wouldn't do that. Ever. You know me. I've always been loyal.'

'Yes, I know. And I'm sure you'll remain so.' Campbell's voice had become a little chillier. 'But even if you do avoid prison, why should I pay an ex-copper when I've several active helpers still on the force? It wouldn't make financial sense.'

Hawkins couldn't answer.

The car had been on the move for around fifteen minutes. Hawkins was nauseous and put it down to fear, but then his head began to spin. Despite these symptoms, he started to feel pretty good. Euphoric, even. Perhaps things would be OK after all? He became sleepy and found it a little hard to breathe. Just as he lost consciousness, Campbell's face loomed over him. He could just make out the words.

'Bye, Bob. You've retired.'

As soon as Hawkins passed out, Campbell pulled a small leather case out of his jacket pocket and unzipped it. He withdrew the syringe inside, ejected an air bubble and slid the needle expertly into a vein in his own left arm. The naloxone coursed through his circulation, neutralising the effects of the heroin he had dissolved in the whisky and reversing the sleepiness he was beginning to feel.

In the seat beside him, Hawkins stopped breathing and died a few minutes later.

Campbell's car returned to Hawkins's house, and the driver opened the front door with the keys from the dead copper's pocket. He checked that no-one was watching, slung the corpse over his shoulder and carried it into the house. Campbell brought in the poisoned whisky and left it on Hawkins's bedside table, together with a small plastic bag containing a residue of heroin. The two men carried the body upstairs and arranged it on the bed.

Campbell and his driver discreetly searched the house for records linking Hawkins with their activities. They knew that any phones, computers or recording devices would have been removed by the police, along with paper records of Hawkins's financial affairs. Nevertheless, Campbell thought it worth checking. Finding nothing, the two men left the house, leaving the keys on a shelf in the hall and closing the door behind them.

Mel knocked on Ellen's door and was greeted by a suspicious stare as it opened on the chain.

'Hello Ellen', she said. 'I dropped by to see how you were, after your ordeal. Sorry it's a bit late.'

Ellen's expression relaxed when she recognised her visitor and she opened the door, looking nervously up and down the street before ushering the detective into her lounge.

'You'd better come in. I suppose you'll be wanting tea. All the coppers on the telly do.' She looked much frailer than she had when she turned up at the police station with George's head.

'No. No. You're all right. How are you coping?'

'Bit more careful about opening the door and I don't get much sleep. I don't go out unless I have to, never after dark, and sudden noises make me jump.'

Mel smiled sympathetically. 'Have you seen the doctor?'

'No point. I don't want pills, and counselling's a waste of time.'

'Well, I may have some good news for you. Charles Osbourne is dead.'

Ellen relaxed visibly. 'Good riddance,' she spat.

'We're certain that he killed George, and we've also arrested Michael Ramsey, one of the thugs who kidnapped you. The other is on the run. Also, we've recovered the jewels, so I'm sure you're safe now.'

Ellen looked sceptical. 'You said much the same when I went to Jenny's, and look what happened.' Her tone lacked the asperity her words implied.

'Well, I'm confident no-one's coming after you. There's no reason for them to do so. Oh, and I've brought your keys back,' said Mel, placing them on the table.

'Thanks, but there was no need. I had the locks changed when they mended the door.'

'Good idea. There's one other thing, Ellen. The gun. I'm not sure that what you told us was completely accurate.'

'Are you sure you don't want that tea?' Ellen didn't meet Mel's gaze.

'Yes, I'm sure. Anyway, we are satisfied that you didn't intend to shoot Ramsey. As to how you came by the gun, we are prepared to accept your explanation and see no reason to involve the Crown Prosecution Service.'

'It'd be a bloody cheek if you did, after what I've been through.'

'I know, I know. It's been terrible for you. No-one wants to make things any worse, so you needn't worry. I'm afraid I've got to go now, but if I can help in any way, please give me a call. You've got my card.'

Ellen looked as though she was about to make a sharp rejoinder, but her expression softened.

'Right. Thank you. And thanks for telling me about Osbourne and Ramsey. I'll sleep a bit better now.'

Mel smiled and prepared to leave. Just as the door was closing Ellen called to her.

'DC Cotton?'

'Yes?'

'You're all right.'

Mel grinned as she walked back to her car. Sometimes this job is bloody great, she thought.

Chapter Sixty-Two

Friday 25th October

'WELL, we may have stopped a leak but we're still not much further forward,' began Fiona at the morning briefing. 'Ramsey's going "no comment" all the way, and Hawkins gave us nothing. He may try to make a deal, but he's doing time whatever happens. He won't last long inside, even if he helps us. Oh, and I've had my results back from the lab. They found traces of GHB in the samples I sent them. A woman bumped into me in the pub and must have dropped it in my drink. That's why I looked drunk when I left. No point looking at the CCTV as she was obviously in disguise. If I hadn't been pulled by Traffic there's a good chance I would have had an accident.'

'A narrow escape, boss,' said Martin.

Mel and Tom made sympathetic noises.

At that point Fiona's phone rang. It was Inspector Winwood from the Traffic division.

'Yes Bill. I haven't seen him. He did what? Oh shit. OK. Thanks for letting me know.'

She turned to the others.

'We won't be seeing DS Jessop again. He was pulled for speeding last night. Just over the limit. He might have got away with it, but the traffic guys gave him a breath test because his voice was slurring. He failed it. Comprehensively. Turns out he had a drink problem in London, which was why he transferred from the Met. He also admitted that he scratched Jack's car. He's now under suspension.'

'No loss,' muttered Mel.

'There's something I've discovered,' said Tom. 'Hawkins was the arresting officer when Martina Baranska was last nicked. He used to work in Glasgow before he transferred down south.'

'Nice one, Tom. Looks like there's been some kind of association going back decades. The complaints guys will be going through his record with a microscope, but it would do no harm for us to take a look as well. Perhaps you could sweet-talk them into sharing?'

'I'll try. But it would probably be easier to talk a tiger into sharing a goat.'

'Now, now. No-one likes the IOPC, but they have to exist.'

Tom conceded the point and agreed to make an appointment.

'One other thing, boss.' Martin looked puzzled. 'If we look at what Tom and I discovered about Maldobourne's activities, the players are much better off than they should be. OK, they have a drugs operation as well as the legitimate businesses, but added together they can't provide them with the wealth we've discovered, to say nothing of any other assets we don't know about. They must be up to something else that generates this unexplained income.'

'You mean something involving this mysterious third man?' Fiona looked thoughtful.

'I suppose so. We'll just have to keep on digging.'

There was little more to be said, and the team went back trying to establish the extent of Campbell/Mackintosh's activities.

A few minutes' research gave Tom the private mobile number he needed.

'DS Jessop? It's Tom Ferris.'

'What do you want? I'm suspended. Didn't you know? I'm not supposed to talk to anyone from the nick.'

'Yeah. Sorry to hear about that.' Tom tried to sound sympathetic, although he had no time for drunk drivers. 'Look, I know I'm not supposed to talk to you either, but I wanted to pick your brains. Can you spare a minute?'

'Why shouldn't I just tell you to piss off?'

'Well, it won't do you any harm to be helpful, will it?'

'OK. Meet me in the Royal Oak in half an hour. And you're buying.'

The pub was crowded with drinkers taking an early liquid lunch, but Tom found Jessop in a quiet booth at the back. He ordered Jessop a double Scotch and an orange juice for himself, the latter prompting a contemptuous look from his companion.

'So what's this about?'

'You worked vice in the Met, didn't you?'

'So what?' Jessop looked wary.

'Did you ever come across a woman called Martina Baranska? She was a working girl from Glasgow who seems to have dropped off the map until her DNA turned up in Mexton.'

'Can't say I did. It's a name I'd remember.'

'How about Marnie Draycott?'

Jessop fidgeted and looked blank.

'Not in London. I know she was Wilkins's tart in Mexton.'

'Kelvin Campbell?'

'There were rumours he was pimping out teenagers and running sex parties, but we never had any proof.'

'Why didn't you tell us this?'

'You already knew we had suspicions. I saw the note in the file.'

'Yes, but you could have given us more, surely.'

'Why should I? You lot have hardly made me welcome.'

'It's the job. That's why. And your attitude was pissing everyone off. Especially Mel Cotton.'

'Got the hots for her, have you? She won't be interested in a twat like you. She needs a real man.'

If Jessop hadn't been so pathetic, Tom would have lost his temper. Instead he controlled his rising irritation and stood up to leave, an expression of contempt on his face.

'I'll tell the DI you've almost been helpful. But, really, you shouldn't be in the job. Not with your alcohol problem.'

'Don't tell me I've got a problem, you sanctimonious little prick. I'm a better copper than you'll ever be and I can take you any day.'

Tom refrained from mentioning his red belt in Tae Kwan Do and simply left the pub. As he looked back he saw Jessop downing the last of his whisky and reaching for his phone. A waste of oxygen, he thought. And who's he so desperate to ring?

Shortly after lunch, Fiona received a call from a uniformed sergeant and quickly called the team together again.

'Hawkins is dead. Looks like suicide. Possible drug overdose.'

'I suppose he couldn't face a trial and the prospect of years in jail, a target for everyone who hates coppers,' said Martin. 'Not sure I blame him. Do we have any details?'

'He didn't report to the station at nine a.m. as his bail required. Two PCs went to fetch him and found him dead on his bed, a bottle of whisky and some white powder beside him. Forensics are there now. Any luck with the IOPC, Tom?'

'No, boss. They wanted to have a go at him but were taking their time preparing a case. I got the impression they had a lot to talk to him about.'

'Well, keep at them. They may know something about his past that could help us.'

'Will do.'

Fiona felt no remorse at Hawkins's death, even though her sting had exposed him. Dirty coppers were a stain on the force, and his actions had not only obstructed justice, they had nearly led to the deaths of two officers and the ruin of two others. Who knew how many cases had been derailed and people harmed as a result? It was just unfortunate, she thought, that the extent of his corruption wouldn't come out at a trial.

Chapter Sixty-Three

Saturday 26th October

THE INCIDENT ROOM was an unpleasant place to be, the following morning. Heating engineers were tinkering with the station's boiler system and, for some reason best known to them, the radiators in the room were stuck on maximum. Twenty sweating civilian staff, plus the rain-soaked clothes they had brought in with them, soon sent the humidity levels soaring. Sweatshirts, T-shirts and blouses rapidly developed dark armpits, and even Jack's suit looked as limp as a week-old lettuce. The team drooped listlessly, and Fiona did her best to energise them.

'I've had the pathologist's report on Hawkins,' she reported. 'His body contained a large quantity of morphine, and his stomach contained diamorphine – that's heroin to you and me. It looks like he took a large dose of heroin, which is turned into morphine and something else. He simply over-dosed. But here's the interesting bit. He had no needle marks, and there was no drug paraphernalia on the premises, so he wasn't a regular user. The plastic bag and the bottle of whisky found beside his bed contained heroin, which ties in with what Dr Durbridge found in his body.'

'So? What's so interesting about that?' Jack queried.

'His fingerprints on the bag and the bottle were smudged, but, crucially, there was no saliva on the neck of the bottle. There was no glass by the bed either.'

'Which means he drank the whisky, from a glass or a cup, elsewhere,' completed Mel.

'Clever girl,' said Jack, earning him a frown from Fiona.

'So it's murder,' said Martin. 'Clearly someone was worried that he'd talk. My money's on Campbell. Perhaps the IOPC will be prepared to share what they've found, now he's dead.'

'Get in touch with them again, would you, Tom?' Fiona asked. 'Either sit down with them and report back or ask them to give us a briefing.'

'Yes, boss.'

'Have we got anything from Ramsey?'

'No. He's still going "No comment" all the way,' replied Martin. 'He's too experienced to give us anything. But there was one thing. We found a receipt from a takeaway in his pocket. Two meals, delivered to the Maldon Club the day before yesterday. Osbourne said Ramsey and Marlow hadn't been there for years, but it looks like he lied. I think it's worth another visit.'

'Agreed. Take Mel with you this evening and see if you can find anything. Talk to the staff again and emphasise it's a murder enquiry. Threaten to do them for obstruction if they don't co-operate. Good luck.'

'Come in, DC Ferris. I'm Steven Chisholm. Do sit down. I gather you'd like to talk to us about the late DCI Hawkins.' The slightly chubby IOPC officer polished his glasses and smiled, his genial manner belying a fearsome reputation for weeding out bad cops.

'Yes, sir. Thank you for seeing me. As you know, Mr Hawkins was murdered while bailed on corruption charges. He'd been tipping off organised criminals about our activities of late, until my boss, DI Gale, set a trap. I posed as an informant, and someone tried to kill me at the rendezvous. Hawkins was the only person who knew about the meeting. He admitted what he had done when arrested, but wouldn't give details of any other involvement with the gang. We wondered whether he had come to your attention for any reason before.'

'Yes, he has, and we have quite a file on him. We've been watching him for some time, although we've never had enough evidence to speak to him formally. There have been rumours, the odd remark from someone. Evidence against minor drug dealers going missing when he's been around and investigations hampered. That sort of thing. Do you know about Scotland?'

'No. What happened?'

'He used to work for Strathclyde Police, in Glasgow, and had a reputation for dropping soliciting charges in exchange for sexual favours from the girls. Nothing was proven, but he knew the complaints department was looking at him. He moved south before any formal action was instigated. God knows how he got a decent reference from his boss, but he managed it.'

'The Scottish connection's interesting, sir. Our prime suspect, Kelvin Campbell, used to operate in Glasgow under his original name, Callum Mackintosh. And a former sex worker from Glasgow was involved with Charles Osbourne down here. Martina Baranska, who Hawkins once arrested. We lifted her fingerprints at Osbourne's flat but can't find her anywhere. She must have changed her name, too.'

'Baranska. Baranska. That name rings a bell.' Chisholm consulted his laptop and looked up at Tom. 'Yes. That's right. Hawkins arrested Baranska for soliciting in Glasgow, in 1999. He let her off with a caution despite the fact that she had a significant record. She should have gone to court. This was one of the cases that raised questions with Strathclyde.'

'I'm wondering, sir. Suppose she encountered Hawkins in Mexton? She would have recognised him and known his vulnerabilities. Could her involvement with Osbourne have been more than just providing sex? If she was a major player in the gang, she could have been blackmailing, and/or bribing, Hawkins for information. We know there's a third person at the top, but we assumed it was a man. Perhaps it's her.'

'Very plausible, DC Ferris. We know Hawkins was getting money from somewhere. When we searched his property, we found details of a bank account in a different name, set up before the current money laundering regulations came into force. Over the years it received modest but regular sums, with occasional larger payments. The larger sums appeared shortly after a raid failed, a dealer was let off or some evidence disappeared. The biggest, two thousand pounds, was paid in after a battle on the Eastside Estate, when some dealers from London apparently tried to set up in Mexton. Their leader was found in the canal. He'd been shot. We suspect Hawkins tipped off the Mexton gang using police intel.'

'That's really useful, sir. Thank you very much. Is there anything else you can tell me?'

'Not at the moment, but we're still looking into things in

Mexton. I'll let you know if I consider anything we find relevant to your enquiries. Good luck, DC Ferris. You have a good reputation, especially for computer work.'

Steven Chisholm closed his laptop and stood up, signalling the end of the interview.

'Thank you again, sir.'

Tom left, feeling pleased. He had no idea he had a good reputation. He just kept his head down and got on with the job. Returning to the incident room, he told Fiona what the IOPC had said.

'Thanks, Tom. That certainly fills in a few gaps. But it leaves us with another question. Who the hell is Martina Baranska? I think we should take a closer look at Marnie Draycott.'

Chapter Sixty-Four

THE MALDON CLUB might have looked sophisticated once, but years of use and lack of maintenance had turned it into a rather shabby dive. Despite the smoking ban, it still smelled of stale tobacco, and no-one had bothered to paint over the tar stains on the ceiling. Mel and Martin spent a fruitless hour talking to staff and the few customers who slouched in, looking for an evening of karaoke and overpriced drinks. No-one knew anything, or was prepared to talk, despite threats of obstruction charges.

The manager, uncommunicative as a pickled oyster, made no objection to their searching the place. Nobody would admit to seeing Ramsey or Marlow on the premises, and the detectives found no takeaway food containers corresponding to the receipt in Ramsey's pocket.

'We'd better check the bins outside,' Martin said.

Mel wrinkled her nose. 'Rather you than me.'

'OK, I'll toss you for it. Heads or tails?'

'Heads. Oh shit. I'm sure that coin is fixed,' Mel grumbled.

Ten minutes rummaging through a bin full of empty crisp packets, waste food and floor sweepings yielded nothing of interest. Despite wearing latex gloves, Mel absorbed the characteristic smell of rubbish, which reminded her of the visit to the landfill. As they were leaving, she stopped and frowned.

'Did this used to be an ordinary pub back in the day?'

'Yes,' replied Martin. 'The Mason's Arms. My dad used to go there. It was converted into a club about twelve years ago.'

'So they would have served ordinary beer, kept cool in a cellar, not just the bottled designer lagers they sell now.'

'Yes, of course. I know what you're thinking. We didn't see any sign of a cellar entrance. Another look, then.'

The obvious place for an entrance to the cellar was behind the bar, so the staff could quickly change a barrel when the beer ran out. But the layout of the Maldon Club was different from that of a normal pub, with the bar located on a raised platform at the rear, leaving space for dancing and tables in the centre. Clearly, it had been extensively remodelled since its days as a pub, and the original location of the bar was no longer discernible.

A section of the ground floor had been partitioned off to form a small office. Although it contained a desk, a couple of chairs and two filing cabinets, the room looked little-used. A thin layer of dust covered the surfaces, and the room smelt musty. A grimy window set in the wall opposite the door admitted little light. A third wall was obscured by piles of beer crates and boxes of paper towels for the dispensers in the toilets, reaching half way to the ceiling. None of these walls bore any visible trace of an entrance to the cellar.

Mel crouched down and examined the floor in front of three filing cabinets that were ranked against the fourth wall.

'Look, Martin. These marks on the floor. Two of these

cabinets have been moved, recently and frequently. Give me a hand to shift them.'

The empty filing cabinets slid aside easily on wheels, and the detectives pushed them in front of the door to the office. Behind them was a small door, and Mel smiled triumphantly.

'Gotcha!'

Martin grabbed the handle of the door and yanked it open. As he did so a figure came hurtling out, snarling. He didn't see the knife but felt a hard knock in his belly, followed by a searing pain, as the blade slipped under his stab vest and into his abdomen. He staggered and fell to the floor as his assailant leapt over him.

Mel knew her colleague was hurt but couldn't tell how badly. But now she was in fear of her own life as the stocky figure of Dwight Marlow turned towards her, his eyes flashing hate. He held the knife, dripping with Martin's blood, in front of him.

'You hurt me, you bitch. Now you're gonna pay for it.'

He swiped the blade towards Mel's face as she flicked open her extendable baton. It missed her nose by a millimetre, and she turned sideways, striking at his arm. The baton only grazed him, and he held on to the knife. Mel stumbled over Martin's legs as she backed away, trying to get hold of her pepper spray. The knife flashed towards her again, this time skidding across her stab vest. She kicked at Marlow and caught his knee. He grunted in pain and sagged slightly but attacked again, this time going for Mel's legs. She whipped the baton around before the knife could do more than scratch her thigh, smashing it against Marlow's wrist. He howled in pain and dropped the knife, then launched himself at her in blind fury, clawing for her throat. Mel struck his knee as hard as she could and felt something break under the blow. He yelled and collapsed, giving Mel the chance to kick the knife out of his reach. She gave his face a dose of pepper spray and then handcuffed him to a radiator. She would argue reasonable force later. Her priority now was to get help for Martin.

Mel called for an ambulance and police backup, and gently unfastened Martin's stab vest. He was losing consciousness, but a moan escaped his lips as she pulled open his shirt. Blood was pouring steadily from a hole in his gut, and a vile smell came from the wound. She rolled up the bottom of Martin's shirt into a pad and pressed it against the hole. Pressure was crucial, she knew, but she had to clear a pathway into the room for the paramedics and also keep watch on her sobbing prisoner. Spotting a box of paper towels next to the radiator, she called to him.

'Marlow. Kick that box over to me.'

'Piss off. I can't fucking see.'

'Kick it over to me now or I'll come over there and smash your balls to pulp. And if he dies, you're looking at murder. A whole-life sentence.'

Marlow reluctantly pushed the box towards Mel with his foot. She managed to open it without reducing the pressure on Martin's belly. Grabbing half a packet of towels, she removed her hand and shoved them firmly over the wound. She took off Martin's belt and pulled it tight over the towels, hoping the pressure would stem the blood flow. After moving the cabinets away from the door, all she could do was wait for help, holding Martin's hands and talking to him, trying to stop him from losing consciousness.

The ambulance seemed to take an eternity to arrive. No-one from the pub appeared to have noticed the noise or came to help. It was that sort of place. As Mel heard the sirens she redoubled her efforts to keep Martin awake. It was what you were supposed to do, wasn't it? But by the time the paramedics crashed through the door, his fragile consciousness had faded and his pulse became undetectable.

The next half hour was a blur. She saw the paramedics fit an oxygen mask over Martin's face and set up a drip feeding a clear liquid into his arm. She was vaguely aware of them starting CPR and lifting him onto a stretcher, and then rushing him out of the room. Their faces were grim, and they didn't answer when she asked if he would be all right.

Although she was more or less uninjured, she was completely shattered, feeling sick but glad when two uniformed PCs took Marlow into custody. She couldn't stand to be in his presence any longer and didn't trust herself not to assault him. She thought back to her mother's death in the line of duty, and couldn't bear the thought of losing a colleague as well. If only she had opened the door and not Martin. She might have been able to dodge the blade. Probably nonsense. Marlow came through that door so quickly they were both taken by surprise. But what if Martin died? How would she tell his wife? And there was the baby, too. Guilt added to the feelings of nausea and wretchedness that overwhelmed her as she sat slumped against the wall.

Jack came in after the ambulance left, weaving past the busy SOCOs, a worried look on his face. He was the last person she wanted to see. He'd probably find a reason to bollock her and she would most likely hit him if he did. But she was pleasantly surprised to find him supportive and sympathetic.

'Are you hurt, Mel? What's that blood on your leg?'

'Just a scratch. Sarge. Hardly anything. I don't need a doctor.'

'You've done really well.' He squatted on the floor in front of her. 'A good collar.'

'Never mind that. How's Martin?'

'Not looking good. No-one's saying anything, but the paramedics said your staunching the blood may have saved his life. They couldn't say whether he'll pull through. That's up to the doctors when they've had a look at him.'

Mel felt sick but was damned if she was going to break down in front of her sergeant.

'As for you, we'll need your clothes for forensics. And you need to get that scratch looked at in A&E. Then you're going home for the rest of the day. That's an order. You can give a formal statement tomorrow. Tom will drive you in Martin's car. If yours is still at the station, give him the keys and we'll get someone to drop it back to you later. Well done.'

He spoke kindly but firmly, and, keen as she was to get back to work, she knew there was no point arguing with him. Jack cleared the room, handing her a paper evidence bag for her clothes and a Tyvek forensic suit to travel home in.

'It's all we've got and it's not very warm, I'm afraid. But you won't be in it long. See you in the morning, and not before. And if you need to come in late, do so.'

'Yes. Thanks, Sarge.'

Mel insisted on going home rather than to hospital. She knew the cut was superficial. On the way, Tom was kindness itself, although he did try to persuade her to see a doctor. He drove smoothly and didn't insist on conversation. When they got to Mel's flat he helped her in and made her a cup of tea, the traditional English remedy for anything short of a nuclear apocalypse. He offered to help her clean the cut from Marlow's knife, but she declined, not sure she wanted Tom to see her without her trousers just yet. Checking she needed nothing more, he collected her car keys and left, urging her to call him if she wanted to talk. Mel knew he hoped she would, but all she wanted to do was drink a large glass of wine, feed Ernie and go to sleep. She'd phone her dad in the morning.

Chapter Sixty-Five

Sunday 27th October

THE USUAL HUBBUB in the incident room was muted at the morning briefing. Detectives and civilian staff had been called in, although, for many, Sunday was their day off. Martin's empty desk served as a grim reminder of the dangers of modern policing, and even Mel's return, to murmurs of congratulation, couldn't lighten the mood.

'First off,' began Fiona, a catch in her voice, 'Martin. He's lost a lot of blood and the knife penetrated his bowel so there is a serious risk of peritonitis. He's had several blood transfusions and been pumped full of antibiotics so they're keeping their fingers crossed. If any of the bugs that leaked out of his gut are resistant, he's unlikely to make it. But he's fit and healthy, so he has a chance. He won't be able to receive visitors for some days, but his wife will let us know when he can. Don't go in mob-handed, though.'

She paused to let the news sink in. One of the more religious DCs bowed his head and muttered a quiet prayer. The others looked stunned and scared in equal measure.

'Right. Let's move on.' Fiona sounded more positive than she felt. 'What did the IOPC have to say?'

Tom reported on his discussions with Chisholm, describing Hawkins's shady past, the payments to his secret account and their links to obstructed police investigations. He suggested that Martina Baranska could be a key player who had a hold of some kind over Hawkins.

'Thanks, Tom. I expect it was him that jinxed the stakeout and tipped off Campbell about the raid. We really need to find this Baranska woman. Spend some time on it when you've got a moment, please. Have you found anything linking her with Marnie Draycott?'

'Nothing convincing, but I'm still looking.'

'OK. What did we get from the Maldon Club?'

'Nothing from forensics yet,' replied Jack, 'but there's some documents we found in the desk that look interesting. A rental agreement for a warehouse we didn't know about, down Southampton way, and purchase documents for a patch of woodland in Dorset.'

'The warehouse sounds interesting. Jack, can you go down there this afternoon with Mel and Tom? Have a nose around. I'll arrange a search warrant and let Hampshire Police know you're operating on their patch. If there's any news about Martin, I'll phone you.'

The detectives arrived at the warehouse shortly after lunch to find a couple of local uniforms waiting for them. The building was tucked away in the corner of a run-down industrial estate close to Southampton Water. Nothing much seemed to be happening in any of the nearby premises, and Maldobourne's warehouse stood out from the others with its high, razor-wire topped fence, a new padlock on the gate and CCTV cameras dotted around the perimeter.

The Hampshire officers cut the padlock and forced the door, leaving the detectives to investigate the warehouse's contents. The building was warm, despite the autumn weather outside, and a mixture of smells assailed them. Ammonia, decay and an overall mustiness. Half-a-dozen packing crates, bearing the Maldobourne logo, were piled up beside the door. Steel shelving ran the length of one wall, divided into sections. They couldn't understand what they were seeing at first. The shelves appeared to be holding rubbish and bric-a-brac of the type left behind at the end of a jumble sale. But, when they looked closer, they saw labels on each section: 'Elephant', 'Rhino', 'Tiger', 'Pangolin', 'Bear', and so on. All names of animals, some of which they recognised and some of which they had never heard of.

When they looked closer at the items on the shelves, they began to identify at least some of them. Rhino horns were obvious. So were the elephant tusks, wrapped in cloth and laid neatly on the floor, and the tiger skin that Jack unrolled. But odd bits of bone, claws and skin were impossible to recognise, and they realised that they needed specialist help.

Various empty cages were lined up on benches on the other side of the warehouse. A heat lamp shone on a box of tortoises, many not moving, on a table in a corner. Some blue feathers, stuck to the bottom of an empty cage, suggested that a macaw had been living in it recently.

'Something's alive here.' Jack uncovered a cage containing a bright red and blue bird. 'Anyone know what it is?'

'It's a female eclectus. A type of parrot. Worth a grand to a collector. And it looks like it needs a vet.' Tom sounded furious as he examined the listless creature, commenting on gaps in its plumage and a pile of feathers underneath its perch. A water dish was nearly empty, and a few seeds were scattered on the floor of the cage, which badly needed cleaning.

A powerful stench seeped from a plastic bin at the back of the warehouse. Jack lifted the lid and stepped back in disgust. The corpse of the macaw, crawling with maggots, was rotting on top of a pile of other animal remains.

Mel and Tom stepped out of the oppressive charnel house, leaving Jack wandering around inside. Tom was red-faced and quivering. Mel had never seen him so angry.

'Bastards, bastards, fucking bastards…' He kept shouting a litany of hate until Mel put her arm around his shoulders.

'I'm sorry, Mel,' he said miserably. 'That stuff really got to me. I don't know what some of it is, but what I did recognise comes from seriously endangered species. Trade in their products is banned, and some are incredibly valuable. Rhino horn is worth more than gold, per gram, all because prehistoric Chinese medicine considers it an aphrodisiac; some sheik wants a fancy handle for his dagger or a charlatan has claimed it can cure cancer. I've been a supporter of wildlife charities since I was a kid, and when I joined the force I realised there were two areas of work I couldn't get involved in. Child abuse and illegal wildlife trading. I can't be dispassionate enough. I don't get upset about gangsters blowing their rivals' kneecaps off, football hooligans fighting or drunks pulling knives on each other, but that stuff is just too much.'

Mel didn't know what to say. She liked animals well enough and hated animal cruelty. She'd intervened once, as a girl, when she saw a couple of boys tormenting a stray cat. They'd jeered at her until she flew at them brandishing a cricket bat. They never came back, and she'd persuaded her parents to adopt the cat. The sight of the tortoises had upset her, too. They reminded her of Ernie. Tom's reaction had surprised her, though. She had always considered him rather placid and anodyne, and this display of passion was unexpected. Despite his obvious distress, it appealed to her.

'OK. I'll phone the DI and let her know what we've found. Where can we get an expert to tell us what all this stuff is?'

'There's a police National Wildlife Crime Unit that deals with the illegal trade in wildlife products. If they can't identify something, they have experts on tap in zoos and universities who can. Ask Gale to get in touch with them.'

'Will do. In the meantime, d'you fancy getting us some coffees and snacks? I saw a drive-through at a petrol station a couple of miles back along the main road. The usual black, no sugar, for me, and Jack drinks latte with two sugars. And ask the Hampshire lads if they want anything. I'm paying.'

Tom smiled gratefully, glad of an excuse to escape from the horrors inside the warehouse. By the time he returned, Fiona had contacted the National Wildlife Crime Unit, who asked them to secure the scene until specialist officers arrived, promising a briefing on their work back in Mexton the following morning.

Jack delegated the task to the PCs from the Hampshire force and asked them to call a locksmith to padlock the warehouse door. They weren't too thrilled at the prospect of staying, but the free coffees and a couple of flapjacks mollified them somewhat.

'It's amazing what some people will do for a slug of caffeine,' murmured Mel as she steered the unmarked car out through the warehouse gates and headed towards Mexton. The others chuckled. Any humour, however slight, was welcome after what they had seen.

By two a.m. the Hampshire PCs were bored, tired, and hungry. The locksmith had long gone and they had run out of lewd jokes and things to say about football. Their boredom was relieved when the radio crackled.

'Robbery in progress, Totton High Street. Anyone available?'

'That's just up the road,' said Colin, the driver. 'Should we take it?' His mate, Malcolm, agreed and notified the control room that they were temporarily leaving their post. They drove off with the gate and warehouse door padlocked shut. The red lights on the CCTV cameras flickered.

Twenty minutes later, frustrated by a false alarm, the officers returned to find the gate smashed open, a black pickup truck backed up against the warehouse and two men pouring liquid from a couple of metal drums under the roller door. The PCs leapt out of the car and ran towards the truck, the smell of petrol spurring them on.

'Police. Stay where you are!' Colin drew his baton and Malcolm readied his pepper spray. One man dropped his drum, spilling its contents on the ground. He leapt into the truck, slewed it round and drove it at the officers, who dived sideways to escape. The other lit a rag and dropped it into the pool of petrol. The fuel flared up in his face, fanned by a stiff breeze, and the man stumbled in surprise, tripping and falling to his knees. A tongue of flame crept along the ground, engulfing his chest and setting his hair on fire. He screamed and called for help, but his mate ignored him, revving the truck, racing out of the gate and disappearing into the night.

The two Hampshire PCs, shaken but unhurt, raced to the burning man and pulled him from the flames by his feet. Colin removed his stab vest and tried to wrap it round the arsonist while Malcolm grabbed a small fire extinguisher from the police car.

They managed to put the fire out, choking at the smell of burning flesh. But by the time an ambulance and fire engines arrived the man was dead, his body smoking malodorously on the tarmac.

Meanwhile, flames were licking up the front of the warehouse door. The smell of blistering paint mingled with the smoke from the burning petrol. It only took a few minutes for the fire service to extinguish the flames with foam, but it took much longer for the door to cool down enough for anyone to open it.

Inside, the warehouse was barely damaged. The arsonists had been interrupted before they could get much petrol over the threshold, and the fire had burnt out rapidly. There was still a smell of smoke, so, showing more sense than they had when they left their post, Colin and Malcolm rescued the eclectus and the box of tortoises, stowing them in the back of the police car. The parrot seemed no worse for its ordeal but they couldn't tell whether the tortoises were harmed or not. The PCs rather hoped their actions would deflect some of the shit coming their way when their excursion came to light.

Chapter Sixty-Six

Goa, India 2019

Avi had been stalking the tiger for hours. He knew there was one in the area, because he had seen its tracks close to the village and heard it in the night. And he was sure he was closing in.

Officially, there were no tigers in Goa. Not because they didn't exist, but because the local people didn't want their lands to be declared a nature reserve, with all the restrictions that entailed. So they poisoned them with pesticides and hid the evidence, ensuring that their assertions couldn't be challenged.

Avi had made a substantial living out of the non-existent tigers. He had a distant relative in England who paid him handsomely for any tiger parts he could acquire, arranging transport for them as well. He didn't have the skill to skin the animals neatly, but that didn't seem to matter. He removed what he could, along with the paws, and packed them in crates for dispatch. No-one worried about the smell. The judi-

cious use of bribes kept mouths shut, and there were no diffi-
culties in getting his prizes to the port, where they were loaded
onto a ship bound for Europe. He buried the parts not immediately saleable in the forest, returning some months later to
retrieve the bones, which rodents and insects had cleaned for
him. They, too, would fetch a good price from his relative.

Finally, a tawny movement caught his eye. He rushed
forward and caught up with his prey. The tiger staggered into
a clearing and collapsed, twitching, the pesticide finally over-
powering it. When it became still, Avi waited a few minutes to
make sure it was dead, then approached. Drawing out his
knife, he smiled in anticipation. But he had miscalculated. As
he lifted the animal's forepaw to remove it, the tiger moaned
once and convulsed. The paw jerked sideways, the claws
ripping through Avi's neck. The jet of bright arterial blood
that sprayed over the tiger's back made a garish contrast with
the tiger's amber fur, and Avi collapsed within seconds. He
was found a day later, killed by a creature that didn't exist.

Chapter Sixty-Seven

Mexton | Monday 28th October

THE FIRST TOPIC for the morning briefing was Martin. His condition was still precarious. Next was the fire at the warehouse.

'We nearly lost all our evidence,' began Fiona. 'Early this morning, two individuals took advantage of the Hampshire officers' temporary absence to torch the warehouse. They poured petrol under the door and on the ground. Unfortunately, the person who lit the fuel had underestimated the size of the flames and fell into the blaze. The two PCs tried to rescue him, but he died of his burns before help arrived.'

'No loss,' muttered Tom, with uncharacteristic venom. Fiona pretended she hadn't heard.

'There was no serious damage inside the warehouse, but it would have been destroyed if the Hampshire lads hadn't returned in time. They rescued a parrot and some tortoises from the smoky atmosphere and took them to Southampton central nick. They had volunteered to attend a reported robbery in progress, which turned out to be a false alarm. Undoubtedly a diversion. Their absence from the scene is being dealt with locally. It's probable that the CCTV cameras around the warehouse sent live footage to someone who ordered the torching. The dead man was from Southampton, and the truck they used, stolen in the city just before the attack, was found burned out on some waste ground a couple of miles from the site.'

Various mutterings around the incident room commented on the Hampshire PCs' competence and parentage. Tom wondered what would happen to the eclectus.

When the hubbub had settled down, Fiona introduced a DS from the National Wildlife Crime Unit, who had agreed to provide them with some background on the trade.

'Morning,' he said. 'I'm Detective Sergeant Damien Attenborrow. Please don't take the piss, I'm no relation.' His light-hearted introduction contrasted sharply with the rest of his talk.

'The illegal trade in wildlife products and living animals is worth billions of pounds worldwide. No-one is sure exactly how much, because most of it goes undetected. Lack of laws, inadequate monitoring and corruption all facilitate a business that is driving many species to the brink of extinction. Elephants, tigers, rhinos, crocodiles, parrots, snow leopards – the list is endless. And the profit margins are huge. Our unit is responsible for tackling all kinds of crime involving wildlife, but I specialise in imports and exports.'

DS Attenborrow went on to describe in detail the threats to key animal species, peppering his talk with horrific images in a Powerpoint display. Statistic after statistic appeared on the screen, and the watching detectives became numb after a while. There was too much detail to take in, but they soon realised that the police and the Border Force, because of austerity and staff shortages, were stretched to the limit in trying to control the trade. People trafficking and illegal drugs tended to attract more attention than wildlife products, and Attenborrow's frustration was obvious. He concluded with some comments on the discoveries in the warehouse.

Tom remained mute during the briefing, his knuckles white on the handle of his coffee cup and an expression of all-consuming fury on his face.

'My colleagues have had a quick look at the items found and estimate the total value, in the right markets, to be some-where north of two million pounds,' Attenborrow went on. 'That's a lot of dead animals.'

The assembled detectives looked stunned.

'Obviously, it's not all destined for the UK market. Some of the rhino horn and tiger bones may end up in Chinese pharmacies in Britain, but most of it will be transhipped.

'Maldobourne's specialist transport vehicles and distribution network are ideal for moving illicit objects around the world,' he continued. 'Most wildlife items are small and could be concealed in a dummy server cabinet or other item of computer equipment. If the documentation is correct, Customs aren't going to insist a shrink-wrapped steel cabinet marked "Extremely fragile" is opened for inspection, especially as wildlife products won't be found by drug dogs or electronic explosive sniffers. All in all, this was a terrific, though terrible, find. Thanks to you all.'

Attenborrow declined the offer of lunch in the canteen and rushed off to join his colleagues at the Southampton warehouse.

'Well, we now know why Campbell and Co. are so wealthy,' resumed Fiona. 'The income from this nasty trade could dwarf the drug operation, even if they are running a few county lines. The trouble is, we still can't find Campbell and we've no idea who this third man is. You look pensive, Tom. What's on your mind?'

'One of those documents from the club, guv. It was for the purchase of some woodland. But what would a company like Maldobourne need woodland for? They're not into forestry.'

'Perhaps it's just recreational,' suggested Jack. 'Or a tax dodge. I think there are grants or something for wildlife habitats too, although they seem more interested in destroying wildlife than preserving it.'

'Maybe. D'you have any details, Tom? I'll look it up on Google Earth and see if there's a decent satellite photo.'

Tom rummaged through the paperwork and found a grid reference for the woods. Fiona typed it into her laptop, and an image appeared on the projector screen. It looked like a sea of trees from above, with the occasional path or track weaving through it. Fiona scanned backwards and forwards across the site, looking for anything significant, when Jack called out.

'Hold it. Just there. There's a building partly concealed by the trees. Where that path divides.'

Fiona zoomed in, and a small slate-roofed lodge, almost invisible from above, came into view.

'That could be it! Where Campbell's been hiding.' Fiona's mood switched from gloom to excitement. 'I think we'll pay him a visit. We know his rifle wasn't in his gun cabinet so we'll need firearms support. I'll brief the Super and arrange a search warrant. Tomorrow we're going down to the woods. And not for a teddy bear's picnic.'

Chapter Sixty-Eight

Friday 25th October

MARNIE'S END game started with a campaign of destabilisation. Her plan was to unsettle Campbell and lure him to the lodge in the woods. Then she would confront him and either leave him wounded for the police to pick up, a handy dossier of evidence beside him, or kill him. She still couldn't make up her mind which would be worse for him. And there was someone else she might need to eliminate, but that could wait.

She had a couple of jobs in mind that needed specialist expertise, and she consulted her mental client list for suitable operatives. Within a few seconds she had recalled the names and addresses of a bent copper in Portsmouth and a former senior fire officer. Both had enjoyed the services provided by her agency when visiting London, unaware that their sessions were being recorded. She made a couple of phone calls, overcame protestations with threats and the offer of financial rewards, and sat back to await results. Finally, she checked that all the arrangements for her disappearance were in place. New identity documents, flight tickets and an appointment at a discreet plastic surgery clinic were all in hand. In a few days' time she would be a different person on paper, and by the New Year she would look different as well. She didn't expect anyone to come looking for her, but she had to be sure. Marnie didn't like taking chances.

Kelvin Campbell's Bentley Mulsanne Speed was his pride and joy. It had cost him a fortune, and he paid a mechanic handsomely to keep it clean and in perfect condition. He rarely drove it in Britain, despite the false registration that prevented it being linked to him. But in continental Europe he could give the 530 horsepower under the bonnet free rein, occasionally reaching the promised speed of one hundred and ninety miles per hour. Unsurprisingly, he was apoplectic and sick to his stomach when his mechanic phoned him early one morning with the news that his precious car was now a burnt-out wreck. The mechanic couldn't account for the fire, assuring his boss that there was nothing wrong with the electrics, the fuel system or anything else that could lead to unwanted ignition. A furious Campbell dismissed him on the spot, with threats of dire retribution.

'I'll make you pay for this, you useless piece of shit. You'll never fucking work again.'

The following day the housekeeper reported a break-in at his luxury flat overlooking Portsmouth harbour. Nothing much was taken, as he kept little of value there apart from a 50-inch TV bolted firmly to the wall. But the intruders had voided bowels and bladders prolifically on the premises and belaboured the TV with a golf club. The housekeeper concluded her account of the mess with her immediate resignation.

Two days later, the barman unpacking a case of tortilla chips delivered to the Maldon Club discovered something strange in the bottom. An alarm clock and battery were connected by wires to a small metal cylinder embedded in a block of yellowish material. As an aficionado of action movies, the barman had no trouble in identifying the assemblage as a bomb. He lowered the box to the floor with infinite care and rushed out of the building, screaming.

'Bomb! Bomb! There's a fucking bomb!'

The few lunchtime patrons abandoned their drinks and stumbled out of the club. Bystanders scattered in terror, apart from a couple of youths brandishing their phones, hoping for an image of a catastrophe that would make them stars on social media. Possibly posthumously. The police soon moved them on.

It took nearly an hour for army bomb disposal technicians to arrive on the scene, during which time the police had cordoned off the street and evacuated buildings for several hundred yards around the club. The army's robot bomb disposal unit rumbled towards the device and inspected it with a TV camera. The corporal in charge frowned as he viewed the images then marched into the club. He returned ten seconds later, carrying the device, and yelled at the police officer in charge.

'Someone's having a laugh. These wires don't mean anything, and the clock isn't even ticking. And this,' he said, biting into the 'explosive', 'is bleedin' marzipan.'

The corporal dropped the fake bomb on the ground with an expression of disgust and stalked back to his vehicle. With the robot back on board, the unit returned to base leaving a crowd of rubberneckers and journalists behind, disappointed at the anti-climax.

The final straw, from Campbell's point of view, was the news that one of his shipments had been intercepted by customs on arrival at Harwich. The consignment, a smallish quantity of heroin, was not hugely valuable, but the fact that a flawless operation had now sprung a hole and his supply chain was interrupted infuriated him.

He phoned Marnie and demanded that she meet him in one of his flats in town, partly to berate her and partly for company.

Marnie arrived at Campbell's flat bearing whisky and an expression of sympathy.

'I'm so sorry to hear about your car,' she began. 'I know how much you loved it. And that business at the club. So embarrassing and bad for business.'

'That's not all,' Campbell snarled in reply. 'My flat's been trashed. And what happened with that shipment? You were supposed to make sure it got through untouched.'

'Yes, I'm furious, too. My man was sent off to cover at Felixstowe at the last minute and I couldn't put anyone else in place in time. It wasn't his fault. Just our bad luck that it was picked up on a random spot check.' Marnie concealed her smile.

'Someone's out to get me,' ranted Campbell. 'It's a campaign. A conspiracy. Who is it? A London mob? The Albanians? The Russians? We could do with someone like George to sort this out. We've got too soft.'

Campbell's raving diminished as the whisky bottle emptied, until he just sat there mutely. For the first time in his criminal career he felt vulnerable. He didn't see Marnie hiding a smile of grim delight.

'This is really stressful for you, Kelvin, I can see that,' she soothed. 'How about popping down to the country for a break? Get some fresh air. Shoot some deer. I'll come down and join you. It could be fun.' She stroked his arm as she said this, and a flicker of lust stirred in Campbell's eyes, despite the fact that Marnie was at least three times the age of his usual bed-mates.

'OK,' he agreed. 'I'll go down there on Monday. When will you join me?'

'Probably the day after. I'll make sure everything's running OK here and drive down. I'll have a surprise for you, I promise.'

Marnie kissed Campbell on the cheek and left him to fall asleep on the sofa. As she drove home her mind was filled with anticipation. She turned over various scenarios in her mind, rejecting or modifying them as the tyres hissed on the rainy tarmac. None of them involved shooting the local wildlife. But they all, most definitely, involved a shotgun.

Chapter Sixty-Nine

Tuesday 29th October

IT WOULDN'T BE LONG NOW. He'd had a good run. Made more than enough money. But all things come to an end, and it was time to wind things up. There were loose ends to deal with, evidence to conceal or destroy, and a credible reason for moving on to set up. None of these presented a problem, but he did wish DI Gale and her team hadn't been quite so clever. They weren't supposed to know about the lodge in the woods, and it was only that idiot Osbourne's sloppiness that led them to it. Leaving documents in the Maldon Club was unforgiveable.

When Gale was given the lead on the case, he expected her to get nowhere. His sources didn't rate her that much. She had a reputation as a good organiser and manager, but he didn't have her down as a particularly good detective. He hadn't reckoned on her team shining at the nitty-gritty of information gathering that had brought them to this point. He knew they would be there later, but his back way through the woods was quicker than the obvious route. He would be long gone before they arrived.

As his tyres swished on the wet road and the windscreen wipers battled with the downpour, he reflected on what had happened. If Osbourne and Wilkins hadn't been greedy and set up the jewel robbery, and Wilkins hadn't tried to keep the proceeds, none of this would have happened. Wilkins's head on his wife's doorstep had triggered the collapse of the whole enterprise, like a row of dominoes falling, and had cost several lives. It would cost another one before the end of the day. He was secure, his exit strategy planned to the last detail. And, to the end, no-one would suspect him.

He pulled off the road and drove along a track through the woods, parking behind the small stone building. He wasn't expected, but that was not a problem. He wouldn't get a hostile reception, especially as he was carrying an expensive bottle of whisky. He put on a waterproof jacket, stepped out of the SUV and walked towards the door. Closure.

Chapter Seventy

JACK CURSED as he peered through the windscreen of the unmarked police car.

'Bloody English weather. I can't see a thing in this rain.'

'You should try Wales,' replied Mel. 'I once spent two weeks in Pembrokeshire on a family holiday and we had a grand total of three hours sunshine.'

'That's not helpful. There's supposed to be a track off to the left along here, but I've probably missed it. Hang on, there's something.'

Jack swung the police vehicle off the main road and eased it slowly along a forest path, glad that it wasn't his own car's paintwork making a screeching noise against the undergrowth.

'They'll never get an armed response vehicle along here. It's too boggy with all this rain.'

'It doesn't matter. They'll be coming along another track, the other side of the lodge, and their vans can cope with difficult terrain,' snapped Fiona, annoyed that the firearms unit would be delayed. 'They're mopping up after another op, according to DSup Shah. They'll contact me when they turn off the main road.'

Progress became slower and slower as they got further down the path. What had started out as a reasonably firm surface gradually turned into a quagmire, weeks of rain having saturated the ground. Eventually the car ground to a halt, the engine screaming and its wheels spinning pointlessly in the mud.

'Switch the engine off, Jack,' said Fiona. 'If there's anyone there they'll hear us coming from miles away.'

Jack complied, leaving only the sound of pouring rain splashing on the windscreen and hammering on the bonnet.

'So what do we do now?' asked Mel. 'Wait for firearms to pull us out? Call the AA? How far is it to the lodge anyway?'

'About three hundred metres, according to my reckoning,' replied Tom. 'We could take a look while we're waiting for the AFOs. Just to see if there are any signs of occupation.'

'Yeah. I'm up for that,' said Mel. 'How about you, guv?'

'No, I think Jack and I will stay here in the dry. Privilege of rank. I'll need to direct the others when they arrive, anyway. Off you go – and don't take chances. If you see anyone there, come back at once. Understand?'

'Yes, boss.'

Mel and Tom zipped up waterproofs over their Kevlar jackets, climbed into wellies, pulled their hoods over their heads and stepped into the deluge. Once they were off the path the rain wasn't as intense, since the tree canopy acted as a giant umbrella. Large drops still found them, but at least the ground was less soggy. The tracks of heavy-duty tyres were visible on the path beside them. As the detectives approached the lodge, which was tucked under the trees like something from a very wet fairy tale, they spotted a hybrid SUV pulled into a clearing.

'We could've done with one of those,' murmured Tom, nodding towards the hybrid. 'It wouldn't've got stuck in the mud and it's almost silent in electric mode.'

'Boys' toys,' teased Mel, although she saw his point.

The presence of the car put the detectives on high alert. They watched the lodge silently for several minutes but saw no signs of anyone in or around the building. There were no lights inside. Cautiously they inched forward, the sound of the rain masking the squelching of their boots on wet leaves.

'You take the front windows and I'll take the side ones,' whispered Tom.

Mel nodded and they split up. They kept out of sight of the windows as far as possible, creeping through the trees. The last few yards were more open. They dashed from cover and stood flat against the walls, Tom on the left-hand side and Mel at the front. Mel slowly moved her head and peered into the window. She jerked back in shock and inched her way along the wall to where Tom was standing.

'There's someone on the floor. Dead or injured. I can't see who it is. His head's hidden by a table.'

'Call Gale. Don't go in.'

'But he could be alive. We're supposed to preserve life, aren't we?'

'Yes, but not at the expense of our own.'

'Did you see anyone on your side?'

'No, I think the place is empty.'

'I really think I should go in,' Mel insisted.

'No, Mel, please. I don't want to see you hurt again.'

'That's sweet. But someone could be dying in there.'

'Yes. It could be us.'

'I'm going in, Tom.'

'You're an idiot. But I'll come with you,' Tom sighed.

'OK. Thanks.'

'This is stupid. Really stupid,' he muttered under his breath, but kept it quiet as he didn't want Mel to see that he was scared.

Mel dialled Fiona's number as they approached the door.

'Guv. There's someone on the floor, dead or injured. Apart from that, the place seems empty. We're going in.'

'Are you sure there's no-one else there? For fuck's sake don't take any chances.'

'It seems clear. We've looked through the windows and can't see anyone. I need to check if this guy's still alive.'

'Well, OK. But at the first sign of anyone else, run. Understand? We'll come and join you.'

'Yes, guv.'

Mel pushed open the door to the lodge, with Tom following her. The building appeared to have two rooms: the main eating and living area, with cooking facilities in the corner, and another room off it, presumably for sleeping. There was no sound apart from rain dripping on to the roof. It could have been quite pleasant as a rural retreat but for the sickly smell of blood in the air and the corpse sprawled face down on the floor. The splashes of blood and grey matter on the wall and ceiling didn't help, either. Mel's stomach turned over and she saw Tom only just avoiding vomiting.

The body was Kelvin Campbell. He'd been shot. Much of the top of his head was missing. But he was the man they thought was armed and dangerous. So who had killed him? She got her answer when a figure stepped from behind the door, levelling a rifle at the two officers.

'Put the phone down, Constable. And come away from the door. Both of you.' Mel complied and Tom silently cursed himself for suggesting this reconnaissance. If Mel died it would be his fault, and he couldn't bear the thought.

'Detective Superintendent Shah,' gasped Mel. 'What are you doing here?'

They stood side-by-side as Shah faced them, his back to the doorway.

'Tying up loose ends.'

'What do you mean?'

'Things have unravelled,' replied Shah, his finger lightly touching the rifle's trigger. 'Campbell was losing it. Osbourne's dead. You found the warehouse. It's time for me to move on without leaving embarrassing traces. When I've finished here, I'll deal with Marnie Draycott. She knows too much as well. Then I'll retire immediately on health grounds. I can pay for a phoney diagnosis. I've had a good run with these clowns, but all things must pass.'

'Shit. You're the third man.'

'Of course. You didn't think Hawkins was the only senior officer on board with them, did you? Someone had to keep them informed about high-level police activity, things Hawkins wouldn't know about. Perhaps you're not as clever as you think you are.

'I joined them shortly after they started up in Mexton. I had a source of tiger parts in India, a distant relative, and Maldobourne's operation was ideal for getting them out of the country and onto the market. Expansion into other animal products was easy. The market is huge, and we made more from that than we did from drugs. Only Osbourne and Campbell knew my identity, and they're both dead. Reluctant as I am to harm fellow officers, I'm afraid you'll be joining them. I have someone in the force who can alter computer records and lose paperwork, so there will be no mention of a third man. And Rowse won't make it. I'll make sure of that.

'Here's what happened, officially. You came across Campbell in the lodge and he shot you both. He realised there was no escape so he killed himself. In fact, I got him drunk and put the rifle under his chin, using his finger to pull the trigger. I'll make sure only his prints are on it. I was never here. No-one will look for DNA, and I'll make sure the investigation is limited. I'm parked behind the building and I'll be away long before anyone finds you.'

'But we didn't come alone. And there's a firearms unit on the way.'

'Yes, I heard your car getting stuck on the track. I can pick off your colleagues before they know what's hit them. I'm an excellent shot. I once brought down a rhino at two hundred yards with one round. As for firearms, they won't be coming. I didn't ask for them.'

'You bastard,' shouted Tom, starting forward.

Shah raised the rifle and aimed at Tom's head. But before he could pull the trigger, they all heard a cool voice behind him. Shah turned to see Marnie Draycott, dripping from the rain outside, aiming a shotgun at his chest.

'So I'm a loose end, am I?' Someone to be dealt with? I don't think so. I know who you are. Charles told me when I screwed him. But you've deprived me of the pleasure of getting rid of Campbell. And I now have to do something about these coppers, which makes things much more difficult.'

Marnie moved into the room and stood where she could cover both Shah and the detectives.

'Why Campbell? You were partners.' Shah was stunned.

'He brought me over from Poland as a young girl with promises of a job. I spent the next four years in a filthy Glasgow knocking shop until I was too old for the perverts he catered for. He then chucked me out on the streets. I've spent years planning the perfect revenge. I was going to blow off his kneecaps and send details of his activities to the cops. OK, he's dead, but that's not the point. It wasn't me that killed him. And I'm very unhappy.'

'I'm sorry about that. But he had to go.'

Shah let the barrel of the rifle drop so it pointed towards the floor, turning away from Tom and Mel. 'There's no reason why we shouldn't come to some arrangement now, is there? I had nothing to do with what happened to you in the past.'

His voice was encouraging, but underneath a current of fear had started to flow. 'I've plenty of cash and I can make sure you're comfortable for the rest of your life. And Campbell's death will look like suicide so there'll be no investigation.'

'I don't need cash. I have plenty. And I've had an exit strategy in place ever since I came to Mexton. You've nothing to offer that I could possibly want.'

With Shah and Marnie focussed on each other, Mel and Tom were temporarily forgotten. Unarmed, they had little chance against a rifle and a shotgun. But their eyes met and they tacitly agreed to at least go down fighting. Mel was closest to Shah, while Tom was slightly nearer to Marnie. She pointed at Marnie and then to Tom, who nodded. Holding up her fingers she counted down from three. At zero she hurled herself at Shah, catching him behind the knees so he fell backwards. Tom made a shallow dive towards Marnie, knocking her off balance as he collided with her legs.

Shah fired as he fell, sending a bullet into Marnie's side. Marnie fired in the same split second. The blast from one barrel took off most of Shah's face, and a pellet ricocheting off the stone wall hit Mel in the earlobe, spattering her blonde hair with blood. The second barrel fired as Marnie convulsed in agony, most of the charge hitting the wall, apart from a dozen pellets that hit Tom in the legs and backside.

Their ears ringing from three shots fired in a confined space, the two detectives slumped on the floor. Blood dripped from Mel's ear and Tom lay on his front, swearing. Shah was clearly dead, but Marnie was still alive, a stain spreading along her trousers where the bullet had carved a channel in her hip.

Mel crawled over to help her, but Marnie waved her away.

'It's not too bad. Good job I've developed a fat arse. The bone's not hit or I wouldn't be moving. You may have saved my life. I owe you.'

Marnie rolled over, grabbed the dropped rifle and aimed it at the detectives.

'I'm leaving. I don't want to hurt you, but if you try to follow me, I'll shoot you. Don't move until you hear me drive off.'

'You're Martina Baranska.' Mel said, through gritted teeth. 'So this was all about getting revenge on Mackintosh, wasn't it? What are you going to do now?'

'I'm moving on. To a new life. Far from scum like these two. I'll get patched up by a tame doctor who's helped us before, and you won't see me again. By tomorrow night I'll be on another continent. I'm not usually a grass, but there's a lot you'd like to know about Campbell and his activities. Just remember the old English saying: it never rains but it pours.'

'What do you mean by that?'

'Work it out, Miss Clever Detective.'

With that parting remark, Marnie limped to the door, one hand pressed against her hip and the other covering the detectives with the rifle. They heard a car door slam and the vehicle drive off, the engine note fading until it was inaudible above the sound of the falling rain.

Mel phoned Fiona again, her hands trembling so much

she could barely press the keys, asking her to call an ambulance and bloody well hurry up. She helped Tom to his feet, clutching a tissue to her bleeding ear with the other hand. Keen to escape the stench of blood, they stumbled out of the lodge, shaking and nauseous. The shock hadn't fully set in, and the detectives tried to make light of things. As Tom hobbled along the track, his backside stinging in a dozen places, he plucked up his courage and turned to Mel.

'I'll get you an earring to go in that hole, if you like,' he joked. She smiled back.

'Good plan. And I'll rub some ointment on your bum when you've got rid of those pellets. If you like.'

'Is that a promise?'

'You bet!'

'You were bloody lucky to get out of that alive. Both of you.' Jack was furious, but there was a hint of admiration in his voice. 'We heard the shots and were shit-scared you'd been hit.'

'Yes, I know, Sarge. You're right.' Mel looked contrite. 'But there might have been a chance to save a life. It was instinct.'

'Well instinct could get you killed.'

'I guess so. Sorry.'

As they waited in the car for the ambulance, Tom kneeling rather than sitting on the back seat, Mel turned over Marnie's cryptic remark in her mind. She obviously wasn't referring to the weather and wanted the police to decipher her clue. Mel cast her thoughts back over the case, from the time Ellen had brought George's head into the police station, as if she was playing a video in her head. Then it clicked: the kitschy statue in the front garden of Marnie's and George's place on Blackberry Way. It was a woman continuously pouring water from a jug into the pond, driven by a pump. Maybe whatever Marnie was referring to was connected with that, in some way? She resolved to take a look after they'd finished with her at A&E. And after that, all she wanted to do was sleep. Preferably for a month or two.

Epilogue

It took nearly three months of co-ordinated effort, involving Mexton CID, the Met, the National Crime Agency, the Border Force, Police Scotland and the National Wildlife Crime Unit, to prepare for the raids. At dawn, on a wet January morning, three hundred and fifty officers raided premises up and down the country. By lunchtime, fifty-three suspects were in custody, and the documents, computers, mobile phones, drugs and other exhibits subsequently seized would have filled two shipping containers. Everything they needed had been on flash drives hidden under the statue.

Campbell's operations in Mexton were swiftly dismantled and his county lines shut down. Maldobourne's assets were seized under the Proceeds of Crime Act, but as the directors were all dead, there was no opposition. Users on the Eastside Estate inevitably found other sources of supply, but, for a while at least, criminality subsided slightly.

After weeks of treatment and rehabilitation, Martin Rowse returned to work, a shadow of his former self. Cadaverously thin, he was confined to desk duties at first, but a diet of canteen food and his wife's cooking slowly put weight on him. Cricket would be some way off, though.

Fiona competed with three other Detective Inspectors for DCI Hawkins's old job and won, despite mistakes made during the investigation. Jack was invited to take an Inspector's course and apply for her job but he declined, preferring to stay closer to the front line.

Mel and Tom were sent on sick leave and offered counselling to cope with the trauma of the shootout. When they returned to duty, they received commendations but were also firmly warned never to take such a stupid risk again.

Tom was allowed to adopt the eclectus parrot found in the Southampton warehouse and eventually found it a mate. The tortoises were re-homed via the RSPCA.

Relationships between serving officers in the same unit were officially discouraged, but Mel and Tom started going out together, semi-secretly. Tom transferred from the Major Incident Team to Cybercrime, where his skills were particularly useful and he was less likely to get stabbed or shot in the arse. It also meant he could agree when Mel suggested they moved in together.

Ellen recovered her old spark and started work with Victim Support, helping people traumatised by crime.

Marnie Draycott disappeared completely.

Glossary of Police Terms

AF: Authorised Firearms Officer
ANPR: Automatic Number Plate Recognition (camera)
ARU: Armed Response Unit
ARV: Armed Response Vehicle
CEOP: Child Exploitation and Online Protection Centre
CHIS: Covert Human Intelligence Source
CPS: Crown Prosecution Service
DVLA: Driver and Vehicle Licensing Agency
DWP: Department for Work and Pensions
ESDA: Electrostatic Detection Apparatus
HMRC: Her Majesty's Revenue and Customs
HOLMES2: Home Office Large Major Enquiry System
IOPC: Independent Office for Police Conduct
MET: Metropolitan Police Service
NABIS: National Ballistics Intelligence Service
NCA: National Crime Agency
PNC: Police National Computer
RIPA: Regulation of Investigatory Powers Act

SOCO: Scene Of Crime Officer (aka CSI)
TIE: Trace, Interview, Eliminate

Acknowledgments

Firstly I would like to thank my wife, Jen, whose eagle-eyed and perceptive scrutiny made the early drafts of this story fit to be read outside the family.

Rebecca and Adrian at Hobeck Books deserve special thanks for reading the manuscript and picking me up as a new member of their select group of authors – and also for commissioning Jayne Mapp who produced such a striking cover and Sue Davison who copy edited the manuscript so effectively. Their support has been amazing.

I would also like to thank the lovely people at Crime Fiction Coach who ran the 'Best first sentence for a crime novel' competition in 2019, which I won. I then had no choice but to write the novel! They also provided support through their Facebook group and Louise Voss produced an excellent, encouraging critique. I would recommend anyone who wants to write crime to join the group.

Thanks are also due to Zoe Sharp, thriller writer *par excellence*, for helping me to shoot people and to Graham Bartlett for his advice on police procedure. Any mistakes or liberties taken with the latter are entirely my own fault.

Finally, I would like to thank Martin Edwards and Dea Parkin, who encouraged me to join the Crime Writers Association, and also the organisers of Crimefest. If I hadn't spotted a poster for the festival just in time to get a ticket five years ago, I would never have realised how welcoming and supportive crime writers are or had the courage to attempt to join them.

About the Author

Brian Price is a writer living in the South West of England. A scientist by training, he worked for the Environmental Agency for twelve years and has also worked as an environmental consultant, a pharmacy technician and, for twenty-six years, as an Open University tutor.

Fair Trade is his first full-length novel. He has also contributed to a number of short stories to a local writing group's anthology, called *Cuckoo*. He is the author of *Crime Writing: How To Write the Science*, a guide for authors on the scientific aspects of crime. He has a website on the topic **www.crimewriterscience.co.uk** and advises crime writers on how to avoid scientific mistakes in their books.

Brian reads a wide range of crime fiction and also enjoys Terry Pratchett, Genevieve Cogman and Philip Pullman. He may sometimes be found listening to rock, folk and 1960s psychedelic music. He is married and has four grown-up children.

To find out more about Brian and his crime fiction writing please visit his website: **www.brianpriceauthor.co.uk**.

Hobeck Books - the home of great stories

We hope you've enjoyed reading this novel by Brian Price.

If you enjoyed this book, you may be interested to know that if you subscribe to Hobeck Books you can download a free novella *Fatal Beginnings* by Brian, exclusive only to subscribers. There are many more short stories and novellas available for free too.

- *Echo Rock* by Robert Daws
- *Old Dogs, Old Tricks* by AB Morgan
- *The Silence of the Rabbit* by Wendy Turbin
- *Never Mind the Baubles: An Anthology of Twisted Winter Tales* by the Hobeck Team (including all the current Hobeck authors and Hobeck's two publishers)
- *The Clarice Cliff Vase* by Linda Huber
- *Here She Lies* by Kerena Swan
- *The Macnab Principle* by R.D. Nixon
- *A Defining Moment* by Lin Le Versha

Also please visit the Hobeck Books website for details of our other superb authors and their books, and if you would like to get in touch, we would love to hear from you.

Hobeck Books also presents a weekly podcast, the Hobcast, where founders Adrian Hobart and Rebecca Collins discuss all things book related, key issues from each week, including the ups and downs of running a creative business. Each episode includes an interview with one of the people who make Hobeck possible: the editors, the authors, the cover designers. These are the people who help Hobeck bring great stories to life. Without them, Hobeck wouldn't exist. The Hobcast can be listened to from all the usual platforms but it can also be found on the Hobeck website: **www. hobeck.net/hobcast**.

CPSIA information can be obtained
at www.ICGtesting.com
Printed in the USA
BVHW080853070921
616214BV00014B/700